Under
the
Stardust

SHERREE BROSE

NEWMAN SPRINGS PUBLISHING
320 Broad Street
Red Bank, NJ 07701

First originally published by Newman Springs Publishing 2022

ISBN 978-1-63881-395-8 (Paperback)
ISBN 978-1-63881-396-5 (Digital)

Printed in the United States of America

Thank you, Mom, Shelia, Cindy, Marcy.

Contents

"When they come, tell them you want to go with them!"
"No way… I don't want to go!"
She heard her three-year-old voice say, "Yes, you do. Tell them."
Her mother insisted, "Tell them you'll go with them."
"No! I don't want to go!"

Stardust

Cyril could see the heat waves radiate off the surface of the desert floor. Inside the old Volvo, the cool breeze coming from the air-conditioning had just rattled to a stop. Cyril decided to open her window when a sharp contrast from cool to hot air assaulted her. The delicate chiffon of her dress flew up in the jarring breeze. She quickly laid her fingers wide onto her lap, smoothing the sheer fabric down gently. Small colorful sticky notes swirled around the interior of the car littering the back seat and floor. Cyril glanced at the cluttered dash; the program read she had forty-four minutes before arriving at the company party.

What an odd place to have a party, she thought. She must be getting closer as small personal jets, helicopters, and cars fancier and faster than hers were all passing her by. All were going in the same direction. Turning off onto a secluded desert road, she noticed a stark black contrast to the new pavement. Approaching a line of other vehicles, Cyril put her hand over her stomach, trying to settle her restless internal butterflies. Who would she see there? Would her new friends from work be there? she wondered. Will she be seated with her friends? Was the dress she picked out going to fit in, or would she be overdressed or not dressed well enough? Her shoes, of course, matched her dress. Would they start to kill her feet? Could she dance in them? Would there be dancing? she wondered. Too much to think about while her internal butterflies stirred.

On the car dashboard in front of her was a row of four hot pink sticky notes, all reminders. These notes were lifesavers. Having lost her memory almost two years ago, now she just had to remember to read them.

1. "PROGRAM DIRECTIONS TO AND FROM PARTY." Thank god for Tully, her helper; she knew how to program this vehicle, getting there, then getting back home. Way over her head, Cyril thought.

2. "GOING TO COMPANY PARTY." In small print read, "Have fun," signed, Tully.

3. "DON'T FORGET BAG." In small print read, "Find Mr. Joy give him the bag; we think this stuff is his 'IMPORTANT ask first.'"

4. It was blank; Cyril had forgotten what she was writing. It bothered her all the way there. She had written a big #4 up on the corner, but her memory was blank. She had a feeling #4 was essential and that she would regret not writing it down. Being independent was not easy. Having to rely on others to keep her life in order was sometimes overwhelming.

Cyril peeled off the dash the first and second notes, placing them on the headliner above her head. She stopped staring up at the headliner, covered with all different colors of sticky notes, thousands of reminders, notes to get her from here to there. Letters to herself, Cyril had already forgotten. All reminders of what she had been doing and with whom. It was hard not having a past. Every day Cyril knew she was building her past one moment at a time. She knew she had a lot to learn, especially about herself.

Before giving the car over to the valet, she grabbed the large brown paper bag sitting atop a stack of binders and half-opened envelopes from work. For a split second, she thought about how embarrassing the inside of her car looked. Books, binders, stacks of case notes and photos, small cracked-screen tablets she had intended to have fixed but had forgotten, information on each she might need later maybe. Shoes of assorted heights and colors were comfortable for the first few hours but then ended up needing to be changed later on in the day. All were ending up in the back of the car, sticky notes that had fallen from the headliner. Crumbled-up litter everywhere, old sunflower seed shells, stale french fries crammed between the seats, so much of her life inside the car now for the valet to see. For that moment, Cyril wished her past could also be so easily exposed to her. But the bag. That was, after all, the only reason she came to the party. The minute she stepped out of the car, glittery diamonds fell from the sky like confetti at New Year's. *Nice touch*, Cyril thought, *for this festive event*. Scanning the other guests as they got out of their cars, she noticed the sparkly stuff was only on her.

Out in the middle of nowhere, grass carpeted the oasis in front of her. A walkway following a dry creek lined with palm trees ran through the middle of the dining area. Tables littered the desert floor, flanking both sides of the trees; also, a large screen and dance floor were set at the edge of the bluff.

As she walked down the path toward the tables, the guests parted and nodded, all saying in their language, "Bonsoir," "Buenas noches," "God aften," "Good evening," "Guten abend." A friendly group, she thought, as they all moved to let her through. Heads turned and stared. In the distance, music surrounded the area. The tune was familiar as she hummed it to herself. *Some enchanted evening, you may see a stranger; you may see a stranger across a crowded room. Some enchanted evening, when you find your true love.* Distracted, she kept the tune in her thoughts.

As Cyril looked intently around for the mysterious Mr. Joy, it was apparent to onlookers she was up to something as she carried the large bag in her arms. Her heart was pounding with anticipation as she had only heard about the mysterious Mr. Joy. Hearing comments from the crowd up ahead, she knew he had to be the center of their attention. The guests parted out of her way, and there he stood. He gasped when he saw her.

She was looking down, struggling to pull her satin stiletto heel out of the soft grass. When she looked up, she said to him, "Is your name Mr. Joy?" Clear to him, she had no idea who he was.

The soft chiffon of her dress slowly floated to rest, settling around her as if she had just landed.

The faint fragrance of lime and sandalwood filled the air as she waited for his answer.

His heart stopped, his eyes fixed. Cyril was his childhood friend; he had known her all his life, appearing different now. She took his breath away.

For the first time in many years, he saw her without combat fatigues or camouflage or wearing all black. The last time he saw Cyril, she lay unconscious on a gurney with a sheet over her. She was stunning. It left him speechless.

"I think this is yours," she said, holding the bag toward him, arms stretched out as far as she could reach. He took the large paper bag into his hands and glanced down at her.

Giving her a half smile, he said, "What's this?" sounding surprised and happy at the same time. Did her face look familiar to him? she wondered. She knew nothing of her past, leaving her ready to discover new parts of herself.

Cyril glanced at the name tag on his lapel. She was right. It is him. Mr. Joy, Federation of Intergalactic Investigations and Communications. In small print below that it read, "President." Yes, this was her boss. Almost giddy inside, she wiped the smile off her face. She had heard all about him so far; everything she could see was correct, tall and handsome and, in her mind, *all that*! But there had to be more. How else could he get where he's at? Not with looks alone.

Glancing at her for a moment, he could see the seriousness in her expression. Cyril wasn't there anymore. His friend was gone; she didn't know him. Cyril's past with Mr. Joy was gone. Like the rest of her life wiped clean. His head turned as he focused on the bag and the shifting weight of its contents. He looked into the bag then quickly looked back at her. He looked at her in a way that only a friend could look.

She found comfort in that. What was cluttering Mr. Joy's mind? Cyril wondered while she looked deep into his expression, trying to read the look on his face.

He watched the stardust gently fall onto her. Like glitter or a soft rain, the magic of the stardust would change everything for her tonight. This evening the stardust was for her only. Every moment she spent under the twinkling lights could hopefully change everything. Maybe even bring parts of her memory back. Mr. Joy watched it fall onto her, sprinkling tiny glitter gently over her, creating a soft glow appearing to be almost like a halo. Cyril recalled three days before about the mysterious powers of stardust. Could it work on her memory loss? She held her hands out to watch glitter particles land then disappear into her skin deep into her memory. Then it occurred to her #4 should have read, "Stardust tonight will show you your past and imprint your memory back." Having never experienced the stardust, she wasn't sure what to expect.

The word "steam" came to the forefront of her mind loud and clear while staring up at him. Cyril said the words over and over in her head. Where were the words coming from? she wondered. She whispered the words again to herself, still searching for an answer. *Steam?* The word echoed inside her empty memory.

Flashing inside of her was a young boy crying. She ran into the room and put her arms around him.

Cyril looked to the sky with her arms out. "Where did that come from?" she whispered then looked at Mr. Joy.

"What do you mean where did what come from?" He had a puzzled look on his face.

"Oh, nothing. I think it was just a memory."

But this time, when he looked at her, he waited for an answer. Cyril saw that look before on his face. It stopped her cold. Was this another memory? For that moment, she knew him. Her heart screamed inside, *Remember me!* for no one to hear.

Confused, she thought, *Maybe I'm mistaken. God forbid it could be just a dream, perhaps only in my imagination.* She collected herself, putting on her most polite face and holding on to the past what little she could manage, even if it's a faint smell or just the look in his eye. It was comforting; but out of nowhere, how could this be happening if she didn't know him, or did she? she wondered.

"My name is Cyril," she said, holding her hand out for him to shake, trying to be formally polite. She was hoping he would hear her voice, then maybe their moments would flood back to him. But she wasn't a party to what was happening to him right then. Not even her name rang a bell.

His legs became weak. His statuesque form fell back like catching his breath. Then righting himself, his ankles crossed like going into a yoga pose. The six-foot-four statue dropped smoothly into a sitting position: Italian suit and all down to the lawn. Suddenly the guests thought something might be wrong with him. They gathered around him, sipping their champagne while trying to hear what was going on. Cyril noticed men in formal tuxedos with French cuff links. Some wore customary robes with flowing sleeves with delicate embroidering, all in their traditional home styles, so many cultures in one spot. Women floated in their finery, adorned with exquisite jewelry—all in the latest summer fashions from whatever their culture.

While he reviewed the contents of the bag, Cyril watched him gently get comfortable.

"Is your name Steam?" Cyril asked, sounding surprised and curious at the same time. It was a long shot, but one she felt confident in asking him. Would he play along with her question? His answer should be "No, I made it up," with a fair amount of sarcasm sprinkled in.

When we were children, it was the answer he always gave people. Cyril whispered it so only she could hear. *When we were children*, it echoed in her vacant mind. Still unable to take her eyes off him, Cyril could only wonder. Then out of nowhere, the thought of him teasing her. *The stardust*, she thought.

He would tease her about how deep her voice was for a girl. He had to remember her, especially the sound of her voice.

It's the stardust, she thought. Did she know him? *The stardust must be working*, she thought.

They were both teased often as children; she remembered they had that in common. She knew why he wanted people to call him Steve. Out of all the people here, she had a clear understanding of what he had gone through. Or at least what she could remember. Bits and pieces like puzzle pieces to put back into her mind. Some parts left by the wayside forgotten forever. At least until someone else picks them up and brings them back to you. If she was remembering, was he also?

His facial features slowly started to change as his head began to tilt to look down. Steam's eyes stayed fixed, concentrating on her shoes. *High heels? She would never wear shoes like that!* passed quickly through his mind. Then slowly, he began to look up her legs. He was examining her from her toes to her head.

He seemed so small now, looking at him at this angle. From the corner of her eye, she could see two men quickly approach them. Steam's left arm went out, his hand, flat fingers, straight palm down motioned for them to stop. The two men kept their distance as they watched on. The guests in all their finery formed a thick circle around them. The whispering crowd kept their distance, permitting Cyril and Steam with a comfortable space between them. It was almost like they were in a glass bubble; no one was favored to enter.

She could see puddles form in his eyes.

Looking back down at the bag's contents, almost childlike in disbelief, he asked her, almost in a whisper, "Where did you find this stuff?" His voice sounded like a curious child, one she remembered fondly. She almost wanted him to say it out loud to her again. Did she hear a child's voice in that question? She could swear she heard a child's voice, the child she once knew.

"It looked important, so I thought I'd try and find the owner."

What was I going on here? The initials on the top of the box, how did she know it was his? What was her first clue? Who was providing her with the answers? She knew the box was his. She would have staked her life on it. How could she be so sure? Where did these answers come from? Not from inside her, that she knew.

Again he asked, "Where did you find this stuff?"

Sincere and grateful in his tone, he looked up again, waiting for her to speak.

"So it is yours?" she said with skepticism, already knowing the correct answer.

Tilting his head slowly up and down, motioning yes, she gathered his reaction then began to explain, "The office manager said to keep the stuff I might need and get rid of the rest of the stuff. I was to make room for my things. That's when I came across boxes of things that looked familiar, but I didn't think they were mine. So I took out the good stuff, stuff I would have wanted to keep. I have other boxes I couldn't bring myself to throw away. They are in a closet in my office just in case I did find the owner. So it's all yours now!"

Cyril's office was piled high with childhood toys, school papers, and pictures he had drawn. One box had all his class pictures up to the time he left for college. Four or five boxes were nothing but trophies and ribbons, from football to track and field. He even had a few as tall as her from sailing. It was his childhood mingled in with her childhood, and all laid out for her to view. Someone put his life in that room for her to find. So she asked again, wanting to know, was it him?

"So is your name Steam? Do you sail?" she asked, looking at the top of his light-brown curls.

She knew he sailed. His father had taken them out many times. One time when they were six or seven, no older than that. The day could not have been more perfect. She remembered the water and wind. Steam's mom didn't come with them. She wasn't feeling well that day. Steam and Cyril packed tuna fish sandwiches and barbecued potato chips for lunch. It was what they always called their provisions. A military term they liked to use.

But now, at this moment, he almost seemed like a lost little boy who had just come in from a bad storm. His skin weathered and kissed harshly by the sun, his hands steady, he was happy and grateful at the same time.

"How did you know my name is Steam? No one calls me that," he remarked.

"Yes, they do behind your back," she quipped.

Cyril stood waiting to see if his mind could be somewhere in his past. Cyril looked directly into his eyes, nothing.

Steam stared back into the bag, reaching in; he pulled out a scarred wooden box, with the letters *SJ* deeply carved onto the top. All the brass corners and hinges ornately clutched the container, holding it together.

He looked up with a sad smile on his face. "Thank you." This was an adult thank you. Not one she heard a million times as a child, not a goofy one you tell your childhood best friend. He was an adult now with an adult mind, adult logic, adult memories. No room for childhood games like "Is your name Steam?" Still no sarcastic answer in return.

Was that more stardust still falling from the sky? How beautiful, she thought, the pieces almost looked bigger. Cyril could see memories flooding back to him. Every item in the box told his story; some of them included Cyril. Moments in his life he thought were forever gone. Now bits and little pieces of his childhood were packed neatly in the brown paper sack. She was lost somewhere inside herself as he was lost somewhere inside of her.

Yes, she said to herself, *I know him, but what do I know?*

"Why do they call you Steve and not Steam?" she asked, still looking down at him.

"It's a long, complicated story," he said with a sort of anguish as if he was talking to a stranger.

If she pried, could she get him to remember? So she asked again like any stranger feeling just a clue would be nice. Maybe even a hint, so with sarcasm, she said the next most common thing people used to say, "Who names their baby Steam?" shaking her head back and forth in wonder.

She could only guess what he must be thinking, but his mind was only about what was in the bag and nothing more. When he opened the box, a smile covered his face like a glow shining on him. His long tanned fingers traced the surface of the sextant, tracing twice over the wood that remained. The brass appeared to have been polished before it was placed to rest. Still beaming, she saw a tear fall from his right eye. There was the emotion she knew when they were eight, almost nine when his mother died.

Cyril noticed the dark red flashing lights shining on her bedroom ceiling. Grabbing her windowsill, she peered out of the cold glass looking toward Steam's house. She counted three police cars and one ambulance; some officers stood in front of his house, jotting things down, taking notes. It was early morning with a thick layer of frost on the grass; the sidewalks were slippery from the cold. The morning sun had just broken through the trees.

She couldn't remember if she put on her robe and slippers. She felt herself running as fast as she could. The ambulance driver stopped her as she ran into Steam's house. She dashed past the gurney right when his mother's body was taken to the ambulance. Cyril's back was flat against the door as she watched. She watched his mother leave for the last time. It was a big black plastic bag; a large zipper went up the middle, enclosing her inside. Her feet left the house first. You could tell where her head was. As quickly as she could, Cyril ran in to find Steam. Past the police then past Miss Lyn, the housekeeper. She was sitting in the hall crying uncontrollably, looking up. She held her hand out to grab Cyril; she said, "No, no, not good time for visit, no, not good time for you!" She waved her hand for Cyril to come to her, holding a tea towel in the other, wiping her tears.

Miss Lyn saw the look on Cyril's face then waved the tea towel toward the stairs. As fast as Cyril could, she ran up the stairs down the hall past more police, all looking like they were doing something important. She pushed the door wide open into Steam's bedroom.

They're sitting on the floor alone against his bed. Steam's head was down, his knees up. Cyril stood in the doorway. She could hear him crying. Slowly his head went up, looking over his arm at Cyril; his eyes fixed on her. Tears filled her eyes as she approached him; he grabbed her and wouldn't let her go.

Her heart was breaking for him and the pain he must be going through. He told her over and over again, "You're all I have left! My mother's gone. She's never coming back, never. She's never coming back. You're all I have left."

Cyril lightly brushed her hand across his cheeks, wiping his tears. "You're going to be all right, I promise you. Everything is going to be all right. Everything is going to be all right."

Inside she wasn't sure if what she was saying to him was true or not. She had never been away from her parents. No one in her family had ever left her, let alone died. She had nothing to compare to the way he was feeling. His father let Cyril stay for three days. Her parents even stopped in to check on them. They dropped off food, including the tuna fish sandwiches wrapped in wax paper with barbecued potato chips they had both enjoyed.

Then as quickly as the moment came, it was gone. Cyril caught herself staring at the top of Steam's head while he looked intently at the sextant.

"It's just how I left it. I thought it was gone forever," Steam whispered. He was talking to no one but himself. Steam held the weathered wooden box open. He was filling his memories with moments, learning to sail with his grandfather. Seeing his mother's long thick auburn hair whip in the wind, he remembered how she always had such a sweet smile on her face while on the water.

"So you do sail?" Cyril still tried to get into his past, trying to find him. "So this stuff is yours, right?" she repeated the question.

Not getting an answer, she then realized the pain it must have all brought on. Cyril knew it was his. His emotions gave her that answer. Now she wanted to walk away. She tried to stop how she felt.

Seeing him in this state, she needed space, then she realized they were the center of attention. The crowd around them was silent, trying to hear their every word.

Whispering in the background caught her attention. Looking up, no one looked familiar. She needed to go. She needed to sort out what was happening to her, who he was, and most of all, who was she to him.

Cyril laughed inside for a moment when she heard the violins and cellos in the distance. "Strangers in the Night." She knew the words and how they all fit so well into the moment. Strangers exchanging glances. Who were these people, and who were they to her?

Suddenly looking down at her right hand, Cyril saw and felt something gently holding her. When she looked at her hand, she jerked back quickly to avoid it. Still holding her hand was a strange greenish-gray hand with exceptionally long pointed fingers. The tips of the fingers curled inward, caressing her gently, then rolling out straight, almost like a pulsing rhythm, rolling in, rolling out. Cyril could only capture the moment as she watched and stared motionlessly. The foreign hand was something she had never seen before. She should be afraid. It was strange, almost reptilian, as she watched the fingertips curl inward then lay out flat against her skin. It almost appeared like it was purring in its slow rhythm. It wasn't warm nor cold. It was just there touching her skin, similar to velvet.

Containing herself, she repeated over and over again, "Relax, just relax." It's the dust. Then if that's the dust, that was part of her memory. What was this?

"Oh my god." She spoke to no one. What the hell was that? The memory was gone, but the feeling upon her skin remained. The touch was almost cool once it left her skin. A thought was left inside her, that of caring and hope. Then the feeling was gone like it was deliberately taken from her.

Realizing Mr. Joy's time was expensive and that she was lucky to find him here, she said finally, "I'm glad I could find you. It wasn't easy to catch you. You're a busy man. I asked your secretary. She was of no help. One of your employees told me you came to this event last year. So on a fluke, I thought you might be here this year."

Bewildered, he asked, "How long have you had this stuff?"

"Three weeks!"

"Three weeks and no one would tell you how to get a hold of me!"

"Yes, that's right. It took a lot of digging. I did have help from another employee.

"Look, I have to go. I'm meeting some friends. I have to figure out how to find them." She collected herself and started to turn away, and the crowd looked up at her to see her next move.

He didn't look up. He didn't move. Softly he said, "Your invitation will tell you where your friends are. Do you have your invitation?"

"No, it's in my car. I was just going to get it."

Keeping his concentration on the contents of the bag, he asked, "Are you staying for the announcements and dinner? There will be dancing later. May I have the first dance?"

Now looking up at her, his eyes centered on hers. His demeanor changed. He looked like they were long-lost friends, like he was happy she was back in his life and that they needed more time to be acquainted. Still, the look was like he was grasping at straws, like maybe it was just wishful thinking. She wanted him to remember her. She wanted him to see her, the woman standing in front of him right now, not the little girl with pigtails and skinned knees with calamine lotion smeared all over her as he would point to touch her like she was on fire. She wanted to remember him. She also wanted to be remembered. With all the fragments, seeing his face, him pointing at her laughing. The moments she remembered, did he remember them also? "I'm sorry, but I have to go. I'm late, and I'm never late."

Looking around her, she remembered the footpath following the long row of trees. That's how she would get back to her car if she could just get through this crowd.

His voice suddenly stopped her.

Steam looked up. "How can I thank you? Please tell me how I can thank you."

She heard a pleading in his voice, one she felt warm to. A small part of his childhood remained in his voice, a moment left inside her.

"Just the look on your face is thanks enough. Really just to see your response is enough. Maybe I'll see you later on tonight."

A pain radiated inside her chest at his coldness. Cyril's Steam would have grabbed her like a rag doll and held her in his arms as you would to a buddy you lost. She got none of that.

Slowly the banding crowd around them parted out of her way. Seeing the footpath at the edge of the trees, she collected herself then started to walk away.

She stopped dead in her tracks, catching her sharp heel again in the soft grass. She could see herself falling and skinning both her knees all over again. Then suddenly, out of nowhere, a hand came out gently and securely, stopping her from falling. The smooth strength lifted her, setting her right, easing her jolt. Her thumb felt the hair across the fingers. The warmth on the skin and a waft of the surrounding scent comforted her. At the moment of the touch, she thought she saw two soft blue lights flash in front of her. Not looking to see who it was, she remarked, "Thank you," pulling her heel from the soft grass. She quickly walked on to the other end of the trees, now out of Steam's sight.

Steam sat there still on the soft grass while closing the box. Reaching into the bag, Steam pulled out a round blue leather pouch cinched at one end, pulling the dark blue cord to open it. Inside looking brand new was a polished brass compass. The weightless arrow swung around then pointed north. Under the black steel arrow was an intricately painted woman's face. Big round blue eyes, the color of the sea was looking back at him. Her full lips a rosy red, in his mind, "Stop, pay attention." She was smiling at him. He remembered his grandfather said, "This is Mother Nature. Be kind to her. She will show you your way." The shiny metal felt cold in his hand.

Then he remembered his tenth birthday party. That afternoon Cyril and all the kids from their class were there. Strewed dead balloons, wrapping paper, ribbons, uneaten cake everywhere. He remembered his father kept saying, "Never again, never again."

Turning the compass over, he read the engraved inscription as his face again beamed with happiness. It read, "Go in the direction of your dreams. Love, Grandpa Steam."

It was a long way to the other side of the park. Cyril had told her friends from work she would try to meet up with them. Earlier, she noticed the other guests holding their invitations, a small illuminated card she had forgotten in her car. It was mandatory to bring for security reasons. Also, it would tell her where her table and friends were sitting. But why was she let in without it, and why wasn't she stopped from entering? Maybe bring the invitation should have been #4, she wondered.

The party was impressive, mostly because of where it was at, out in the middle of nowhere.

In the distance was the sound of helicopters still landing; people were still arriving from who knows where. The sun was just about to set, and the sky was an orangish gold. She had always tried to look at the sun setting to catch the second it turns green, and then it's gone. She couldn't remember who told her she did that...someone who knew her well. Cyril missed it tonight as she watched it pierce the dusk.

She thought about how worried she had been over the last few days, thinking she would never get a chance to give the bag to him, but this encounter changed everything. She needed to get back to her car to think and to try to put her pieces together. She had questions that needed answers, like how did she get here? She couldn't even remember applying for this job, let alone getting the job. And why did they let her in without her invitation? What kind of security was this?

At the end of the path, a drone approached her and softly asked her, "Where can I take you?"

"I need to go to my car," Cyril said clearly so there was no misunderstanding.

The soft male voice took a moment to read her then said, "Cyril, you're in section 37A. We will arrive there in two minutes." Floating along the outskirts of the canyon area, she could see Steam in the distance. The crowd still gathered around him. Or would she call him

Steve like everyone else? The crowd watched him as he pulled other memories out of the bag.

Cyril thought it rare to see Steam out in public. She hadn't seen him since he moved away with his father a few years after his mother died. Was that the stardust again?

Cyril heard the employees' stories of wild encounters along with how mysterious Steam was. His reputation always lingered long after he left the building. He was like a mirage: the stories they heard were unbelievable. One story was about a close friend of his who had a relationship with the Grays. They got into a fight one night with the Grays when they were kids. Steam's friend tried to introduce him to the Grays for the first time, and it didn't go well. His friend used to play with them as a child. That was the night Steam found out that the Grays, or what his friends would call little green men, were living among us. It was hard for him to believe, but they were both visited continuously by those strange little men often. A person once said, "Haven't you ever been in bed and you couldn't move or speak? Then the next thing you know, two to six hours later, you're back in bed, looking up at your ceiling, wondering where the time went." His close friend once said, "You can't judge something you know nothing about. You need to take time to understand them first before you can change what's happening around you." Rumor has it the friend to this day still contacts them regularly. People would say a lot of crazy things about Steam and his friend. He's Steam, kind of invisible but everywhere.

Looking at the edge of the park, thinking about how he seemed grateful, inside she felt happy and hurt strangely at the same time. She understood how vital things of sentimental value were to her. Those things linked her to her past, a past she didn't have anymore. To see Steam drop to the ground and cry right there in front of all those people. Okay, maybe they didn't know about that tear, but she did, and that's big, that's really big.

The drone stopped. The soft voice asked, "Should I wait for you? Are you going back?"

She answered back, "Please, just a minute. I need to find something." The drone hovered, keeping its lights on, and waited for her, not leaving her in total darkness.

Digging through her stuff inside the car, she tried to find her invitation. The minute she thought, *Where's my invitation?* a small glow came from under a stack of binders and folders from work. The invitation became illuminated so she could read it in the dark. Little red illuminated arrows directed her to her table. The invitation highlighted a picture of her table with a massive bouquet of soft pastel pink orchids and light-orange spikes of gladiolus. At that moment, it showed the people sitting at the table drinking their champagne, talking, and looking around at the other guests. Once the drone dropped her off back at the event, small arrows directed her toward her table. She scanned for her bouquet through the ocean of tables. She saw purple violets and white roses, red dahlias and pink peonies, yellow sunflowers, and green chrysanthemums—every combination you could come up with. Then a few yards from the creek, there were the pink and orange flowers that marked her table. Every table had a beautiful fragrant bouquet.

As she approached the table, her coworker Mimsie saw her from a distance and came walking quickly over to her. Cyril could see Mimsie's high heels stabbing into the lawn like she was aerating it. The soft powder-blue silk organza of her dress floated in the air around her, making it almost invisible. This woman knew her planets and beyond. She had studied every aspect of them.

"What did you do to him? He has people looking for you everywhere!" Mimsie said as her head tossed back and forth, looking for the two men.

"You mean Steam, our boss." Cyril scrunched her nose in disbelief.

"Yes, you gave him the bag, finally. Was it his?" She too had wondered for three weeks who was the owner.

"Yes, it was. I'm surprised how glad Steam was to get it."

Cyril kept her feelings to herself. She couldn't let on how she knew him. Their stations in life had dramatically changed. Steam's was so far above hers. How could she have ever known him, and who was he now? Suddenly out of nowhere, two men approached her.

"Excuse me, is your name Cyril?"

Mimsie's elbow indiscreetly gave her a jab, nodding. "Oh, here they are. These are the guys looking for you," she said as both her hands went out to present Cyril like a gift.

They asked her as if they already knew the answer. The shorter of the two asked while the other looked off in the other direction.

"Yes." These had to be Steam's men, she thought.

"My name is Westlund. This is Atwood. We work for Mr. Joy. Mr. Joy would like to talk to you. Can you come with us to his table?" Westlund held his hand out, directing her toward the foot-bridge just yards away from her table.

Westlund fit in nicely. Black suit tailored, expensive fabric fit perfect. He appeared to be polished with manners. His height was 5'8" at most. He walked with confidence, sounded educated, held his head high, had tanned manicured hands, and had a simple thick tight silver bracelet around his left wrist, perfect teeth, and friendly smile. She couldn't be sure if he was threatening or not. Was that his personality showing keeping her unsure?

For some crazy reason, Cyril didn't like the sound of those words put together like that. "Come with us." Why did it sound so ominous? She needed to keep her control. She needed to act on how she felt. Cyril just needed to relax.

Kind of surprised at their names, she asked, "Are those your first names or your last names?"

"Both first names, ma'am," Atwood replied. Atwood was tall, maybe 6'2", beauty marks on the outside lower left eye, probably worked out in a gym somewhere, bald, no facial hair, looked you in the eye when he talked to you. Atwood was wearing an impeccably tailored black suit to fit his muscular form. He had a friendly smile. Again, Cyril was unsure if he was threatening or not. Strong hands. He might have clear nail polish on. She couldn't be sure. Italian leather shoes might be custom made. *Nice package*, Cyril said to herself after examining him.

"Please don't call me ma'am. Cyril, just Cyril, okay?"

"Yes, ma'am, sorry. Yes, Cyril."

"Right now, I'm going to get something to eat and enjoy the moment. Please tell Steam maybe later on this evening. I'm hungry and tired. It was a long drive, okay? Thank you."

She thought they would leave once she said thank you in a way to dismiss them, but they just stood there. Stunned, both men walked over to the small footbridge that separated part of the festivities. Both men not knowing how to respond, she guessed no one told Steam no. She watched the two men. The short man was talking to his board. *I'm sure explaining to Steam why I'm not coming.* Westlund held his board up toward her; he must be showing Steam where she's sitting. Atwood clutched his hands still like a pillar of stone, not looking at her but looking at everything around her.

In the distance, the music softly surrounded the area coming from maybe the stage. Playing in the background was a familiar tune. Cyril heard the words in her head, a song by Sting. "I'll be watching you," the lyrics played in her head. She heard the words coming to her like a message from a long-lost lover whispering in her ear, "Every move you make, every vow…" It stopped her. Every word was a message she heard before clearly from someone while they looked into her eyes. Stunned, all she could do was listen.

Just ahead, a vast ebony dance floor was softly lit around the edges with small torches, flames reflecting off the shiny, invisible black surface.

The stars sparkled on the surface like large glittery diamonds. The sea of white tablecloths was like clouds dotting the surface. A beautiful bouquet graced each table in a colorful softness.

Cyril looked closely at tiny small particles of stardust still falling from the sky.

Suddenly feeling the heat from the desert, a gentle breeze touched you the minute you felt warm, cooling you gently. Suddenly out of nowhere, waiters wearing black-and-white tuxedos with one white towel across their arm appeared holding large trays. Suddenly every table, every person had their plate set in front of them at the same time. Even their drinks appeared at the same time. It was all so precisely done. She couldn't begin to count all the tables and how many people were at each table. Their waiters draped white cloth napkins over their laps. Then they were asked if there was anything else they might need. Then as quickly as they came with their food and drinks, they were gone. The music changed. It seemed softer and gentle, almost like it was coming from above them or maybe around them now. She couldn't be sure. Seven of them were at the table.

Mimsie was to Cyril's right with her husband, Wen. She had coal-black hair, transparent white skin, almost like she had never gone outside or seen the sun. She stood maybe 5'5", curvy with a sweet personality. She's in First Eleven Section 1 or F111, a department having to do with the planets around them.

Cindy, to Cyril's left, blond, 5'8", family first, couldn't weigh over 140 on a bad day, loved her job, and nothing shocked or surprised her. She worked in Anomalies Earth 1 or AE1. Her department was odd. Anything you have trouble trying to explain on earth went to her. It was a lot of fun hearing the new stuff. She brought her daughter Megan. Across from Cyril was Norie, 5'11", a very handsome man. He worked in Not from Earth 1 or NFE1. It was interesting going into his department. A lot of the stuff that happened there was hauntingly familiar to Cyril. Norie's wife was very tall for a woman, maybe 6'3". Her name was Alice.

Mimsie couldn't stop talking about the men standing at the footbridge.

"They're waiting for you. You know that, don't you? He's having them wait till we're all finished eating, then what do you think happens?" She waited for Cyril's answer.

Norie looked at Cyril and pointed his fork toward her. "I can't believe you got him to sit on the ground," he said as he began to laugh out loud. His ultrawhite shirt and teeth contrasted against his beautiful dark Indian skin.

"Steve," his wife interjected, "Steve, are you kidding? I can't believe you were able to surprise him like that! Nobody gets things past him, nobody!"

Cindy told them all, "Tonight we're calling him Steam." She waited for them to agree, nodding yes, when suddenly her eyes followed the stardust floating in the air. Cyril also watched the particles, keeping it to herself, but wondered why anyone wasn't saying anything about it. Cindy was the only person she noticed who looked right at it.

Norie held the conversation, still orchestrating it with his fork. "No, his name is Steve. Don't say that out loud. It's Steve or Mr. Joy. Do we all understand? I'm serious, you guys, this is important. Do we all understand? I hope those guys don't tell him what we're saying about him."

Cyril looked at Norie. "I called him Steam right to his face. He either didn't hear me, or he was too wrapped up in what was in the bag." Cyril had always called him Steam. It's his name. She knew him by nothing else, she said quietly to herself. "I asked him why we call him Steve instead of Steam. He said it was complicated, a long story, but I got no answer from him."

Cyril looked around the table once the servers were gone. Every plate was different.

Mimsie had some kind of fettuccine pasta in a light-green sauce with cheese sprinkled over it. Her husband, Wen, had shellfish-like cioppino legs and claws sticking out of a huge white bowl with another plate of sour French bread with iced butter.

Cindy's plate was colorful, with grill marks on fresh garden vegetables, while her daughter had a bacon cheeseburger and fries. Norie's plate was piled high with saffron rice and spicy lamb, while Alice had what looked like a Cobb salad, everything you could put in a salad on a large platter.

Cyril's dish had a three-inch-high elk filet mignon seared perfectly. It sat on top of garlic and sun-ripened tomatoes in polenta next to barbecued zucchini rounds burnt just right. It was perfect.

"Polenta," she repeated to herself as she watched the water start to boil in the pot in front of her, her hand stirring in a circular motion. A hand came in front of her, broadcasting salt across the water surface. "Keep stirring," the voice came from behind her, filling her memory. "Do you think the water's ready?" the voice behind her asked.

"Yes."

"Okay, here it comes, so stir fast. Don't let it get any lumps," he said as he poured the dry polenta in slowly. He turned, taking two signif-icant cuts of butter off the cutting board, drop-ping them into the yellow paste. Then two big handfuls of grated cheese were sprinkled over the top. Cyril looked over to him while still stirring. "I love how you make this stuff."

Cyril's eyes blinked as she looked around. Who was she making polenta with? Who was that man? The stardust, she thought and smiled. Everyone at the table was silent, their eyes closed, savor-ing every bite. Cyril took her last bite and leaned back in her chair. Comfortable, not stuffed. She took in the moment, not wanting to forget any part of the evening. Glad inside that she had reconsidered, not wanting to come by herself. Cyril had decided at the last minute to go but only because of the bag and only because he might be here. Cindy insisted, in her gently forceful way, "It would be good for you to participate in the company's biggest yearly event."

Even if Cyril was only there for less than a month. Cindy was the one who researched Steam, finding out if he would be there or not. She was also kind enough to go shopping with Cyril to find something to wear at the last minute. Not knowing Cindy for very long, Cyril felt very comfortable in her company. There was an uncanny sense that she knew her. Once in a while, they would even joke, "Are you sure we haven't met before, maybe in a previous life?" Now that Cyril thought about it, she would always just smile and laugh but not answer her.

Off in the distance, in front of the dance floor, was Steam's table. Cyril didn't recognize the two men sitting with Steam. Also at the table were three empty chairs; maybe those guests weren't coming or late.

To Steam's left was Ezek. He watched Cyril at a distance, notic-ing the two men at the footbridge waiting for her. Ezek, grabbing his long thick black beard, stroking it downward, asked Steam, "Why are A and W over there? Are they waiting for her? Did you send them?" His eyes went up with a glare, waiting.

"Yes, I had them ask her to come and join us. She refused. Hey, don't call them A and W. It's Atwood and Westlund, okay? You know, I haven't seen her since her accident. I can't begin to tell you how much I've missed her. It's been hard not having her here. I saw her in Stockholm at the Karolinska Hospital, where she was recovering. You were right to send her there. She got the best of care, but they couldn't help her. The tests were so hard on her. Nothing helped, no explanations of what it is. It was hard to see her lying there, helpless. She never came to while I was there. I don't think she even knew I was there waiting for her to wake up. I was there for only a few days." Steam looked in her direction, remembering the moment.

To Steam's right was Sven. He looked over to Steam and asked, "With all the tests they ran on her, you think something would have come of it? Is she on any medications? So you think it was an accident, huh?"

Ezek held his beard then asked Steam, "The part I don't understand is why you haven't contacted her all this time. Come on, man, she's your friend!"

"I wasn't allowed. I got my orders. Cyril's very stubborn. She doesn't like to take pills, so no, she's not on any medication. Come on, man, she was working when it happened. My orders were not to disturb her or distract her in any way while she was recovering. I don't think what happened to her was an accident. I think it was to stop her from speaking at the forum. We still have no idea what they used or who did it," Steam admitted, not liking how it was out of his control.

Ezek turned to Steam. "But you guys are old friends. What's wrong with showing her you're there for her? I saw how you treated her when she gave you the bag. Aren't you even glad to see her? You never answered one question she asked you. You didn't even acknowledge that you knew her. What kind of game is that? You, of all people, know she doesn't like games. She has always shot straight with you. What's going on?"

Steam felt for a moment like Ezek was poking him with a sharp stick and not caring about the repercussions.

"Of course I'm glad to see her. You forget we spent a lot of time together. It's complicated." Steam's words drifted off as he stared over in her direction.

"That's your answer to everything: it's complicated." Sounding frustrated, Ezek stared back at him.

"You don't understand. She doesn't remember most of what has happened. It was made clear to me it would take time. She's not even able to program her car and make it to work by herself. She's almost independent. If it weren't for Tully, we would have to put her in a facility. She still has big pieces missing. It's hard to see her like this. I can't fix it. That's why she gets so frustrated at home and work. That's why she's here. Hopefully, tonight will make a difference. Some of her life will come back to her."

Ezek dropped his head then took a deep breath, holding tightly on to his beard. "Yes, I know she doesn't recognize anyone. Each day she gets new memories, but nothing from her past. Now that makes sense." Apparent stress saturated his tone as he looked over in her direction again.

Sven closed his eyes and then opened them, looking directly into the sky. "You're giving her the stars tonight, aren't you? That's why she's here. That's why the dust is following her." He stood up quickly, almost in a rage.

Ezek looked at Steam. "How much of this does she remember?" Deep in his mind, Ezek knew she could never ever forget him. For a moment, could it be true or just his own personal vanity?

Steam softly said to Sven, "Please sit down. Let me explain. She's just now starting to remember me, and that's in small fragments." He turned, facing Ezek. "I'm not sure how you're going to take this, man. I know how much she means to you and how you have cared for her all these years, but she doesn't remember you at all."

Was he saying it to be mean, or was it a fact? Ezek tried to sort the unbelievable information. He knew her, and who she was now was a sharp contrast to who she once was. Deep inside, she had to be there somewhere. No one could reach her. She just needed to be found, maybe even rescued.

Sven looked off in her direction then asked, "I haven't seen Mikel or Virginia. Aren't her parents coming this evening?"

In disbelief, Ezek snapped, his voice raised. "So that explains it. I took her hand this evening while she walked away from you. Her heel was stuck in the grass. I stopped her from falling. I took her hand. I thought if I touched her, she would feel me. All she did was thank me. She never even looked up." He shook his head. "She never even looked up. She doesn't know who we are. I could walk right up to her, and she wouldn't recognize me. She has no idea of all the things she has done, her accomplishments, her sacrifices. How she's made a difference."

"Man, look at you. Sometimes I don't even recognize who you are. Relax, man, you know I don't think I have ever seen this much hair on your face, let alone your head. Your hair has never been this long, has it? I've known you forever. What's going on with you? Have you heard from her parents? I don't think anyone has." Steam waited for him to respond or maybe even react.

"No, her parents are still off the radar. I was hoping they would show up tonight, but no word still. Hey, when are you going to tell her who her real boss is? I'd like to be there for that moment just to see the expression on her face. No, really, I want to see how she's going to respond to that. Why can't something be done to help her? Steam, this has gone on for way too long." Ezek rubbed his thick eyebrows, holding his forehead in disbelief. It couldn't escape him.

"I've been with her most of her life. I feel I'm a part of her. How can that just be erased?"

Anguish and pain distorted Ezek's face. Then with both hands, he covered his face, collecting himself.

Steam understood Ezek's and Sven's anguish. "It's important tonight. She will see her past. It will come from the stardust. It will come at random. There's no telling how she might respond. So keep your eyes peeled. She might need our help. Depending on what she sees and experiences, it will seem like only seconds to us. To her, it could last minutes, maybe even hours, even up to weeks similar to dreaming. She will be inside her moment. It will be like she's right there, reliving it all over again. I'm going to her table. I've asked her for the first dance."

The table went silent as they all remembered their moments with her.

Sven asked, "Will she remember everything?" Concern more than curiosity in his voice, Ezek noticed. Ezek turned and waited with Sven for Steam's answer.

"No one knows. It's been almost two years since it happened. If Cyril could only tell us who did this to her and why. Whoever it is, they need to be caught. It has to be someone she knows to get that close to her. What was used is not from this Earth, so it's hard to say how to reverse it. So tonight, we'll try stardust. It started falling on her the minute she got here. The tiny bit of dust started first, then bigger particles will happen on the dance floor. I have everything ready, but just in case, please be prepared to help. I'm not sure how she's going to handle it. Maybe if she sees you later this evening, it will be easier for her. I know all her reports show there are six people she misses the most. The thing is, she doesn't even know it." Steam kept it to himself; he just couldn't let Sven know he wasn't on that list.

Ezek looked up. "But Cindy is sitting at her table. She hasn't put that together yet either?"

"No, she has no idea who she is." Steam looked over to the creek.

Ezek paused, then asked, "What have you told Cindy?"

"She is to act like they meet here until her memory returns. She's kept a close eye on her, helping her adjust to her new job. All of this has been very hard on Cindy. She told me she has so much to talk to her about but can't. So much of their conversations are classified. She said it's hard seeing her like this. She wants to help get her back also."

Ezek almost interrupted. "Is that why you moved her office next to hers? You didn't change anything in her office, did you? She did some of her best work there." Ezek just tried to put the pieces together.

"I needed her to be comfortable here, so it's just a start, and no, her office is just like she left it. The only thing I've changed is I took her name off the door."

Ezek looked Steam in the eyes. "Man, when she snaps out of this, she's going to be pissed. We all know what that's like. I don't want to be here for that moment. The first thing she's going to ask is why did it take us, and I mean all of us, why did it take us so long?" Then Ezek stopped and lowered his voice. "I'm glad she went back into her home. I've been watching her from a distance, and she's happy there. It's very confusing for her. We spent a lot of time there, as she would call it her happy place. Tully's been on top of it. She's been very patient. It's not easy for Cyril to be around someone that can't hear. But she knew that when she hired her years ago, they have always been close until this. Thanks to Tully, she's keeping things together."

"What do you mean you've been watching her?" Steam snapped with a sharp tone.

"Yes, like I have watched her most of her life most of the time. She doesn't see me."

Steam's tone of voice changed. "And when she sees you in her house, what the hell happens then? How do you explain that to her? What do you say then?"

Ezek smiled and remembered all the moments in her life when they were together alone while he was her big brother and guide. "I let her only remember me as a dream-like when we were children. It was so easy then." He recalled watching her get ready for the party that day. It surprised him she was wearing makeup and a dress but most shockingly high-heeled shoes, making her much taller than she had ever been before. In her bare feet, she stood all of 5'3". He watched her study her face before applying her makeup. She found that purple made her green eyes pop. He found it fascinating only because she had never put makeup on before. "Makeup, who has time for that girly stuff?" she would say. When she held the dress up to herself, admiring it in the mirror, Ezek noticed a proud look upon her face. The look told him she had made the right decision on her dress choice. He had only seen her in a formal frilly girly dress once before. It dawned on him that he didn't know her anymore; this was the new person she had become. Where was his Cyril? he wondered.

Over the months and years, Ezek couldn't shake the feeling of loss like someone had died. "That's why I can't believe she doesn't remember me. I never erased any part of her memory. I put it all into a dream. She's aware there is that fine line that has separated us." For that moment, he regretted all their moments he had to shelve into her dream section. How he wanted her to remember it all, every joyous, every tragic, every quiet, every warm moment with him. He kept it all locked inside him, never to forget her like she had forgotten him.

"Please wait, don't rush this. I need her! I need her back the way she used to be. It all has to be done right." Ezek almost sounded like he was pleading with Steam like maybe Steam might even have some kind of control over the matter.

"So we all agree this has to go well tonight. I have to make my announcements. Then I'm going to ask Cyril to dance. The minute we're dancing, the larger pieces of stardust will start dropping. Those pieces will open her memory and stay. So whatever she sees will be put back into her memory but only that moment, not all the details that go with it. The dust that's been following her has so far only confused her. I'll explain this all to her once we're dancing."

Ezek looked down, then slowly tilting his head, he looked from under his thick eyebrows at Steam. "Let me get this straight: you're going to explain what's happening to her while she's dancing? Why don't we all just sit down and discuss it like we would in one of her meetings? That's not the way Cyril would have planned it. She would have wanted the person to know what was going to happen to them before it happened, or maybe she just doesn't like surprises like everybody else?" Ezek's voice was loud and clear, heard by many of the surrounding tables. Still in a lather, Ezek looked at Sven. "So you're okay with her seeing you for the first time in one of her dust moments. Let's hope she gets all the right details first before she's dropped into a moment that could mess with her mind. Man, you guys, she's been through a lot. Cyril's done a lot of really messed-up stuff and might not look so good out of context. I don't want her to think she's a monster. Let's face it, we all have a monster inside us.

Hers always came out for a good reason. I'm not sure the person she is now will know that person exists inside of her. I'm not sure she can handle that. Who she is now is very different from who she used to be."

Steam knew Ezek was right and could see he was trying to protect her like he always had.

"Will she remember everything with the stardust?" Sven asked again, seeking an answer he wasn't sure he wanted. "Is it possible she'll remember us after that?"

"I can't be sure. We still don't understand what happened and why her memory is void, but if it's what I think it is, she should get some of it back. We just don't know what parts." Steam looked directly at Sven.

Placed in front of Cyril appeared a small stemmed glass. Delicate cut crystal Waterford, perhaps? Inside the glass seemed to be frozen sheets of thinly shaved ice, like small square pieces of clear glass, sharp at the edges. She noticed the delicate sheets of ice didn't seem to melt in the surrounding warm temperature. No liquid formed at the bottom of the glass, no condensation, leaving her to think she didn't need to hurry and try it before it melted. By touch, it felt ice-cold. Whatever it was, it was refreshingly light like snowflakes on her tongue. It melted quickly once touched. Cyril remembered hearing the flavor was discovered by NFE1. They all got to try it if they wanted to. It would be the first time NFE1 introduced the dessert to the public. She thought the taste was truly heavenly; how refreshing!

Flashing in her mind like a memory, she saw the gray hand and the fingers unfurl again. This time the thought was comfort and tranquility. What was it? She also wondered, still thinking about how she reacted the first time, not afraid. The touch this time had no temperature of its own, not cool or warm, just there. As she saw it in front of her, it became strangely familiar. Then suddenly it was gone.

In the distance across the creek, the music stopped. The enormous screen on the stage slowly turned to the color green focusing, showing billions of tiny blades of grass whispering in the wind. Then it appeared to change into a very calm ocean; small white caps showed its current movement.

Then while looking at it, you realized it had changed again. What appeared to be soft clouds in the sky suddenly darkened, becoming galaxies. Now it was space, outer space. Stars and planets and galaxies went on forever.

Colors so beautiful and vibrant, real pictures coming in live feeds that very moment from satellites belonging to the company. Everyone looked in that direction except Atwood and Westlund. Both men were waiting at the footbridge.

Then a man began to speak. It was Steam. He seemed so tiny next to the enormous screen. His voice was commanding, making you want to hear him, almost hypnotic, soothing in a way. He started by saying, "I hope everyone is having a wonderful time. How was the food? I thought it was amazing how they served us all at once." Sounding surprised, he commented, "My dinner was perfect. Hey, thank you all for coming." He clasped his hands in front of him. "As you can see, we have friends from all over the planet. Thank you for coming from so far away." Steam held his arms out wide to the audience. He walked to the left of the stage toward Cyril's table. Then he stopped and said, "This evening, someone asked if my name is really Steam or Steve. For the record, to answer that question"— Steam pointed to the crowd—"and you know who you are! Yes, my real name is Steam. No, it's not a nickname. I was named after my grandfather on my mother's side."

Cyril got the strange impression she was the only one he was talking to at that moment. Almost like he was asking for his past back. Steam was his past.

"Before I get any more sidetracked, I need everyone to pick up their invitations. What did you think of the dessert from NFE1? Did everyone enjoy that? I found it very refreshing, so I thought it would be nice to share it with all of you. Okay, on the invitation will appear a question on it with multiple-choice answers. There's no right or wrong answers. Just your opinion, that's all we're looking for, so go ahead and touch your answer.

"We'll be collecting your answers right now. Behind me are the findings." The enormous screen showed the four answers and the percentage that answered each. The question was "What does the shaved ice taste like to you?"

1. Lemon 12 percent
2. Salami 14 percent
3. Dirt 0 percent
4. Licorice 74 percent

Norie shot Cyril a sharp look while he watched her see the percentages. She was not to know what the meanings were. No one was, but judging by the look on her face, she did know.

Norie's face had a sort of panic look on it, almost like he was reading her expression. Then his head motioned in an ever-so-short *no*, shaking back and forth so only she could see. She signaled back to him with a disgusting answer of okay, kind of rolling her eyes toward him. She was mentally letting him know she won't say a word that she knew what this all meant.

She thought to herself, reiterating Steam's words. He did say he also found it refreshing. They both found it refreshing; that meant they were the 12 percent. She looked around to see who else could be a part of that 12 percent, but how could you tell? Wasn't that the point of this so-called dessert? She knew each card was reporting the answer. Also, it said who was answering it. Steam talked for almost twenty-five minutes. He went on about the projects, the success that had occurred during the year, and new funding than exploration. Then he awarded individuals from different departments for their inventions and their discoveries. Then he came to the moment of the night, the breakthroughs. When Steam finished speaking, each employee's invitation illuminated in front of them. Their fingerprint affirming it was them releasing all their personal information for them to view. It was showing their yearly bonus, which had just been deposited into their account. It offered everything about them when they started, what department they worked in, the discoveries, and their breakthroughs.

Cyril's was short, having started three weeks ago. There at the bottom of her card was a note written in beautiful red old-fashioned cursive: "I am deeply in your debt. I can't begin to thank you enough. May I have the first dance? Steam J."

Cyril looked around the table, seeing smiles on everyone's faces as they read their cards. Steam thanked everyone for coming and insisted they all have a wonderful evening as he stepped off the stage. The screen behind him showed live satellite feeds. They displayed everything the company satellites were viewing that very moment. It was beautiful and fascinating. Space like you could reach out and touch it. The guests all clapped and watched him walk offstage as their eyes all followed Steam to his table.

He stopped for a quick moment, dropping something off. Then he kept moving. He was going somewhere, weaving through the table shaking hands with guests. He came to the footbridge. Standing there for a moment, he talked to Westlund and Atwood. His head went up, and he saw her. That very moment, everyone at Cyril's table looked past her, which told her someone was behind her. Cyril took a deep breath for a second.

She thought she saw two blue lights blur quickly by her. Blinking her eyes to focus, she waited for him to approach. A gentle breeze wafted his scent toward her, and it was almost hypnotic. Did he do that on purpose? she wondered as she was stuck in her chair. Coming around so she could see him, he asked, "So how was your dinner? Did they prepare it the way you prefer?" Towering over her, she felt small and insignificant.

Looking up, Cyril said, "Yes, it was perfect, just what I thought it should be."

He thought about what she said and tilted his head, for that moment they both knew how everything worked. He smiled then held out his hand. "So you already know how this is going to work. Can I have the first dance?" Every table was buzzing whispers and nods. Necks stretched to see what Steam was doing and whom he was talking to. No one at her table could say a word, just listen.

Then she held her hand out, and he touched her gently, lifting her from the chair. The men at the table stood when she did. Cyril smiled then glanced over to Mimsie. She was beaming. Cindy could only smile as she whispered, "Have fun."

Let's Dance

Steam led Cyril to the footbridge, then they weaved through the tables, then past his table toward the dance floor. Before setting foot on the dance floor, Cyril stopped; it was beautiful, black polished, no seams, reflecting the stars from the sky. It was one big sheet of glass, like stepping into deep space. Cyril felt a kind of magic stepping on to it, then she looked around to see what other unexpected things were about to happen. The minute Steam put his arm around her waist, the music surrounded them. It was soft and slow. They both glided into it; Cyril felt almost fragile, delicate, as if she could suddenly be broken. By his touch, even she sensed him to be afraid.

"How has your evening been so far?" Steam leaned down, waiting for her answer. Cyril's first thought being this close to him, *He smells good in a comforting kind of way, almost familiar.* Cyril didn't know where to start.

Everything had happened so fast, so she searched for what to say. Steam stopped and looked at her, holding her a short distance away. "Are you all right?" he asked, sincere concern in his voice, almost like maybe he sincerely wanted to know.

"Okay, I'm just going to put it out there!" she said.

"I heard you were like that," he said with a relaxed smirk.

"By who?" Cyril jumped in for an answer. "Hold on, I have some questions. I don't ever remember being interviewed for this job, and who told you I was like—what? I have my own office." She was startled and in disbelief.

"Yes, you do. You have two," Steam stated the fact.

"While I was going through all the boxes in the office next to mine, I kept getting flashes of my childhood."

"You should. We grew up in the same neighborhood. We met when we were infants. We were born at the same hospital on the same day, September 24. We have a few mutual friends also." He said it to her as if even he was remembering it for the first time, reciting it like reading it from a list.

Okay, she said to herself, *I forgot who told me my birthday is on the twenty-fourth of September. He got that right.* Then it occurred to her that she didn't even know her own birthday; someone else had told her. What else was reported about her life that now became her truth?

"So what do the NFE1 dessert percentages mean?"

Steam was amused that too was gone from her memory. It had been her idea from the start. She wanted to know how many people worked at the company from the old planet. Also, how many were mixed, and maybe there were those from somewhere else. This dessert she thought would give her some of the answers she was looking for.

"It breaks down the possibility of who's from here and who's not without written permission for testing all the employees' blood. Besides, they're people who don't want to know. Then some don't believe any of it in the first place. It keeps it secret from those trying it."

"That was a good idea. Who came up with that?"

Steam stopped and smiled at her. "You did!"

"Wow, what else have I been up to lately?" Smiling while shaking her head, Cyril was proud of herself. Following Steam's eyes, she saw the moment a much larger piece of stardust was about to pierce her. Little did she know she was about to be thrown back into her own life.

A thin cloth felt stuck over her eyes. Her hands were tied tightly behind her back; she had no will to struggle as she sat there calmly. Through the darkness, she kept seeing the light flashing before her eyelids. Bright then gone, then blue-like swirls quick across her eyelids again. Could this be her forever state in the stillness? For her, it felt like she had been there forever. Again the light, then a calm whisper brushed her ear.

"I'm here, sweetheart." He carefully removed the zip tie, cutting into her wrists, rubbing her skin gently. "I'm taking you to a hospital, so try to stay calm."

Whoever it was didn't remove the blind-fold. Voices in the room were talking quickly in a language Cyril didn't understand. Next to her, she felt something brush against her right side. Then footsteps shuffling as something was being dragged across the floor away from her. A pounding high-pitched noise came from outside, one she didn't recognize. As if she was weightless, he was carrying her toward the sound. It began to frighten her, but he told her to stay calm. She heard a door creak open quickly then hit the wall behind it.

"Yalla yalla" came from the man holding her.

"Yalla yalla," she heard him repeat over and over again. Sharp, strong winds took her breath away, catching short breaths. The noise was now on top of her. She felt him gently lay her flat onto a soft surface. His hands took her legs, moving them straight, patting them gently. He laid her hands across her chest as she felt straps across her, tightening her to the surface, covering her ears; he adjusted a headset over her head. Then from the headset, she heard, "Can you hear me okay? Just nod," but she said nothing and didn't respond.

Then the same voice whispered, "I'm here to protect you. You don't need to worry. I'm here."

She could feel the quickness in the travel up and away lifted from the earth's surface. Then quietness in the others surrounding her; no one said a word. She had the overwhelming feeling they were all staring at her. Again, a blue light raced across her eyelids even through the blindfold. The light appeared, making itself known to her.

When she woke, she heard people to her left talking in a language she didn't understand. She was startled by the touch of a cool cloth wiping around her eyes and forehead with a solution she didn't recognize, but it smelled fresh and clean. She could feel someone behind her begin to untie the blindfold. Slowly and gently, the tugging of the fabric felt stuck to her eyelids and temples. She felt a hand softly dabbing the solution across her skin. Her skin felt tight and cold at the same time as the cloth began to lift off. Her eyes felt cool and did not want to open. Someone took her hand. The same voice as before. "You're going to be all right, sweetheart. We just have to figure out what this stuff is. Do you know what this stuff is? Can you tell me what happened?"

She felt the warmth of his hand while he waited for her to speak. She had no words inside. She had no emotions to relay. She had no idea anything was wrong. She lay there speechless as if in a trance. She was someone else somewhere else. She had no agenda, no moment to share. She was void. She didn't exist inside herself. She was gone. Her eyes saw the blue light again. This time, the light stopped and hovered against her eyelids, then dashed away. Slowly her eyes opened, now looking outside herself. In front of her stood a man looking into her and saw she was gone. He had looked into her eyes many times before, but now she was vacant; this disturbed him. Her eyes darted all around him. She heard someone say in English, "Her eyes are open." She repeated it to herself. "Her eyes are open, her eyes are open," as it became a whisper. Then inside her head, she heard someone speaking only to her.

"Yes, sweetheart, your eyes are open."

Cyril saw the white tile walls and the two huge round spotlights hovering above her. She examined the face in front of her. His skin was smooth as if he had recently shaved; he had dark skin, tanned with coal-black hair tied tightly in a ponytail with a black ribbon. She watched his light watery green eyes and long thick eyelashes as they darted back and forth, trying to find her somewhere inside herself. She concluded that he was taller than the others in the room. His suit was not off the rack but tailored comfortably in its cut; it appeared he had slept in his clothing. His shoulders were broad, his hands strong. His finger-nails appeared well kept. He carried himself with authority from the others in the room. He spoke a variety of different languages to the doctors and nurses surrounding her bed, none of which Cyril understood. He seemed comfortable in his surroundings, but Cyril noticed he was exhausted.

Collecting herself, she whispered to herself, "I didn't say that out loud, eyes open." The first words she thought in almost three months. He felt for a moment she might be in there somewhere, so he asked her again, "Do you know what happened to you? Do you know what this stuff is? The black stuff on your eyes? Can you tell me what your name is?" Someone had referred to her or called her sweetheart. So her name must be "Sweetheart, Sweetheart." She did not say it out loud but only thought it to herself.

She told herself for only the two of them to hear. What he heard was her as a child. She was very proud of herself for giving him what she thought would be the right answer. But the other question had no answer. She thought for a moment, *Did what to me?* It was hard to understand what people around her were saying. All aspects of time didn't exist. She knew days were starting to pass only because the day went into the night. The nurse brought in a tray every day to take blood samples. It was like clockwork. Cyril stretched her arm out, ready for the nurse; she knew the drill. Her hair had been cut and sent off in small vials. Every other day a nurse came in and would scrape her skin's surf, always in a different spot on her body. Cyril never knew what to expose for the samples. It wasn't painful. It was regular. Every morning a bright light was shone quickly into her eyes. While her nails were being trimmed, she watched how careful they were not to cut her. Every cutting went into the small glass container, even her toenails. Every day she heard the same voice, "How are you today, sweetheart?" It was in broken English, a language she understood. At the same time, he was there. In the corner of her eye, she thought she saw a blue haze zip past her.

She noticed the blue light at night when all the lights in her room were out. Then in the morning, she would see it again. After what seemed like weeks, she was still unsure how long she had been there. She was taken on walks around the halls. Then one afternoon, the nurse came in and told her she was going home. Cyril said over and over to herself, *Home! Home? Where is home?*

Moving in a half circle, she stopped Steam, her hand gripping his. "What just happened there?" She still felt the blindfold across her eyes. She still saw the sharp white light from the walls pierce her retina, only being calmed by the soft blue light and the voice calling her sweetheart. Her hand went up to touch her eyes as if it had just happened. She felt the cold; she could smell the solution across her skin.

"What was that?"

The large particles of stardust had started, and now he needed to explain. "We're trying to restore your memory. The bigger particles will show you parts of your past. Those parts will stay, and hopefully, the pieces will all come together and make sense to you."

"Why was I in the hospital?"

"You've been in the hospital a few times. Do you know what hospital it was? Now that I think about it, you've been in hospitals all over the world—the Karolinska in Stockholm. You spent a few months there. That's when your memory was scrubbed. Then there's the Sheba Intensive Care Unit in Israel. We heard it was the best in the area. You were there for a few weeks before we got you back to the States. The doctors and specialists did amazing things for you there. They saved your life that time you were severely burned. You also had a broken arm. You needed 126 stitches on the back of your legs. You can't even tell by looking at you that you have been through so much. Oh, also the hospital in Geneva, the HUG, and the Mayo here in the States. I'm sure I'm leaving a few out."

"Tell me about the people in my life and what you know about me." She tried to say it quickly before something else happens.

"We both know Ezek and Sven. They have been with both of us for, let's see, since we were three or four, I'm not sure I know, since we were very little."

"Ezek and Sven," she repeated the names to herself. The names didn't sound even remotely familiar.

"Why, who are these people?" She racked her brain, trying to find any clue but nothing.

"They're sitting at my table. Ezek has the beard. Sven's the guy in the tan suit next to him."

Startled, she kept moving, gliding across the floor with ease, trying to compose herself. Her dress floated softly like air in their movement together across the dance floor.

"I'm sorry, that's a lot to give you at one time, but let's get it out there. Do you want to sit down?" Steam slowed and waited for her answer.

Cyril enjoyed dancing with him. It was romantic and fun at the same time and strangely familiar. She needed answers. Internally, she tried to collect herself.

"Tell me, who calls me sweetheart? How do I know them?" Cyril asked, frustrated, trying to get closer to herself.

"Ezek has been with you the longest, I think."

"Does he call me sweetheart?" she asked.

"I think he only calls you that when you guys are alone. I don't think I've ever heard him say that to you in public. Sometimes he talks to you for only you to hear. You two can have complete conversations and arguments just in your heads with each other that no one else can hear. That is, you used to before you were scrubbed. I think he's always trying to talk to you. You just can't hear him anymore."

Scrubbed, Cyril thought. Her memory was scrubbed! So yes, she did know him before giving him the bag. She only thought she might know him. Now she was sure. The small stardust particle gave her memory little flashes of Steam's mother after she passed away. Or Steam and Cyril playing in the fort they built in the big bay laurel tree in her backyard. Or spending the night at each other's houses. Or the language they made up that no one else knew. Moments of pinkie swear promises they had made to each other never ever to be forgotten for as long as they both live.

"Yes, I remember you up until the time I was ten. Then you were gone. You vanished. You just left me."

"No, that's just part of it. I kept in contact with you. We even saw each other when we went to college. We all met up during school breaks. We worked at the same company before your incident. You've been out recuperating. It's taken almost two years to figure out how to help you. Every team we have here has been working on it. We all want you back. Most of what we tell you, you forget. We were told you need to see it in your own mind. You know the saying: seeing it with your own eyes is believing."

Cyril tried to take in what he was saying, trying to understand the process, then asked, "So…what do you mean when you say 'every team we have'? I have or we have a team? Okay, who is this so-called team?"

"It's everyone, all the departments at this company. Each having a specialized field. Hopefully, with their research and knowledge, they might come across something that might be found to help you, like the stardust. That came from NFE1. One of Norie's colleagues found it and has been testing it for a year now. Tonight they were confident it might help you."

Cyril smiled, holding his gaze long enough to make him smile back, then look away. "Just how do you being on the outside show me my life so it sticks? Just how does that work?" Steam not skipping a beat centered his attention only on Cyril. His smile beamed. It was magic. What was it within that smile, that beam that came from his eyes? She had seen it before she knew it from somewhere else.

Then out of nowhere, it was as if she was given some strange elixir to make everything crystal clear. Was it something he said to trigger it? She looked at him suddenly as if she had an aha moment. As clear as it was yesterday, she said out loud to him, "I do remember you. I was confused at first when we first met this evening."

"What do you mean?" Steam asked.

"It was the way you smell. I saw flashes of moments I had no memory of it. It caught me off guard."

"I'm sorry. They said it would be an adjustment."

"Who are they?" she said in a frustrated tone.

"I can see we have a lot of catching up on." His hand spread wide across her back, holding her like he had held her before. "Go ahead, say it."

"Say what?"

"Say what's on your mind. It's always been easier for you to think out loud. Talk to me."

"I do remember you, your face, the way you move, the way a waft of you tells me you're there even when I can't see you." A calmness consumed her like a soothing blanket. She felt safe all of a sudden. Strange this feeling being safe; she wasn't used to letting her guard down. It was almost uncomfortable.

"It's almost like you're touching me everywhere, at the same time. How strange." Cyril could feel his hand on her back. His fingers spread and adjusted themselves, turning her into the music. She thought she had closed her eyes, but everything was wide open. She was seeing clearly now. Small glittering dust blanketed everywhere she went. The music slowed, almost like everything was coming to a close. It occurred to Cyril the silvery stardust was following only her.

Like diamonds or falling stars from the sky, the dust was unavoidable, all around her, covering her. Some particles were bigger than others. As she watched it piercing her skin, the stardust sent her back into herself for another memory. Then the music was gone...

Her ears rang with numbing pain. Black specks of hot gunpowder burned, piercing across her skin. All her breath had been knocked completely out of her. Cyril struggled to catch her breath. She asked herself, *Am I dying?* as an uncontrollable panic rolled through her.

The air was gone. Cyril struggled to catch her breath.

Gasping again and again. There was no air.

She could smell gunpowder, burnt hair, and skin at the same time. Was it hers? she wondered. Raining from the sky, rocks, sand, and other debris fell with a driving force. Cyril held her arm up to shield herself. Falling fast, a large branch hit the center of her left forearm. Other debris piled around her. She felt her body overwhelmingly heavy, unable to move.

Pain radiated over her as the rain of rocks and debris kept falling. Smoke filled the surrounding area, making it hard to see. Far in the distance, she could hear a high-pitched noise coming from what sounded like a large metal tube. Sounding like something was offtrack, unwinding, coming to a slow stop. Then she felt a hand come under her head. Then another hand clutched her legs, lifting her effortlessly. A sharp pain came from the back of her legs. Cyril let out a screaming shrill. She was unable to see the man holding her in his arms. Her right arm held him tightly.

He put his mouth to her ear. First, she couldn't make out what he was trying to say. He was speaking so fast, in a language she didn't understand, then he said it in English. All she could hear was "They're going back. They're leaving. You're going to be all right. I'll get us out of here. I've got you now. You're going to be all right." There was a trusting feeling that washed over her at the sound of this person's voice. She felt like she was dying; but she was comforted knowing this person, whoever they are, was there. Who was leaving? Who was it that caused so much pain? Were they retreating from them? Was the violence over? Then suddenly another strong blast threw both of them into the air, landing deep into the sand, feeling like she had just been molded into a bed of clay. Cyril couldn't feel her body, her ears filled with deafening pain. She knew the security of that person's arms was no longer holding her.

The leather protecting her skin was gone. Heat rolled over her skin, charring it with pain.

What happened to the person holding her, the person who gave her comfort and security? Reaching her arm out into the void, Cyril was unable to see. Sand and stones raining from the sky filled her hands. There was no one there. There was no one within arm's reach. She was alone, and so was he. A wave of heat radiated over the surface of her skin again. The smell of burnt skin and hair surrounded her senses. She felt she had died. Had he died trying to save her? Was it all just another bad dream? It felt real. She could smell it.

Her body felt the pain radiate outward toward her skin.

The banging metal slowed, winding to a stop. Then the smoke slowly cleared. A vast crater was off in the distance.

Body parts littered the area; some human shapes were not familiar to her. Nothing was moving. There was no sign of life for as far as Cyril could see.

The moment felt like an eternity.

Then far off in the distance, she thought she heard a high-pitched whistle, a tune familiar to her, just two notes, one high and the other flat. Cyril thought for that moment she might be smiling, having recognized the tune. Then she heard it again. Now she knew for sure it was that tune, that whistle. Only one person called her from a distance like that. A hand gently wiped the blood across her face, moving her hair out of her eyes. Then to her neck, two fingers stopped after finding the spot. Feeling for her pulse, she sensed to herself. Then they put their arm under her legs then stopped. He noticed the back of her legs had been sliced. Blood was pouring through his fingers. His broad hands pressured the wound.

He grabbed her, lifting up and away; she felt the movement. Cyril struggled to stop him, but her resistance was weak.

"Where are you taking me? Find him. Don't leave him here."

"We have to go. You're injured. He can't be helped," the voice said quickly.

"Don't leave him here. Stop!" She tried to move but couldn't. "Put me down! I can't leave him. Put me down!" Her voice faded. "He can't be helped?"

She repeated it to herself, *He can't be helped. Was he dead? Was he saying he's dead?* She was crying inside, but no tears showed. They were all gone. As she tried to free herself, his arms held her tighter as he moved quickly.

"Put me down!" she tried to yell as she struggled.

He stopped and laid her on the ground, gently lying on top of her so she couldn't move or be detected. Holding her down, he whispered in her ear, "*Stop!* this is going to get you killed. We need to get out of here. I'll come back for him, I promise. You have already killed most of them. How much revenge do you need? Let's go."

"Can you see how many are left?" He could barely hear her voice. Cyril knew her arm was broken. Also, maybe a few ribs, but what was wrong with her legs as she tried to move them to get up and walk? Her legs were not cooperating. Blood kept getting in her eyes, running from the top of her head. She repeated to herself again, *He can't be helped. What the hell does that mean?*

"What's wrong with my legs? I can't move my legs." As the pain faded, now she could not feel her legs at all.

He laid her left arm across the front of her chest, setting it just so. Then his body pressed against her as he whispered, "I'm getting us out of here. Hold on," giving her no choice. She could no longer give orders or make demands. She was at the mercy of Ezek.

She knew she would be all right as she slowly lost the energy to hang on to him. Ezek felt her leave her body, her arm no longer holding him, her weight suddenly different. Had she died in his arms? he wondered as he raced to the helicopter. They fell into the open side door. "Get us out of here!" he demanded.

Cyril stopped, catching herself now, feeling both feet firmly on the floor. Her eyes searched the tables behind Steam, who was the person who tried to save her. She stopped Steam, turning him to look at the two men at Steam's table. They stood up from their chairs. Was it a salute? Was it a moment to retreat? What could they be thinking? Were they worried about what she was remembering? One of the men at the table, tall, handsome, dark hair and beard, glanced at her, then back at Sven; then suddenly Steam realized what was happening. As he held her close, the music changed a little faster this time. They moved quickly, both her feet firmly on the floor now.

Steam, holding her close, whispered, "What did you see? Tell me." She felt comfort in his grasp, a calmness in his tone, but something wasn't right.

He wasn't the man she just saw, nor were the men at the table. Who could he be? Was the empty chair at the table his?

Was he late getting here? Was he coming at all? Was he unable to be helped? Was he dead? Who was he?

Cyril watched a piece of sparkly stardust float softly in the air. Then she watched it pierce her skin, melting in quickly, like snow on a warm surface.

Cyril heard water splashing under her boots. The room was cold and damp. She listened to the water running down from the ceiling along the walls. She was on the fourth floor in a vast empty warehouse.

Sunlight illuminated the entire south wall of small metal-framed windows, some still holding glass. Splashing footsteps echoed down the empty building. Behind Cyril was someone running at her pace, staying close to her. They both stopped against the broken glass wall.

Six panes of glass were empty. Cyril pulled from her pocket what appeared to be a small silk-like scarf but stretchy—placing it tightly across the open panes. A large grid of illuminating colored strands began to pulse, twisting like rainbows showing to the outside. It appeared like a screen on a window. It was beautiful, but she knew once stretched, it was deadly. Looking through the grid past the darkness off in the distance, she could see a large what appeared to be a building moving toward them in short strides.

Energy pulsed off its surface like a beacon warning everything in its path. Its warning couldn't threaten Cyril. All she understood was they were there to eliminate it. Behind her, the stern voice said, "Bend it." Was it a suggestion or an order? She wasn't sure.

"Bend it," he repeated louder this time. Then again, with urgency. "Bend it! Bend it *now!*" It was loud and clear.

She reached over to touch the grid in front of her, examining it slowly. When she saw the right color combinations twisting like rainbows, some colors faster than others came together in an intersection. She touched it, pressing it toward the large object with her index finger.

Quieter than wind, the object was gone. A haunting stillness took the air away. The tip of

Cyril's index finger felt like a sharp needle had pricked her. Rubbing it did not relieve the pain.

Cyril carefully removed the fabric, tucking it into the right side of her bra. She turned and raced out of the room, splashing through the shallow puddles.

Cyril's boots echoed off the cement walls and floor while she tried to read the colorful graffiti artistically sprayed along the way.

The words told her she was in the deepest part of Germany. The propaganda was all the same, even down the empty stairwell. Once out of the building, she ran toward the open field where the object had disappeared. She felt the vibration of moving molecules in the atmosphere still humming. She sensed no danger but kept her eyes moving, waiting for retaliation. Dropping to her knees, she touched the sand in front of her. Her hand lay still for a moment.

Her mind wondered, did the occupants know what was going to happen to them? Were they aware of how they would be stopped? Did their extinction occur to them the second the energy touched their surface? Her mind wondered what their last thoughts might have been. Were they even told of their risk? Cyril's eyes focused around her to see if anything was approaching. She dug deep into the cool sand, filling her hands, letting the small particles fall through her fingers. In among the sand were large chunks of powder-blue turquoise. Sifting through the sand, she collected a pile of turquoise stones, leaving them exposed on the surface. Turning to see the only witness was Sven standing behind her. Sven tried to catch his breath, trying to get the words out. "If you leave them there…" His words broke as he caught his breath again. "Everyone will know it was you." He took in a deep breath. "Do you want the repercussions of that?" He knelt down on his knees beside her, trying to catch his breath.

He said, almost answering the question for her, "Hell no, you don't." Did Sven think she was going to hide or sneak off?

Laying the turquoise stones on the surface was like leaving her calling card. She turned to Sven and made herself very clear.

"I want everyone to know it was me. I don't want the Grays to have any doubt who did this destruction. I can't begin to estimate how many of their lives I have taken this time, but they have to know I am answering them loud and clear. I am solely responsible. This can't go on anymore. We have to find a way, or they need to leave. They need to go somewhere else. We got here first."

Cyril felt justified and terrified at the same time. This was the Quiet War. She was right in the middle of it without really realizing it up until then. Either the Quiet War would eliminate us or someone was going to have to leave. We would fight to our death. Now the casualties on both sides were uncounted and hard to believe.

No one saw this war on the news. It never made any front page anywhere in the world.

It was current and quiet and affected every living person on the planet. They had an answer for all the missing people, all the deaths from the flu and other illnesses, all the shootings, all the violence All over the world. It affected everyone. Excuses were made, so it didn't take on its actual appearance. No one could handle the truth. It wasn't sugarcoated. It was just a lie, a lie everyone had heard so many times before. They were immune to it. They were used to hearing about the massive death tolls or the missing planes filled with innocent people. One or two killings were happening everywhere.

But let's do a head count, now we're overwhelmed by the ongoing deaths. The Quiet War had to stop. The sneaky unseen enemy was everywhere and nowhere, at the same time. This one building was an enormous advancement in our civilization but not enough. Cyril swore to herself she would remain in the dark to quietly fight to save all that she could. This wasn't over, but she couldn't let Sven know that.

Cyril could feel a warm large hand spread across her back, holding her gently, moving her to the music she had just begun to hear.

Steam's voice whispered in her ear, calming her. "Are you back? Tell me where you went. What did you see?"

Would there be retaliation? Inside her, she felt devastated. The losses were huge, and she was solely responsible. She knew what was happening inside the building; she had been in one of them before on tour. Her mind stopped. *On tour*, she repeated to herself, *on tour?* For a moment, she tried to remember the inside of the building. The massive structure held thousands of Grays and human bodies. But for what? The moment wasn't clear to her.

Who was that? Did she have that in her, she wondered, just to kill to murder? Was she really capable of that kind of carnage? Apparently she was. What kind of person was she, who was she, and what else was she capable of? Finding herself took on a new meaning: who was she really? *Oh my god.* She stopped for a moment to collect herself.

Am I really capable of such things? Yes, apparently I am. She nodded her head up and down in agreement with herself.

The box, that massive box, or should I call it a building? Oh my god, it just vanished. It was just gone. I could feel in the moment all the energy, all the lives gone, just gone. That cloth, that beautiful, soft, silky, lethal... She shook her head, having no idea what she had experienced, looking up to Steam.

"Wow, what the hell do I do for a living?" she asked.

Steam smiled. "It's okay. It's all right." As he moved her hair from her face, he saw she was upset.

"That's all part of what you do, and you have a good reason why you do it. We all understand. It's okay."

He gently moved her into a turn as the music went on.

She wasn't sure her feet were touching the ground, then on the top of her hand, she saw the speck of stardust pierce her like an arrow disappearing into her skin.

Before she could finish what she was about to say, Cyril saw a faint blue light peeking through the thick oak forest, like a beacon. It felt like early morning with the dew in the air. A crisp coldness surrounded her. Steam and Cyril had agreed they would meet at the big oak tree had they been separated. Cyril wasn't sure if he made it out okay or not. She felt like she was traveling alone. Cyril took the long way home. In case she was being followed, her direction home would not be understood. Her thoughts were *He's my best friend, my friend. He has to be there when I get there.* She was immersed in her thoughts. She knew everything she was thinking was sent into the Grays' brain waves. Others around her could hear her thoughts, including all of the Grays they had just left. Then as she approached the tree, she could see Steam sitting in the crux of the branch waiting for her. She could only go so fast on her bike, pedaling as quickly as she could once she saw him.

Jumping off, she leaned the bike against the tree. Then she climbed it like a ladder. Steam's arms reached out for her. He took her hand and pulled her toward him then grabbed her. Cyril thought to herself, *I like to feel him grab for me. It makes me feel loved and secure at the same time.* She got comfortable and sat on the inside of the branch, glad to know he was okay, happy to just be with him.

"Hold still! Stop! Hold still!" He put his hand on her face, turning her to face him. Then he said, "You're bleeding," as he wiped the blood from her eyebrow.

It was only then that she separated the cold from the pain. She had no memory of the injury until he mentioned the cut above her left eye.

Cyril looked him in the eye. "Man, they don't like you. I think they just tolerate you because of me. You have to remember they can hear everything you're thinking. Let's face it, you really should not have thought that, man. You sure know how to piss them off. Had Yike been there, I'm not sure you would be here right now. 'Cannibals!' Do you even know what that means? You called them cannibals. They don't eat each other. They can't even think how that can happen, but once you said it and once I thought about what it meant, man, that was all it took. They value their lives and personal energy more than anything. Cannibals, *wow*, that cut them deep. Don't let that pass in your head again, or we won't make it out next time."

"I don't think there will be a next time! I don't like them. I can't understand what your deal is with them."

Cyril looked at her fingers, shocked they were dripping with blood. "Can you get home? Would you prefer to walk?"

I kind of like his concern, but a little gash on my eyebrow isn't going to slow me down. Looking at Steam, she had to repeat back to him, "Please don't ever call them cannibals again. Please. I'm tired. Can we rest here for a while, at least until the sun comes up? I just need to rest." Cyril smiled at him. It was her way to let him know she forgave him for his comment and that she's okay, really. "I'm okay." Their legs dangled off the branch, relaxed with his arm around her, securing her to him as her eyes became heavy as she fell asleep.

The warmth from his words brushed her ear. "Tell me what you see. What's it like going back?" he whispered. Steam waited for her answer as they glided slowly across the dance floor.

Cyril could feel inside her she had been on her bike for hours, and inside, worry remained in her thoughts. The idea before seeing Steam in the tree, not knowing if he had been harvested like the rest.

The Grays were not easy to get along with; she at least had their attention and respect, which was the only thing that kept her alive. But she knew Steam was not the easiest of company to them; he knew too much and had no patience for them or their needs. It had felt like a very long night, so she had to ask, "How long was I gone? It seems like a long time for me. How long is it to you?"

"Maybe ten seconds, maybe less, not very long at all. You see more than time can handle. The details are what's important." Steam was trying to gauge her moment.

She explained, "We were riding our bikes down to the river where the cliffs stop. It was late. We knew some young Grays were meeting there. I like to watch them from a distance. They confronted us." Cyril wiped her left eyebrow, stopping her fingers at the scar that went vertical, tracing her finger up and down, then asked him, "You were there when I got this scar. Tell me how it happened. Tell me, what happened that night?"

"We got into a situation with some young Grays. You know I don't care for them. That night you made it clear to me that they do have feelings and emotions for each other. I'm afraid to say it out loud or even think about it after that night." Before he could finish, Steam's eyes followed the stardust as it touched her skin, melting deep into her thoughts...

Lying under the Christmas tree looking up, Cyril squinted her eyes so all the beautiful-colored lights would fuzz together. "Look, it's beautiful," she heard her little three-year-old voice to the person kneeling next to her. The lights blinked and sparkled off the ornaments her mother had collected for many years. Then Cyril saw a familiar hand scoop two blue lights from what appeared not connected to the string of lights. The hand brought the two blue lights down to where Cyril was lying on her back. In his palm, the lights hovered close to his skin but not touching him. Then the person said, "This is Cyril. She's with us. I'd like you to keep your eyes on her and make sure she's safe." The lights blinked and sparkled like they were excited or maybe answering yes. She couldn't be sure.

"This is for you to keep with you always. You might not always see them, but know, they are always there. Blue lights can communicate with other colored orbs. They will warn other orbs of who you are. They will also tell me and show me what's happening to you or where you're at." He reached down while the blue lights stirred around in a circle then hovered over Cyril. One got larger than the other, then both got very small, then blended back in with the other Christmas lights. It was hard to make out which ones were which.

Then moments flooded back to her. She was seeing her blue orbs, her very own. They were everywhere she went. Her first day at school, they got tiny and hid under her collar, watching every encounter without her mother there. Cyril's first kiss was under a blue light. The first time she went swimming, the water around her was blue. The first time she drove a car, the blue lights were just like the officers' blue lights giving her her first speeding ticket. The blue lights followed her everywhere. It was something she never questioned. Once in a while, she would hear someone say, "Did you see that it was like a blue light moving very quickly?" Then the other person would say, "You're seeing things."

In the palm of her hand, she felt the warmth of his hand as she looked up at Steam. She asked, "Do I still have two blue orbs following me everywhere?"

Steam whispered, "Well, hello, you're back. Blue orbs, ha, yes, you do. It's the other color that bothers you. But yes, they stay close to you. They always have. Sometimes other people can see them. You always act like they're not there, so people second-guess themselves if they've seen them or not. Most of the time, people don't believe what they've seen anyway." Cyril glanced up at the large screen, showing the galaxy and all the unexplored vastness, making her feel small and insignificant, so why did she need two blue orbs?

Suddenly the extremely handsome very tall man who had been sitting at Steam's table tapped Steam on the shoulder.

"Can I have this dance?" His voice flooded her, touching every emotion, catching her off guard. The stranger looked only at Cyril with a gentle smile. He made it sound like he was asking, but the real message was "I'll take her now. You can go away."

Steam did not want to let her go. Cyril could feel the tension, but it was only coming from Steam. Who was this handsome gentleman? It was clear this man didn't answer to Steam.

"Cyril, may I introduce Ezekiel? I mean Ezek." He had an intense look in his eyes, almost like he was talking to her with his gaze. She kept his stare, looking back like maybe words could have been exchanged but weren't. Tall, that was the first thing she noticed about him. Confident as if he was trying to be polite in asking; what she was hearing was like an order. Cyril suddenly found herself caught in his gaze, stuck, while she noticed it was creating a smile on her face she couldn't control. Guilt came over her like she was doing something wrong, but her eyes were not giving up. He carried himself with style. Could it be from the way his suit fit him with perfection or the way the color on his tie made you melt into his eyes? No, it was the smile. That smile stole her heart. Feeling her insides flip, she broke the stare then glanced back up at him.

Then Steam released her hand, but keeping his other hand on her waist, he said, "I'll be at my table. Will you join me later?"

"Okay," she said with reluctance, unable to take her eyes off Ezek.

Keeping his hand on her waist, she saw their eyes both follow the stardust that was about to land on her wrist. Then before it touched her, she looked over into Steam's eyes...

Sweetheart

The damp forest floor under her feet was soft with a salty smell of the ocean air. Cold and out of breath, feeling excited and happy inside, she kept running while looking down at her beautiful muddy, sequined white shoes. She could feel they were drenched and becoming heavy.

The drizzling rain suddenly changed, now falling even harder. Cyril clutched her dress custom made of white chiffon covered with tiny white pearls, laid over tulle covered with down feathers peeking underneath. Dragging it through the muddy path, she followed the meandering row of giant sequoia trees. The roar of the ocean to her right mist floated upward as the waves crashed against the rocks. It was dark now, but deep inside her, she knew he would wait for her. Finally, seeing the light coming from between the trees highlighted the rustic building far off in the distance past the row of dense ferns. Running up the stairs and out of breath, she pushed the doors wide open as the coldness followed her in.

The guests turned and stood. Cindy was standing by the open door, holding a beautiful bouquet of fresh fragrant white gardenias with fern leaves. The bottom was wrapped in an ivory satin ribbon. Cindy wore a beautiful lace dress she had purchased while visiting friends in Bordeaux earlier that year. It was a trip Cyril and Cindy had planned for months. They were to become tourists for two weeks and get in some girl time; only Cindy made the trip. In Cyril's mind, she felt the disappointment of missing the trip and a moment of regret having disappointed Cindy. They both knew business always came first, but another trip was scheduled for the following year, but to where? she wondered.

Cyril was soaking wet. She wiped the rain and hair off her face, grabbing the bouquet from Cindy. Cyril stopped, looked at Cindy, and smiled, whispering, "Thank you. You were right. It is possible. It's all possible. You look beautiful." She touched the lace on Cindy's sleeve.

Cindy hugged her and whispered in her ear, "Where have you been? We've been waiting for you."

Looking around the room, Cyril saw Henry looking back at her. At the end of a long table stood Bernard and Steam, both looking over simultaneously. Looking over the heads of women standing in front of him, Ezek watched Cyril enter the room. Ezek smiled at the women while Cyril heard his pleasantries. He was walking toward her with a drink in his hand.

She heard him whisper in her head, only to her, "There you are. I thought I'd have to go find you." He gave her a half smile as his gaze dropped to look at the floor. Setting his glass down on the table next to him, he walked over to her. Taking her hand, he asked, "Are you ready?"

Collecting herself, she looked around the room at all the familiar faces smiling back at her. Some strangers she had never met before all with welcoming smiles, smiles of love. The pastor motioned to her to step forward, his hand waving toward him, his other hand clutching his Bible.

In the distance, she heard a familiar man's voice, stirring her heart. He had whispered a thousand other times in her ear. This time it overwhelmed her. "Where's the ring?" he asked.

Steam took his hand from her waist and motioned to Ezek. The second he touched her, she felt like she was home. The cold and wet were gone. His warmth consumed her. There was comfort in this stranger's touch; it was like her head had laid on his chest before. She felt she was right where she should be.

Not looking up considering how tall he was, she said, "Do I know you? Are you real or from my dreams? Are you a part of what's happening to me tonight?" There was an ease in asking him. She could almost feel him hug her.

"No, I'm not a part of what's happening to you, but I do understand it," he said with a gentleness in his voice. His scent made Cyril's eyes close.

There was security in all that was happening to her right then. *Security, what an odd feeling*, she thought. *Almost like my soul gets a moment to rest. How strange.* The thankful feeling came over her. She took a moment to examine how it felt, relaxed, secure, at peace, no reason to keep looking over her shoulder to defend herself. Still not looking up, she asked again, "Do I know you?"

In his arms, they glided across the floor effortlessly. Feeling for a moment like together, they were music.

"Yes, you know me; and yes, I know you. I know all about you. I have known you most of your life."

Cyril thought for a moment, *Most of my life?* "That's kinda scary. You know everything, everything about me!" she whispered so only he could hear.

"Yes, I do." He stated it as fact.

"Okay, then tell me what you know about me that no one else knows."

"Humm, that no one else knows, let's see," he repeated to himself. "I was the only one with you when you learned how to use color strands. To this day, you can't believe how deadly they are. Also, you like to meditate by sitting among your beehives on your property. In case you're wondering, the other chair is mine. I often sit with you. I find it also relaxes me. Before you were erased, I could hear your thoughts. Now I get bits and pieces of your thoughts or what you're thinking about. It's not like it used to be. I can also feel you. That hasn't changed. It's strange to say, but I can feel your pain like no one else. It doesn't matter how far away we are. I'm always with you. Oh, you like sun-dried tomatoes and cream cheese and salted sunflower seeds on your toasted everything bagel with tea when you get up in the morning. You get up at 6:00 a.m., no matter what day it is."

Cyril had to ask, if he knows everything, and she feels this way in his arms. It just came out. She said it out loud.

"Are we married?" she asked, not knowing the answer.

He paused before answering long enough for her to wish for her own answer. "Sadly, no, we are not!" he said slowly with painful regret in his tone. "You asked Steam earlier who calls you sweetheart?"

Startled, Cyril's first thought was *How does he know what Steam and I were discussing?*

But the moment the word came from his lips, Cyril's eyes swelled. She was overwhelmed, and an enormous part of her heart filled to the brim. She was exactly where she should be at that moment. She knew it was him.

"I think I'm the only one that calls you sweetheart."

"So you know everything about me, and I know nothing about you. Tell me about you. Are you married or seeing someone? Forget that. It's none of my business. Who are you most of all? Who are you to me?"

"Let's see: no, I'm not married, I am seeing someone, I have been for many years." Ezek tried to hold his smile as he read bits of Cyril's thoughts. "I have a unique relationship with her. I would never betray her trust. I would do anything for her. She's my best friend. Years ago, I was sent here to grow up with you, but I often visited you in your dreams."

Cyril looked up and had to ask, "Sent here by whom?"

"From the way I understand it, it was an agreement made between our parents after my mother died."

"I'm sorry about your mother. How did she pass?"

There was a moment as if maybe he didn't want to open that door. To remember was to relive it all over again, and that was painful to him.

"My mother was harvested when I was almost seven. That's when I came to, as my father put it, to watch over you. Because your father didn't want you to know"—he paused again—"about, let's say people like me. I only came to you in your dreams at first. Then after my mother died, I came to live with your family. Most of the time, I would erase our moments together when we would study and just hang out. It helped me string to you. It was easier for you to cope, knowing it was a dream."

"What do you mean by string to me?"

"I hear you no matter how far away we are. I feel what's happening to you also. We have been through a lot together all over the world. I have saved your life almost as many times as you have saved mine. I could tell you every aspect of your life, but that won't make you remember. You have to go back and experience it yourself."

Feeling the bond with him, she had to ask, "What kind of relationship do we have? Are we in love?" It was apparent to her, the way he spoke to her, the way he looked at her, the way he touched her. "Have you ever told me you love me?"

He heard her thoughts all broken up into fragments like a radio with bad reception. "I have never felt the need to tell you I love you. I have always tried to let you know in every action I take. I find that sometimes words are simple. Time spent with someone is the greatest love of all. That's only my opinion. But it's what I believe." His head turned away at the seriousness of having to say it out loud to her.

"Tell me what I was running from in the rain that night."

"You mean, what were you running to? Your dress couldn't have been more you. Beautiful, delicate but drenched and covered with mud. It was perfectly you. You were running from me."

"What? Why was I running from you?" Startled, Cyril needed the answer.

"You were to stay in the cabin on the coast that night. You wanted to be alone. It was your last night of freedom, you said. I had all your favorite munchies and the best champagne on ice waiting for you."

Cyril looked up into his eyes. She saw the pain inside him as he explained. "You got that all ready for me?"

"Yes, you arrived just as I was leaving. It was the gladiolus. You asked me to take the flowers away."

"Why? What was it about the gladiolus?"

"Your words were 'They would remind you of me, and you couldn't have me.' Then you caught yourself and said, 'I mean, you couldn't have the gladiolus there.'"

Cyril looked up, giving him a grateful smile, then closed her eyes and whispered to him, "I love my husband, don't I?" For a moment, he didn't know if it was a question or a statement.

"Yes, you did. You loved him very much."

He could feel that the question disturbed her. He turned her into a dip. Then he held her for a moment, looking at her as her hair almost touched the floor.

She felt confident in his hands as they stayed posed for the moment. Then her eyes followed the stardust, dropping slowly onto her chin.

Ezek's hand spread wide across her back. He knew she was leaving for another moment of her past. He hated every minute of it, not knowing where she was going but going without him. This he could not control. He knew it had to be done. He wanted her back. He just didn't like the process.

The stillness and quiet of the night were eerie. No wind, no sounds at all. Cyril lay flat to keep herself from any surveillance in the area. Someone was lying next to her; they both kept silent while trying to stay awake. She just needed to be patient. All she knew was to be in the desert

70

at that time. She was going to share information with her colleague and friend. Then off in the distance, she heard the heartbeat of an approaching helicopter. Its lights were off, flying low and only by radar. She put her hand out, touching the person lying adjacent to her. Out of the darkness, the sand stirred in front of her. The helicopter hovered then tilted to one side. She felt his hand around her waist, popping her up into the open side doors, landing onto the floor. Hands grabbed and held her as it quickly tilted up and away. She screamed, knowing her partner was left behind. Looking out, she saw Ezek running after them, yelling in a language she didn't understand. "Her karma will have you! Her karma will find you! I'm coming! I'm coming!"

She knew he would follow them. She had never seen him in such a rage. Struggling to get to the controls, someone grabbed her, preventing her from going into the cockpit, when suddenly she heard a commanding voice tell her to "sit down and shut up!"

Sven was taking her somewhere.

"Where are you taking me? Why did you leave Ezek? Who are these men?" Hands clutched her and strapped her into her seat. One man put a headset on her as Sven looked back at her. "We'll be landing soon. Just relax," the words came from the headset. Cyril looked at the controls. They were going due north toward the Mediterranean Sea. If her bearings were correct, they would be approaching the Gulf of Sidra. Cyril couldn't be sure it was all memory. The darkness concealed her fate. Her thoughts went to Ezek as she was strapped tight in her seat. Her headset hummed in her ears. Everyone on board was silent. Cyril

was terrified. Sven was someone she trusted,
someone who knew her well. All she could do
was wait for the sun to come up; it might give her
a clue to where she was going or where she was.

The music was still playing as she was being uprighted from her
dip.

Ezek held her close like you would during a slow romantic
dance. "Are you all right? I felt your heart quicken."

There was genuine warm concern in his voice. Cyril believed
what he was saying to her as he waited for her response.

"Anything you want to share? Where were you? What did you
see?"

"Sven had just separated us. We had waited all night alone in
the desert for him. I had just been picked up by a helicopter. He left
you there in the desert alone." Cyril shook her head, trying to put the
pieces together, but she had no other details.

"Why didn't he wait for you? I was afraid to be away from you.
I couldn't tell where I was going."

Ezek gave her a warm smile. "No, that's not exactly right." He
shook his head. "There are not many things that frighten you. At
that moment, you weren't flying the helicopter. It's one of your control issues."

"Where were they taking me? Man, you were mad. You followed us."

"Of course I did." He smiled. "I have followed you to the ends
of the earth literally, and now here we are."

He said it in a way that stopped her from worrying. Stopped her
from thinking about where she had just been—hijacked in a helicopter
somewhere in the world. There was comfort in his voice, reassurance
that it was over and in her past. She repeated it to herself, *Her past.*

"What's wrong?" Ezek slowed. All his attention focused on her.

"I don't know who that person is. Sure, it's me; but everything
that's happened to me, all the things I've seen so far, I'm not her. I
could never be her, whoever she is. That scares me to have to walk in
her shoes. I really don't think I can do it."

Ezek felt the fear in her voice. She was now the child he once knew, but knowing she would experience more of her life that evening, how could he make it easier for her? How could he prepare her for who she really is?

"Do you ever lie to yourself? I mean, deliberately make something up in your head so the moment doesn't freak you out. Yeah, it's lying to myself." She shook her head up and down, agreeing with her word choice, but still finding it hard to describe.

"I'm not sure I know what you mean. Where are you going with this? What did you lie to yourself about?" His watery green eyes stayed focused on her.

"While walking down the path to find Steam, something took my hand."

"Something like what? Describe it to me."

"It was delicate. It didn't hurt me. The appearance of it startled me."

"What did it look like?" he said with caution.

"It was greenish gray. The fingers were multijoined and stretched in front of me so they could wrap around my hand. The fingernails at the tip of each digit were round and sharply pointed, rather lethal-looking. It was almost reptilian. I didn't see the body connected to it, thank god! Let's just view a little bit at a time. Velvet! It was smooth like velvet, tiny, thin transparent hair like fur all over it. It transfers a feeling to me of hope and love." Shaking her head while looking up at him, she said, "Weird, ha! So while all this is happening to me, I'm in my head making up some kind of game I'm playing to make it fit into my life, to cope. You know my real life with weird shit like that in it. How do you make that fit into your life? But to lie to yourself."

Ezek's first thought was *He's here.* Could he tell her, or would the night and the stardust reveal him and who he was to her? As his thoughts raced inside him, Cyril looked at him; having received parts of his thoughts, she said, "You know who it is, don't you? I just heard from you."

It had been a few years since he had to shield his thoughts from her. She caught him off guard.

"You read my thoughts?" he said quickly in surprise.

"Is that what I just heard?"

Then gently falling from the sky, she didn't see this speck of stardust hit the top of her head.

Her head was on her pillow, and she felt the coolness of the sheets on her face. Suddenly she felt a bump hit her bed. She rolled over, noticing her favorite flowered sheets she had when she was eight or nine. Sitting on the edge of her bed was Sven. He put his hand on her leg and asked, "Hi, my dear, how are you?"

"I'm fine. Where have you been? I ask for you before I fall asleep. I wanted you in my dreams. Where do you go when you're not with me?" She sat up while rubbing the sleep from her eyes.

"I have an important job to attend. Other people rely on me." Sven's English accent made him sound authoritative and snobbish at the same time. While smiling, he patted her leg, reassuring her he heard her request.

"Do you want to go to study the stars tonight? Or would you rather go count? I think it's a good night to count."

"Can we, can we go right now? Do I need to change my clothes?" Cyril jumped inside with excitement.

"No, you're fine. I think you'll like the new craft I'm in. This time we'll sit inside and count." Traveling with Sven was an education. They spent most of the night going over the names of all the stars and planets in the sky. It was like a road map, he would say. Depending on where you were in the world and at what time of the day or night, you could read the stars to tell you how to get to any planet. He explained where his planet used to be and where the black holes were surrounding her planet.

Most nights, they studied the location of black holes. Sven would say, "It's critical learning." He explained that if you look at two or more lights from a distance that circled each other in a constant rotation, you can be safe to bet their orbit was caused by a black hole and that, within time, they would all be swallowed up eventually like his planet was. He always made it very clear you cannot escape the vortex or pull of a black hole, but you can if you're lucky to be propelled by it. But don't count on it, he would always say. It's like a spiderweb. It will take you in with no way out.

He said the reason they kept going over it was that they were invisible, similar to a vacuum that sucked planets up. So it's essential to know where they're located. He said all this would make sense once Cyril was older. He said he never wanted her to get lost once she was out there by herself. So it wasn't a dream, or was it? They never went far from the house. He would always race her to the top of the hill at the end of the canyon road. Most nights, it was windy at the top. You could hear crickets rubbing their legs together and the coyotes off in the distance. This time he flew her to Point Reyes Station, then they followed the water north to Bird Rock. They parked on the tip of Tomales Point to watch the water. The moon was sleeping that night, so it was very dark everywhere. They counted strange lights going in and out of the water.

The darkness surrounding the area made it easy to see the fast-moving crafts. Break the water's surface like peregrine falcons going into the water, cutting the surface sharply, not creating a wake. When they came out of the water, breaking the surface, it remained still like glass with no sign of any disturbance. Like everything in their presence, it remained still as if it flew at a speed, almost faster than their eyes could see. She counted the ones going into the water; Sven counted the ones going out of the water. That night more lights were going out than coming in. Sven reminded her to keep it in her little book. Cyril always wondered how he knew what nights to watch the lights and where.

When they went home, she very gently opened her bedroom window, balancing the lead weights that made the window go up; both hands were trying to keep it balanced. The old Victorian house was asleep. She noticed her bedroom lights were still off. Startled, she saw Ezek was sitting on the edge of her bed, facing the window as if he knew she was coming. His hands were in his lap. He smiled and asked calmly, "Where have you been?"

Sven stuck his head into the window and replied, "We went to count lights." Sven took her hand and told her, "You're doing very well. You're beginning to understand your surroundings much better." Sven nodded his head up and down, smiled, then squeezed her hand and said, "See you next time."

He then looked over to Ezek. "She has numbers to put in her book." Ezek leaned over, lying backward on the top of her bed, and opened the top nightstand drawer. He pulled out a small pink notebook with decals of planets stuck all over the outside. He slid the pencil out of the binding then opened it to the next page for entries as he handed it over to Cyril while never taking his eyes off Sven.

Cyril wrote the entry that night 36 in 92 out then the date. Ezek pulled back the blankets and gave her a look; she had to ask, "What's that look for? I can't hear you."

"I'm just glad you're safe. Can I go with you next time?"

"You already know everything."

"How can you say that? I have so much to learn."

Cyril understood him. She knew he wanted to learn. He just didn't like her out there by herself without him.

"I'll ask Sven next time, okay?"

"Come on, go to bed. It's late." He stood and waited.

Cyril got in between the sheets as Ezek covered her. Standing at the door, he stopped to ask, "Are you having more company tonight or going out again this evening?"

"Good night, Ezek." She did not answer his question, rolling over with her back to him.

Cyril knew he was in her head, and he had his answers.

Their bodies stopped; so did the music. Cyril hadn't noticed it before, but other people had also been dancing. Ezek whispered down to her, "You look lovely this evening, but tonight you sort of radiate. Share with me where did you go that time? What did you see? I hate it when I can't go with you!" At that moment, hearing him share how he felt brought her close to him.

"You realize this is supposed to be helping you regain your memory?"

What was it that made her believe everything he said unconditionally? "I went to count. I was a little girl flying in a craft new to me."

"Who were you flying with?" He acted as if he didn't already have the answer.

"Sven."

She could feel the atmosphere change at the mention of his name. So she asked, "Are you and Sven friends? Do you know each other?" Then out of nowhere…

Cyril had one arm around Roca, giving him a deep scratch.

Suddenly she heard a faint peep in the distance. Roca stayed seated but barked. Then a bright light shone on the living room ceiling, telling her a car was coming up the driveway. Ezek got out of the way while Roca ran to the front door. She sensed from Ezek no fear, so she also got up to see who it could be. They weren't expecting anyone. Immediately she registered all the information, getting some of it from Ezek, but noticing Roca's not barking.

Looking from the living room window, Cyril gathered, *Black car nondescript; two men wrinkled suits, no threat; both men feeling remorse, tired.* Ezek went out into the rain to greet them; as Cyril looked on, she wondered why he didn't ask the men to come inside.

The men got out of the car. Ezek made no gesture to ask them to come in out of the rain. The conversation was short. One man took a folded paper from his breast pocket then handed it to Ezek. Shaking both their hands, the men got back into the car. Ezek stood in the rain for a moment. Cyril sensed Ezek's thoughts were his own; she can't read him.

Frustrated, Cyril opened the door, yelling out, "I hate it when you do that!"

Looking up, while the rain was falling on him hard now, Ezek asked, "What? You hate it when I do what?"

"Why do you ask that? You know what I'm talking about." Slowly Ezek walked back into the house as Tully, the housekeeper, made her short strides across the kitchen toward him. Tully looked up to read his lips. Her head went down. Then she looked toward Cyril with a saddened face. Cyril looked into Ezek's eyes, trying to read him. His thoughts remained his own.

Then he said aloud, "Your parents' flight home over Greenland has been lost."

"What do you mean lost?" Cyril's voice weakened at the thought.

"Their flight went off the radar at six two this morning. There are no signs that the plane went down. They're just gone."

The folded wet paper stuck together as the ink started to blend the words. Carefully unfolding it, Ezek began to read it aloud. Cyril snatched it out of his hands, tearing the soft mushy paper. The only words she read were "Lost, no wreckage found, off radar 6:02. No survivors." She reread it. No survivors.

The world had stopped spinning. The moment lingered as she waited for it to change. Cyril looked around her. Ezek, dripping wet, wrapped his arms around her; but it gave her no comfort. Tully stood, holding a cup of warm tea in front of her. No amount of consoling could make it better. Her parents were gone, just gone, as he put it, "off the radar," not on the planet. Releasing herself from Ezek's grip, Cyril went out onto the patio into the pouring rain. Ezek followed behind her, taking the chair next to her.

They both looked up into the pouring rain. Ezek took her hand, trying to console her. Ezek knew her heart was broken. He knew her uncontrollable pain would make her cry. It had to be hidden by the rain for her to cry, so he waited with her, while Cyril sobbed uncontrollably. Cyril knew too often when something just vanishes or disappears, it has to go somewhere, but this time it was her parents. Could she say it out loud? Could she think her parents were gone? Could she say it out loud, taken or dead?

After almost an hour, Ezek felt the chill in his bones and knew she must be feeling the same, drenched and cold. He got up and lifted her from her chair and took her into the house. Cyril knew that everyone had already searched for any sign of her parents or the others on the plane. She felt it was out of her control.

Ezek felt Cyril shiver in his arms. "Are you cold?" he asked.

"No, it was the moment when you told me my parents were missing." She was still unable to accept the fact they were probably dead. Cyril could feel the cold from the moment and the rain. Wiping her cold face where she felt her warm tears had fallen, the sharp contrast of the bone-chilling cold and the hot tears sealed the memory.

"Why can't I get only good memories? This is like walking into someone else's life, someone else's nightmare. My god, what's next? Thank you for being there for me. I had no idea just how important you are to me." Cyril felt Ezek relax and gently hug her as they glided across the glass floor while the stars twinkled underneath them.

"Sweetheart, here comes another one." As Ezek's eyes watched, it melted into her skin.

Her skin felt damp but cool. She was lying naked on a cot facedown. Her wet sticky hair twisted in a knot atop her head, ready to unravel.

The temperature inside the tent had to be at least 120 degrees. She had been to the Libyan desert before but didn't remember it ever being this hot. Small gentle breezes outside the tent were gently stirring the sand that surrounded them. Armed guards quietly stood at every corner of the tents. Small camouflage sectors radiated from the tent, keeping her location undetermined.

Stillness surrounded the desert compound. No one was moving. Almost a whisper, "What's wrong with me?" she heard herself ask out loud to the person in the tent.

She heard water trickling on a wet surface. Then large cold hands gently wiped the surface of her skin, cooling her.

"You need to try and stay cool. Please try and relax."

The cot she was lying on was saturated with a combination of water and her blood.

His wet hands glided down her legs for just that moment. She felt him lightly blow on her damp skin, cooling her for a second.

"We'll be out of here soon. We need to wait for nightfall, then we'll go into the desert. They have your coordinates. They'll be here tonight, and by tomorrow at this time, you'll be home. Did you hear me? You'll be home," he whispered into her ear again.

She wondered to herself, *Am I dying? I feel no pain. The heat, the sweltering heat. Is this feeling heat stroke? Am I hallucinating? Is this all really happening?* For that moment, she felt she was out of danger. Only a small relief came over her. She was relieved she was in the hands of someone who made her feel safe. There's that safe thing again asking herself, what is safe anymore? Just the thought of it filled her with resentment and anguish.

"Sweetheart, stop worrying. You are safe. Please relax."

Sweetheart, she said the word over to herself, *sweetheart*.

It was almost like he was inside her head, listening to her every thought.

"Give me your arm." As he placed her palm on his hip, he gently wetted her arm to cool it, his breath like the wind across her surface. His hair moved, wafting his scent across her. For that moment, she felt a chill. Everything that was happening seemed like it was in slow motion.

"You haven't answered me," she said aloud, with what energy remained inside her.

"What, sweetheart?" His voice was gentle, trying to calm her. He knew she needed to know and searched inside himself for the right words to not escalate the situation. Keeping his thoughts to himself was always a challenge with her. She too could walk into his thoughts and hear him thinking, but only if he opened it to her.

He had never taught her how to close her mind to him; he left it as an open door.

"Am I dying?" she said slowly, wanting to know what time she had left.

Her mind searched for answers realizing that when Ezek didn't answer, she knew it could only be because he had nothing good to tell her.

With anger and weakness in her voice, she said, "I am dying. I won't make it into the desert. They won't find me." Her voice emptied.

Ezek realized he was losing her, and her hallucinating thoughts were making it worse. The heat wasn't the problem. It was her lack of blood; her casualties were severe. He had saved her before, as she had saved him before. This time Ezek sent all his thoughts out for help. He whispered to her, "Sweetheart, I am praying in the only way I know how. You are not dying!" He said it as though saying it aloud would make it true. Ezek's words radiated to as far and wide as he could pray.

She barely heard his words but knew for him to pray, then yes, she really was dying. She felt his breath across her wet skin, and his emotions felt raw to her, creating panic inside of her. The cool wetness of her skin while feeling the warmth of his wide hand was her only connection to life as she fell into the darkness.

Ezek felt her body suddenly go limp in his arms, and caught her, preventing her from falling. Her eyes slowly opened. Effortlessly he held her and smiled. "Hi, is there anything you want to share with me?"

Suddenly she felt the floor under her feet. "I need to sit down… please." Saying it exhausted her breath.

From a distance, she could see Steam and Sven stand up at the table, both realizing something had happened. Ezek had his arm around her, casually walking with her to the table. Steam quickly pulled out a chair, taking her arm, helping her to sit.

Sven asked Ezek, "Is she okay? What did she see?"

She looked up at him wanting to say, "I'm right here. Why don't you ask me?" But she composed herself then darted him a look and said, "I just need to take a break, Ezek. Would you introduce me?" She already knew it was Sven, her teacher, then she looked directly into Sven's eyes. For as long as she had known him, he hadn't aged a day: straight blondish brown hair, no gray. Tall, always stood up straight, slender like he would be a good yoga teacher. Eye contact with Sven was always quick; he was always looking at something else, something more important. He dressed in an old style, his suits made only of silks or tweeds in fall colors no matter what time of the year it was. In his left pierced ear was a thick gold ring, his only jewelry. His eyes matched his wardrobe sometimes, kind of light-brown-reddish green color. Sven's eyes changed with his mood.

She never knew what color they were at any given time. His skin was never tanned but fair; big light-brown freckles covered a path over his nose and cheeks. His cheeks were easily flushed with an embarrassing conversation. His voice was deep, and his accent was from the far north.

She felt an uneasy look from Sven. What was it about him that so much conflict jumped into her heart when their eyes met? She had always trusted him; he taught her how to be safe when she was little. He taught her how to read planets and black holes. He was her friend. She remembered calling him before she went to sleep sometimes. He would show up; sometimes he wouldn't. She felt close to him. Then it occurred to her she cared for him, but what was the difference between the feeling of love versus hate? Did she have anyone in her life she hated? But this feeling while looking into Sven's eyes felt like love. But it was different; it wasn't the way she felt with Steam, nor was it the same with Ezek. Could it still be love? Was the feeling of love and hate different, or were they? Was the passion the same? Was one more accepting than the other, maybe more cautious than the other?

When she saw Steam, then when she met Ezek, it was overwhelming how her heart suddenly felt love. Who was this man? Who was he to her? Why was he so concerned about what she saw? Why was everyone so worried about what she was seeing? This was her life. Why was it so important to them?

Ezek handed her a glass of ice water and asked, "Do you want to go home?"

"No, why can't I see just the good stuff?" Looking over to Ezek, she asked, "There are good parts, right? I had a good life, didn't I? Please tell me there are good parts. How long does this stuff last anyway?"

Before anyone could answer her…

Her eyes were closed, and she's lying on her left side facing her bedroom door. The sheets were warm, and there's a smell in the room that's hauntingly familiar but from long, long ago.

Examining the moment before opening her eyes, she pictured her bedroom. The door was just ahead, maybe ten feet away. Then running along the wall were all her favorite artists all framed in a variety of frames. Then the bathroom door, across the foot of the bed, a row of three floor-to-ceiling windows looking out onto the rolling hills. Then a small corner wall displaying a copy of the oil painting by Van Gogh (*Cafe Terrace on the Place du Forum*), a place she often met? Then her memory stopped. Who did she meet there? How many times had she been there as her mind searched? Arles, France, on a warm afternoon sipping a cold drink while watching the tourists waiting, but waiting for who? she wondered.

Feeling the cold spot on her sheets, she's sensing someone was in front of her face. For a moment, she imagined them on their knees at the side of her bed. Then she heard them ever so quietly breathe in as she breathed out. Concentrating on their ability to do it ever so quietly, she kept her eyes closed. She did it, again and again; they breathed in. Now she knew someone was in her face breathing her exhale. Then suddenly, someone got in bed behind her, spooning themselves in, cozying in close with an arm around her waist, wafting their scent. This fit was familiar. *If that's Ezek's arm around me, then who's in my face?* Sensing no threat, she decided to open her eyes—startled because of the closeness. Suddenly she jerked back only because he's too close to see, smacking herself into Ezek's chest.

Then she heard Ezek say, "Would you get away from her? She needs to wake up," as the warmth from Ezek's skin surrounded her. Twyce, with his watery almost-white blue eyes, stared into her. His skin was flawless and touchable. His shiny short finger curls reckless atop his head. Looking like a lumberjack in his red plaid shirt and tight Levi's. Lying still, she asked Ezek, "How long has he been here?" Inside she was thrilled to see him but started wondering how long he had taken in her breath. And morning breath besides. Still staring at her, his eyes never moving off her, he told Ezek as if she's not there, "I love this woman. Why won't you let me have her?"

Cyril smiled, flattered, still staring. "Good morning, Twyce, how are you?"

Twyce leaned in and kissed her on the forehead. "I was doing really good until I got caught by this guy."

As Ezek shoved his brother away from the edge of the bed, Cyril rolled onto her back; and before she knew it, Twyce was lying on top of the covers. Roca ran in and jumped on the bed, always staying at the foot where now there's very little room. "Down, Roca, get down," Ezek ordered him.

"So what are your plans for today? Are you two working?" Twyce asked while kicking his shoes off onto the floor.

"The last time I saw this dog, he was just a puppy. Where did you say you got him? Didn't you rescue him off the freeway or something?"

"Yes, he was just a puppy. Someone left him in the medium. I think they were hoping he'd get hit by a car and be done with. He watched all the cars go by. He didn't move, so I went over and grabbed him. He doesn't look so bad now, does he?"

"No, he turned out to be a nice dog," Twyce said. "Smart too, though."

As she stared back at Twyce, she too wondered if he's anything like his brother.

Owning her thoughts, she waited for Ezek to read her mind when he sent his thoughts to her. "No, he's nothing like me!" He made his point clear to her.

From years ago, she remembered Ezek's first description defining his only brother: "He's a cocksman. You need to be careful of him."

Cyril asked, "What's a cocksman?"

Her hand still feeling the surface of the cold glass, she fell back in her chair. Ezek smiled at her, having read her moment. She still felt the touch of his skin against hers. The waft of his scent against her sheets as his hair fell around her. Reading her thoughts about Twyce, Ezek gave her a shy look, but she didn't read it back.

As she brought the glass to her lips to take a sip, she looked straight ahead at her right index finger. On top of the glass was illuminated by the stardust that just hit the top of her finger.

The window went down. Cyril heard the air rush in. She opened just one eye, her cheek against the door. Looking out for as far as she could see flat dry nothing. The desert went on forever. Looking over to Cindy with both hands on the steering wheel, she appeared to be in a trance. Her eyes fixed on the white broken line in front of her that seemed to go nowhere forever.

"Are we there yet?" Cyril asked, knowing they weren't.

"Do you want to stop and walk around?" Cindy slowed the car.

"Yes, please. I have to stretch my legs. Do you want me to drive for a while?"

"We should be there soon. I'd like to get water out of the back. Do you want one?"

"Yeah, that would be great."

Yawning with her mouth wide open, she began to pull her hair back. Cyril looked out in the vast desert of nothing, yawning again, catching her breath.

"I hope we find something. I hope this trip isn't a waste." Cindy stood drinking her water, leaning against her blue Subaru. She looked out, thinking, *This is where it all happens. This is the place no one comes to look.*

"So how are you going to answer when asked, 'So what did you do on your spring break?'" Cyril smiled at Cindy, both knowing there would be no answer to that question, maybe a lie.

Out in the middle of nowhere, they followed the long fence line waiting to see if they would be discovered. After spending most of the day watching planes and helicopters leave the central restricted area, they decided to wait for the cover of nightfall. With the half-moon waning knowing every night would get darker, they would enter uninvited, memorizing how they got in and out, hoping not to get caught.

After two days, they discovered the weakest spot in the security. They did their homework and had already studied the security system intensely.

The guards' scheduling was a little more complicated; they found the shifts hard to predict, but each guard's location stayed the same. They were mapping out their plan, making it into what was lovingly called Area 50. After comparing the traffic in both places, 51 was where the public went to snoop. Just a few miles away, even more remote, was another fenced compound. Only a few went in; its traffic was small.

But after finding out who was in and how long they were staying, it left them with more questions than answers. After months of research, the traffic going into this remote area compared to the famous Area 51 was where they needed to go.

Cindy and Cyril were convinced that Area 51 was just a distraction to the public. They decided this was where all the good stuff was hidden. Both science majors had their own truth based on their personal experiences. Cyril's heart was pounding, breathing in slow, long, quiet breaths. Cindy's eyes were like radar catching every movement surrounding them. Past the guards and into the lobby down the hall to an inconspicuous door with no distinction. They examined the outside of the door. Heavy traffic on the floor. The foot traffic stopped here at the front of the door. The doorknob was polished from use, the paint on the sides rubbed constantly. They both agreed this was the door they heard would take them to the elevator. Down the dark hall, one light went on. It was displayed on the elevator door, one button showing an arrow pointing down.

Cindy and Cyril knew this was it. Once in the elevator, it occurred to both of them now they were in uncharted territory. Who would be on the other side of the elevator doors when it opened? After all the time they spent researching the facility, they both knew now they were crossing the line inside the point of no return. When the elevator door opened, lights went on one after the other, going deeper and deeper, spotlighting all the past visitors' transportation. In awe, they stood with so much to see it overwhelmed them.

They had been on some of the ships before; but at the moment, when it was happening to them, they had to call it a dream. How else could they deal with it otherwise?

"Who flies in ships like these?" The words slowly came out of Cindy's mouth. Some were flat disks shaped, some long metallic or black, all different shapes and sizes; some made a faint vibrating sound when you would approach them. Still, when you got a distance away from it, it would stop silent. Strange fluorescent cones went around an empty circle. The minute you stepped into its circle, it appeared almost round like a ball blending into its surroundings once you could see it. When you approached another ship, it began to glow only on the bottom so you could see your way into it.

Walking through the rows of the first five ships, Cindy took Cyril's arm and quietly motioned. Cindy started pointing toward the floor. She was insisting they go deeper. Cyril acknowledged as they both went back to the elevator. Cindy was pressing the button to go to the next floor. Again, that terrifying moment when the door would open. Who would discover them? Looking at the interior of the elevator, they noticed no camera. There was a phone and a panic button. Cyril pointed to the panic button and whispered to Cindy, "Just in case."

The door opened. The lights were already on large glass tubes displaying bodies suspended in a clear fluid. The room smelled of a combination of formaldehyde and fresh oranges. In the distance, you could hear a small fan and a faint beep every twenty seconds. Cyril understood the sound to mean something needed to be rebooted. So she walked over and touched it like she would have under the circumstances for that moment, not thinking. Cyril whispered to herself so Cindy could hear her, "Oh shit, what have I done?"

Then out of nowhere, oxygen began to circulate into the first three cylinders.

The inhabitant's eyes began to turn deep purple with a bright mustard yellow color spiking in the iris.

Inside the first tank was a long slender body; it seemed strangely familiar to Cyril, almost haunting. The head was larger than most; its eyes slowly began to open. The eyelids went from the top down, opposite from anything she had ever remembered seeing.

They were large and appeared to be black.

Cyril knew that they were a dark purple with fine yellow lines in the iris striking outward without looking closer. Its skin appeared to be smooth but with extremely fine transparent hairs like velour or velvet. Cyril recalled touching it at some time or other. She knew it was smooth and soft; its light green-gray surface always felt cool to the touch.

Where its nose appeared in front was actually its hearing, and on both sides of its neck was how it would smell its surrounding area. Its front and back were a green-gray color. On its front was a soft white circle; this represented its sex. You weren't able to tell what sex it was until it wanted to have sex. Either it protruded, or it opened whatever was needed at the moment.

This sexual situation is also known as gynandromorph, having both sexes in one physical form.

On the back, running along the spine, were small oval brown spots flanking both sides from the top of its head down to its feet.

Its hand was missing a finger, only having three fingers and one thumb. This one's right hand had all the fingers chopped off, with only a thumb remaining. The fingers were multijointed and could extend twice their length. At the tips where our fingernails are, they have lethally sharp pointed nails; the same occurred on its feet.

Along its sides, the skin appeared white and thin you could see when it was breathing. A faint puckering-like kiss noise came from its mouth, almost like the noise a fish would make when breaking the surface of the water to get air. The other two in the tanks were smaller. One seemed older; the gray on its skin appeared much darker than the others. Cyril touched Cindy and pointed to the tube, both not making a sound; then Cindy pointed back to the elevator for them to get out of there. Cyril nodded as they both went into the elevator to go to the next lower floor even deeper. This time it took longer as the elevator descended faster than before, almost ten minutes; and unable to stop it, they waited. As it dropped, it began to slow down; then it landed on what felt like bumping into a cloud. This time when the doors opened, both stood ready to defend themselves. Terrified, they gave one last look at each other just before the doors opened. Again, the lights were already on. There stood a man half of Cindy's height wearing a white lab coat. He smiled and said, "I've been waiting for you. What took you guys so long?" as he turned to walk away from them both. They left the elevator to follow him.

Cyril looked at the white cloth covering the table: it was like the white cloth of the man's lab coat she had just followed out of the elevator with Cindy. Steam smiled as his arm went up, motioning for assistance. A beautiful young man leaned in to hear him; he then nodded, smiled, then left the table.

"You said something about oranges. I've sent for some. They will be here in just a minute."

Ezek asked, "Cyril, did you say you wanted oranges?"

"What?" Cyril looked around the table and realized she had said something out loud while in her moment, something about oranges.

"No, I don't want any oranges. I want you to tell me about Cindy. Who is she?"

Placing the glass up to her lips to sip, looking to her right there on her wrist, she saw the stardust sink slowly into her skin.

She felt a cool morning breeze across her face when she walked barefoot out the French doors onto the stone patio. Roca ran out from behind her, darting into the trees that lined the patio, sniffing each tree one by one while Cyril looked out to the rolling hills. The large oak trees shaded her from the morning sun. Startled, she noticed a man sitting at the table drinking something. He quickly stood up, put his cup down, and smoothed the creases from the front of his long burnt-orange *thawb*. "Good morning, Cyril. How did you sleep?"

Looking over to Roca, he said, "Your dog, Roca, you call him? He knows everything that goes on around you. He's a good dog." Roca ran past him like he posed no threat.

Then Roca went to Cyril, almost like asking for something he had smelled on the table.

Cyril took a chair across from him to sit down when Ezek dashed up behind her, scooting in her seat leaning in; he said, "This is—"

Cyril interrupted him and said, "I know who you are. You're my mother's friend. I remember seeing you when I was little."

"Yes, that's true, but he's also my father, Cyril. This is Henry." Ezek stood behind her, interjecting, completing what he was about to say. "Your father, why didn't you tell me he was coming?"

"I just found out last night. Tully had everything ready for him. Nothing to worry about."

"I'm sorry to intrude," Henry said in a guilty tone.

"No, please, you're always welcome here. I just wish I would have been prepared."

Ezek put his hands on her shoulders, gently pulling back her hair. "It's okay. We were ready for him." Then, with sarcasm, he glanced at his brother. "But I had no idea you were coming too, Cyril. You remember me telling you about my younger brother Twyce?"

"Twyce," she interjected, "of course, how could I forget?" as her eyes took him in.

"Yes, he's the troublemaker, but I couldn't live without him." There was a playfulness in his voice as his brother came up behind him, giving him a bear hug.

Cyril was noticing both men were both the same height and weight. Their skin was similar to their father's but lighter touchable. Their hair was completely different. Ezek's coal-black, soft, thick, full of body, Twyce's brown finger curls; you wanted your hands in both. Their eyes one watery green, the other watery blue, both strikingly handsome. The minute Cyril realized what she was thinking, and around these guys, it was like talking aloud. Ezek looked at his father, knowing his father could hear her, then over to Twyce. While sliding his hand down the back of her neck like a short massage, her thoughts went directly to him. Stopping her thoughts about comparing them, suddenly she was exposed almost naked in what she was thinking. The three men smiled. Cyril felt the smile and felt the thank you as their eyes dashed around to each other. Henry was amused.

Needing to change the moment, "When was the last time you saw each other?" she asked.

Almost feeling embarrassed and exposed, but then owning it, *Yes*, she said to herself for the three of them to hear, *yes, you three are all very handsome.*

"So what brings you here, Henry? Finally came to see where your son spends most of his time?"

Henry darted a look at Ezek, as if saying, "Should we talk about it?" He looked to Ezek for permission before he spoke.

"I came to clear things up." Henry walked slowly. She didn't realize how tall he was. Her eyes stayed on him while he walked around the patio, looking out onto the hills. He was a handsome man. The color of his eyes matched Ezek's, a soft, light celadon green. His long white hair rippled down his back; it's a sharp contrast to his perfect almost-black skin.

"It has been reported by the council that you're getting ready to tell the world that we're here, and now you're able to prove it."

Twyce pulled out the chair next to her and sat down to listen to his father while Ezek remained behind Cyril.

"Your scientific evidence is conclusive and, most of all, credible and compelling, which is why I'm here. Your mother told me years ago you would be the one to find the answer if she were here right now. I would love to tell her, 'You told me so.'" Looking back at Cyril, he smiled and said, "I miss your mother. I love her very much."

Cyril adjusted herself in her chair, turning toward Henry to ask, "One answer I don't have is why are you here mixing in with us?" Henry sent a sharp look at Ezek, kinda shocked, then said, "You say that like you're not one of us!"

Twyce smiled and said, "You're kidding really with all the research you've done. It's always been right there in front of you." A half laugh jumped from his voice.

Ezek shot him a "shut-up stare." Catching it, Twyce shut up and just gave Cyril an "I'm sorry" half smile.

It suddenly occurred to her what was happening.

She could talk to Ezek just by thinking about him. Most people couldn't; she aged slower than her classmates, always looking a little bit younger than people her age, but then so did Steam and Cindy. She was left-handed; and with Rh negative blood, she had spent so much time researching all the factors, not once looking at herself. Was she getting ready to rat out on her own race? Was this the big secret her father didn't want her to know, but her mother did? Henry turned and walked up to her, taking both her hands looking down on her. "To answer that question, yes, your mother wanted you to know. She wanted you to see the advantages of it all. But at the same time, to be like all the other children, she wanted you to fit in. She wanted your life to be normal here on this planet." Henry turned to walk around the table, looking back at Cyril. Twyce and Ezek watched as their father explained. "Cyril, your father was totally against you knowing your species. This was your parents' biggest conflict. But you need to know they did work together on a project for years, and we're getting closer to implementing it throughout the world. Your mother wanted our presence kept a secret, always knowing the threat it posed to her family and the rest of us here. She knew the scientific advantages of how our knowledge could help this planet. But at the same time, it creates conflict with other species, including the Grays. She knew you would want peace and, in your line of work, would strive to achieve it. In your conflict, the Grays were not capable of keeping the peace as you wanted it. The harvesting would always continue for the Grays to survive. Your relationship with them has been admirable." Henry turned to smile at Cyril while clutching his hands.

"The separation of Grays and your recent studies on them shows like humans and us— there are always bad apples in every bunch. Your mother found this out early on and knew the Grays would have to go. And that our species could stay in the shadows leaking our technology to help humankind here. Your mother and I have a strong bond. It led me to believe in her convictions. I think she found her answer, one I know you have also been looking for. The secret has to remain just that, a secret. We have always mixed in well. We hope it remains that way."

For a moment, Cyril stopped; every thought in her mind raced to only one conclusion: her mother had the answer, one she had also been looking for. She knew her parents saw her fight the Quiet War, as she would refer to it, separating them from the Grays and the others. Cyril was sorting the good from the bad. She knew the planet was not big enough for everyone, and only one race needed to go. The harvesting had to stop. She remembers lying in the hospital with a broken arm and bandage covering over 70 percent of her body. Her mother explained that she would find a way to get the Grays off the planet.

Her father, on that visit, found a moment alone with her. He was angry. "I've told you before, but you refuse to listen. You need to drop this. This has nothing to do with you. Go back to school, get married, but do something else. You're going to get yourself killed. Look at yourself. How many times do you have to end up in the hospital before you learn? Ezek's going to get tired of saving you, then what are you going to do?" She felt her father's words. Words in her mind went on a list of what else she was told *not* to do. That list just got a bit longer.

She looked at Henry. Before she could say it out loud, he answered, "Don't worry, we'll find your parents. I'm sure they're just finishing up loose ends. I don't feel your mother is gone from us. There is a part of her I hold in my soul. I feel she's still there." For just that moment, Cyril's heart melted. Henry knew her parents were alive. He had the courage and reassurance to say it out loud, almost like a confirmation.

"And to that other burning question you have wondered about most of your life, he's shy. He has a big heart."

Henry smirked and gave her a half smile, trying to lighten the mood. Cyril looked at Ezek. "So what you're saying is not everyone can swim. Ezek can't swim. I have always wondered why not."

Henry looked down at the stones on the patio floor, saying slowly, "His mother was the same way." He shook his head. "She always sank like a stone in water. I wish she had learned to swim."

"Tell her why you don't swim, or should we have Twyce tell her the story?"

After all these years, Cyril remained shocked. There was a reason, and he'd never shared it with her.

The cold glass wetted her fingertips as she set it onto the table.

Ezek put his hand on her arm then looked into her eyes, making sure she was back. "Please be patient. This can't be easy on you, but it will help to get you back."

She could see and feel the trust in him. It was comforting, but still, she wondered just how much of her was gone and what parts of her life escaped her.

Ezek said, "We all know who you are and what you have accomplished. What we don't know is how this happened to you and why." Running through her mind, she searched for who these men were to her.

Ezek, faint accent; he also spoke eight languages fluently. Loyal, educated with a few PhDs, patient, thoughtful, considerate, trusting, easy to talk to with a great sense of humor. Tall, dark, and very handsome. She had already asked if they were married. No, he's not her husband. But she had an unarming way of trusting him. He answered to no one except maybe to her, but why?

Steam's extremely intelligent, a doctor of oncology, and a few PhDs. He spoke three languages fluently. He owned his own business. He had a big heart. Also, Cyril found him to be very handsome, tall, trusting, born at the same hospital on the same day, now her employer. How did that happen? she wondered.

Sven, a man of few words but intelligent. A doctor with one PhD and two master's. Personable, again handsome, freckled ivory skin, muscular, spoke with an accent, sometimes hard to understand when he got excited or mad. He'd always been in her life. Not aged a day since she first met him. She was not yet getting a clear picture of him, still a lot of blank spaces. *Why was he there when I was little?* A lot of questions still needed to be answered.

She looked around the table, feeling uncomfortable at what was going on, when Sven said, "Cyril, here comes—" before he could finish his sentence.

Suddenly Cyril found herself lying in tall wet grass. Just ahead she saw a dark figure in the distance. The same dark figure she had hunted for two days, only this time it was before dawn and just outside her property. Upon the hill, she watched as the figure set the high-powered rifle toward her home.

She knew Ezek and Tully were inside the house. Then it came to her he's going to shoot toward them. This figure wasn't spying on them; he's an assassin. She put her thoughts together and said to Ezek, "Please lie down *now*. I'm here on a hill across the house. Someone is here to kill you. I'm here to stop them. Be careful. Please be careful. *Lie flat now.*"

Every part of her had to remain calm. She had to take him out first. She quickly calculated his distance. Quietly walking through the tall wet grass, she estimated the .338 Lapua rifle would be her best choice, under the circumstances. Cyril quietly took the rifle from her trunk. The ten-round magazine was already in the rifle. She aimed it toward the target. She lay flat on her stomach. The bipod legs extended down, resting the barrel, balancing it just so, quietly focusing. She put the crosshairs on her target, squeezing the trigger halfway. Suddenly the tracking system followed the dark figure. The target was tagged.

As she watched the blue lights follow the target, all four arrows lit to red.

She thought about the temperature; it was cool. The wind was almost calm coming from the north.

She slowly inhaled. Focusing, the dark figure stayed still in the red crosshairs. *Perfect*, she repeated to herself, knowing Ezek could hear her thoughts. It all had to be perfect. She pulled the trigger back slowly, hitting the hard spot, then she stopped. She exhaled. All four red arrows aligned before she could finish praying, her finger pressed to complete the shot.

She saw the dark figure drop their rifle and slump over, not hearing any shot from him. Cyril laid the buttstock of the rifle on the grass and began running toward the target. Slowly approaching, she heard nothing while her ears were still ringing. The target lay still.

In her left hand, she held her 9mm pistol toward the target. Cyril was ready for any sign of movement. Coming from behind, she touched his warm neck to feel a pulse. Blood wetted her fingertips. The target was still, no pulse, no movement. Rolling him over slowly, she saw the bullet's entrance and the massive exit to one side of his head. Collecting herself holstering her pistol, nestled in the grass Cyril saw the screen of a cell phone fade to black, she ran back to her spot and threw the rifle up against her shoulder, holding the buttstock in the palm of her hand. Carefully she walked back through the tall wet grass to her car. No thoughts came to her as she rounded the country road then up her driveway.

When she entered the house, Ezek stood casually leaning against the kitchen counter, his ankles crossed. With a cup of hot tea in one hand, while he held the string dunking the tea bag into the hot water, he calmly asked, "Hey, was that you I just heard?"

He pointed with his thumb toward the hallway. "Tully is lying on the floor in her room. Strange how she never asks why she just does it. Do you want to go in and tell her she can get up now?"

Cyril stood in the middle of the kitchen; her words came out slowly. She said, "I shot a man."

Ezek stared for a moment, having heard every word she said, then slowly walked up to her.

She repeated it, only this time she heard what she was saying. She repeated it out loud, not believing a word of it.

"I shot a man. He was going to shoot you, and I shot him first."

"Where is he?" There was an intense look from Ezek.

"He's close by, over on top of the ridge." Cyril's head nodded to the north.

"I heard the shot from here. Are you all right?"

"I just shot a man. Sure, I'm okay." She shook her head in disbelief.

"Why did he want to shoot me? Who is he?" bewildered, Ezek wondered.

"I don't know."

Ezek put down the cup then slowly walked over to her and held her in his arms. He whispered, "It's over, sweetheart, it's over. We're all right. Everyone's all right. I'll take care of it. You stay here. I'll be right back. Don't leave."

"I'm coming with you!" she stated.

"No, go in and tell Tully she can get off the floor. I'll be right back."

"I'm going too!"

"Please, you've been up all night. I'll take care of this and be right back." He saw that there was no arguing with her as they both jumped into her car.

She put her hand on Ezek's arm, looking up into his eyes. She heard Steam say, "She's back. What did you see?"

Ezek smiled at her. "You're okay, you're okay, sweetheart." He nodded in a yes motion.

"Yes, I just saw the moment I shot the man that tried to kill you."

"You can breathe now. That's all over with. Breathe, sweetheart, breathe." It was like he washed the moment away with his words.

It hadn't occurred to her she had stopped breathing, as if she was still readying for her deadly shot, not making a move, steadying herself, knowing that if she missed, he would die; and then she might be next.

To breathe was a liberating moment. It separated her from being terrified. Terrified of missing the shot, terrified of losing him, terrified of all the things that went with the moment. As she exhaled, she could still feel the pain in her left shoulder from just one shot.

Sven stood then walked around the table holding his hand out. "Can I have this dance?" Hearing the music softly in the distance, she felt Ezek stir. Glancing at him, she thought for a moment Ezek was going to stand up and deck him. She felt his tenseness as she stood to take Sven's hand, putting her other hand on Ezek's shoulder, letting him know quietly.

"Please don't."

Ezek's eyes looked toward the floor, as he brushed the sparkly gold chiffon from her dress off his chair, as if dismissing her; feeling his moment, he looked over to her and smiled almost as if saying, "I'm sorry for that."

Was that the old Ezek that was so much a part of her life, the one who protected her, the one who kept her safe? Did he catch himself grabbing at his past, her past when she was his and only his?

Touching Sven's hand gave her no response, like feeling a stranger, like feeling something dead. Cold in his demeanor, she searched for any kind of feeling; then when they arrived on the dance floor, his arm went around her waist. Sven saw the moment the stardust hit the top of her head, falling into her hair into her past.

Deep

Looking up, she watched the passing numbers of the elevator drop her and Sven into the deepest part of the desert. She looked over to Sven and whispered, "I hate coming here."

The lights of the elevator flickered off and on, falling deep into the desert.

"Why are you afraid? Do you think they're going to keep you here?" He looked down his nose at her, thinking it was a joke.

"Well, it is sort of a prison, don't you think?" She swallowed deep, trying to get her ears to pop from the altitude.

"Yes, for people like you, you mean."

"I'm not one of them, and you know it. Look at yourself, calling the kettle black or should I say Gray." She glared at him. After almost fifteen minutes, she felt it begin to slow down. Then it softly stopped. The doors opened; her ears popped while she tried to yawn again. The altitude was different; you could feel they were deep into the earth's crust.

"We've been expecting you. The new residences are this way." The short man in the white coat turned and began to walk forward down the well-lit hallway.

"How many did you get this time?" Cyril was hoping for a large number as the faint smell of oranges filled her memory.

"Four hundred twenty-seven, but it wasn't easy. We lost 410 of them. They don't want to be discovered. It's rather weird how they can go through glass. It took us a while to figure it out, thanks to your colleagues in Anomalies. That ladies got all kinds of answers. We've been working with Cindy, the head researcher. She said these are very young rogue Grays. She called them the Harvesters. They're responsible for the red orbs we keep getting reports about."

Cyril remembered the night Cindy called her. It was late.

Cindy's voice was frantic; she was talking ninety miles an hour. The first thing she said was "They were here."

"Who was there? Calm down, relax, just explain it to me. Who was there?"

"Okay, listen, I was trying to turn over in bed. I was stone cold, dead asleep, and couldn't turn over. I didn't realize it, but while I was asleep, I had sat up. I don't sit up while I'm asleep… What's that all about?"

"Okay, calm down, just tell me what happened."

"Okay, okay, when I realized I was sitting up, I felt that something was holding my hands down, making it hard for me to move. I felt like I had just been put there. Do you get it? Like I was just put there! Like I had just returned! I looked over to my right and saw one in front of me. Another one was at the foot of my bed. When they realized I was waking up, I heard inside my head like *Oh shit, she's awake,* and that's when they both dashed out through the closed sliding door right through the glass. They were short, a little bit taller than the height of a doorknob. Did you get that they went right through the glass?"

"I'm listening."

The next day, Cindy had all the glass replaced in her home with chicken wire glass. To this day, they can't figure out how to get through it.

"The biggest problem is these Grays are dangerous. We attribute them to most of the missing people reports. You're familiar with Harvesters?" He stopped, turned around, and waited for Cyril's answer.

"Yes, I have toured their facilities. They can harvest thousands of humans in a single day. And all they want is their plasma and the white blood cells. Apparently, it also helps their immune system while they're on this planet. Strange, they only need it while they're here. I see you've replaced the glass."

Cyril looked through the fractured chicken wire glass to the first Gray's cell. This one was short in stature. His arms seemed to be longer than most, you would almost think he had a smirk on his face. His skin was a medium gray-green in color. Along his back were very small brown oval spots that flanked his spine. His fingers were uncommonly short, but the tip of his remaining three fingerlike extensions were lethally sharp. His thumb was gone on his right hand.

His feet were wide, and his toes appeared to be chopped off except for the small one on the outside left.

His mouth appeared to be saying something.

"The first one we see here is the easiest to communicate with," the man explained, looking back at Cyril.

"Yes, I remember how it works. It started the minute the gray saw her."

"Really, it's taken me almost two weeks to hear them. Have you noticed they kinda smell almost like oranges?"

"You should have called us sooner. We're all able to communicate with them. Yes, I noticed that. The orange smell, weird, huh? Wow, this guy's mad. Can you get him something to eat? Go to the local pound or slaughterhouse and feed these guys. Oh, keep water away from them. It's not their favorite thing."

Sven quietly looked into the cell and smiled at the Gray. Cyril knew they were talking to each other. Only she couldn't hear what they were saying. Both had locked out their thoughts to her.

Suddenly the Gray's voice was unmistakable. He interrupted her thought and told her it was none of her business what they were saying to each other, as he glared at her with his vacant purple with mustard spiked eyes.

"I'll sign off on the seventeen you have in custody and transport them to our new facility. Sven, do you have any questions before we go?"

"I want to see the rest of them. Where are they?" Sven asked as he walked down the corridor.

As Cyril walked with them, she remembered the first time she toured their harvest facility. The hall was a green color, and the smell was unmistakably that of death and blood. Her escort was a Gray half her size; he explained inside her head how the processing there worked.

"First, we strip them, then rest them, with their arms and legs extended straight out resting their head and neck; then they're quickly lanced. Once the flow starts, it takes maybe an hour for them to drain. Then after that, we change them out for fresh ones."

The small Gray turned and asked, no sound coming from its small opening we would refer to as a mouth. "See anyone you know?" he quipped as he walked away.

Cyril looked out into the room; she could see the round tables go off in the distance, thousands of them each holding ten to twelve bodies each. Grays of all sizes were helping the corpses lie comfortably as each was cleanly lanced. The flow started, echoing under the floor, dripping faster and faster. All the heads went to the center tilted down inward toward the center hole where blood dripped to the floor below.

"The blood is collected in the large vat under the floor. It's constantly churning as we try to keep it cool zero degrees Celsius," the Gray explained.

Cyril remembered walking to the railed viewing area looking over the side; she saw an ocean of churning blood as she gripped the rail. When Cyril turned to leave the room, she was stopped. For that moment, panic flooded her. She wanted out now!

"Look, they're changing out," said the small Gray, happy to see more coming.

Tethered by their feet, each body rose to the ceiling, their faces emotionless; then up they went out of sight out of mind, returning with fresh full corpses to be drained.

Bodies of all sizes. Large and small, white, black, yellow, red, men, women, even small children, mothers, daughters, sons, loved ones. This was the ultimate melting pot. Blood was blood; it apparently didn't matter who it came from at that moment. We were all the same, whether rich or poor; we had only one value now. She remembered thanking the Gray for the extensive tour. The smell of blood lingered in her clothing for the rest of her trip.

On their way back up the elevator, Sven wrote a note on his board, his thumbs moving faster than any conversation out loud could be.

"What did the Gray say to you that was none of my business?" Cyril said in a friendly tone, hoping to get an honest answer.

"You were right. He is hungry. He doesn't like to be confined. He needs more sunlight to stay alert."

Was he complimenting her to distract her from their conversation? Then she commented, "You didn't tell them we figured out about the sunlight, did you?"

"No, but he will be asleep in a few hours because of it. It will be easier to transport them."

"What haven't you told me? Why was it so easy for my thoughts to be cut off? Why were you leaving me out of the conversation with him? It's imperative I know what they need and what they are saying. Don't you understand that? Why are you turning the tables on me? What's going on here?"

Cyril walked quickly down the hallway to the elevator. She needed to get to the surface as soon as possible.

She sensed fear and radiated her thoughts to Ezek. Miles down below the surface, she recalled her words to Sven. "It feels like a prison," he said back then, "for people like you." For that moment, she felt like she was underwater, not being able to catch her breath to reach the surface, then quickly she felt a wash come over her. The words that came into her head were "Breathe, breathe, you are in control. Breathe, you will arrive on the surface in fourteen minutes. I will be waiting for you. Breathe. Now smile. I said *smile*. You're not *smiling*. Smile." The voice became louder in her head.

Cyril smiled and looked up at Sven. She showed her confidence and relaxed her stance while she felt her body move through the earth's crust. She steadied her breathing; then it all came to a stop. The door opened quickly, and before her was Ezek.

He smiled while ignoring Sven.

Ezek handed her his board, for only her eyes to see. "I thought you might want to see this." He deliberately left Sven out of the conversation.

The music was slow as she felt her eyes open. Feeling blind, the dim torches surrounding the dance floor made it almost romantic. Only a few couples were dancing when suddenly she stopped. Sven seemed so distant and cold; no, he was cautious and seemingly calculating. Cyril tried to evaluate him; she just didn't have enough to go on. What did Ezek see or know about him that gave her such caution? She needed more answers.

She said to herself, knowing Ezek was listening, "Are you having a lovely evening? I've missed you! You don't remember me or anything about me, do you?"

Sven smiled.

"I know you're handsome." Feeding into his vanity, she waited for his response when she followed his eyes down toward her right shoulder.

She could feel the green leather under her hand, rubbing it back and forth. Nervous, she glanced at the table next to her where her drink sat and a book of matches that read Petersburg, nothing more. She knew immediately she was in Bonn, Germany, where the last summit was held.

Ezek came into the room wearing a suit that caught her eye. She remembered the fabric she picked out. It all happened in a little bespoke shop on Savile Row in Mayfair, central London. A friend told them about the Taylors there. This suit fit him perfectly. How could a man so handsome be more handsome in a tailored suit? she stared and wondered. Ezek gave her a half smile, or was it a thank you after hearing her every thought?

Taking the seat next to her, he said, "I have everything ready for you." He smiled. "Are you ready? Let's go for a walk. We have a few minutes before we need to go in."

"Do you think they'll let me speak this time?" She glanced up. "They know why you're here. That worries the counsel. They have given you the floor for ten minutes. That's a lot longer than most. Just make your point, and then all we can do is wait for the vote."

A young man opened the double doors; while walking through, he repeated, "Paging Mr. Narrow, paging Mr. Narrow." While walking through the gardens looking off to the Rhine river, the young man repeated his call over again. Then he approached Cyril and Ezek and asked if his name was Mr. Narrow. "Yes," Ezek said, kinda annoyed.

"Sir, you have an important call at the main desk this way." He turned and walked away, thinking Ezek would follow.

Staying where he was at, he looked at Cyril then asked, "I don't understand. Who would be calling you here?"

"But most of all," she said to him for only him to hear, "who would use a landline?"

She looked at the young gentleman and asked, "Who is it that's calling? Did they say?"

"No, ma'am. This way, sir." He turned again to be followed. Ezek looked puzzled. "I'll get it. I'll be right back."

She was thinking to herself, *Hmm, important call, no idea who it is, leaving me alone, an urgency to get him to the phone. None of this sounds good.*

When her eyes opened, she was in the back of a car with her hands tied behind her back as she lay on the seat with a cloth tied tight across her eyes.

Cyril looked down her nose at the only gap of light.

In the back of the car lay litter and dirt, crumbled parking tickets, and leaves all over the floor. Suddenly the passenger window went down. The cold, moist air rushed in when she heard the person spit out the window. Suddenly three sunflower seed shells flew back into the car and onto the floor. Cyril looked through the gap running alongside her nose at the other objects on the floor. Sitting up feeling light-headed, holding her head back, she tried to look out the extremely thick window, trees, lots of trees, and a thick forest rushed by the window. She must have been in the car for quite a while. Moisture had accumulated onto the glass, making it hard to see out.

Where's Ezek? She jerked, feeling her confinement, seeing a faint blue light from under the front seat.

"Ezek, I've been taken. Help me!" she whispered to herself. *The summit!* she thought. *I have to be at the conference.* Racing through her, she knew this was going to be bad, very bad. Then a sudden heaviness came over her eyelids, trying to peer out to see anything that would tell her where she was at or where she was going. Then her eyelids shut like steel traps, trapping her inside.

She was still as Sven was standing straight in front of her.

"What's wrong? What happened?" Sven seemed worried about what she saw.

"Nothing, I'm all right. Let's dance." Holding him in close, she could smell his cologne as she rested her head on his chest. She tried to remember how it felt in his arms, how it felt to be with him. Nothing, absolutely nothing. Had they ever been close? Was he just her teacher or a mentor? She couldn't begin to ask him. Then he would know the coldness inside of her. But she could ask Ezek.

The screen upon the stage showed the universe, the unknown. She stared into it as she glided in his arms.

Cyril tried to remember the ache she felt inside, wanting to be held. She was wanting to understand the loneliness while she was recuperating. Now three men in her life were all closer than she could have imagined.

She heard him whisper, "Here comes another one…"

All the roads were blocked and dusty, so getting to Henry's took longer than expected. The Arab summit was that week; getting around Jordan wasn't easy.

Henry had a white Land Rover waiting for them at the airport.

They approached the main gate and could see the house in the distance. A tall two-story home blended in with the desert landscape. Spiraling up fifty feet, a long row of date palms almost looking out of place lined the driveway and surrounded the landscaped compound.

Henry greeted them at the door, taking his son in his arms, kissing him on both cheeks, then kissing him back on the other cheek. Servants came out quickly to get their bags. Henry smiled then put his arms around her, holding her for longer than usual, like maybe he was going to say something but didn't. Then he gave her the traditional three kisses. Of course, she kissed him back. She was thrilled to see him.

The inside of the house was enormous, cool, clean, and very empty, almost stark. A very faint aroma of sandalwood welcomed you.

"Let me give you a tour." His voice was excited. Everything here was enormous; the floors were like glass, shiny, and new, at least one thousand four hundred years old. The glass on the windows appeared thick, more than just double-paned.

While in the living room, she noticed a collage of pictures, the only cluttered place visible. On it, she saw a photo of her parents, then an image of just Henry and her mother. Both were laughing hard about something. So she had to ask.

"Henry, this picture of you and my mother, what made you both laugh so hard?"

Henry approached the gallery wall, looking at the picture and remembering. Before answering, he asked, "Are you sure you want to know?"

Cyril heard a laugh in his voice, as if the moment was suddenly brought back to him; the smile on his face also made her happy. She was glad to have asked him. He gave her no answer.

Henry quickly went into the other room; it appeared to be maybe his office. When he came out, he held a white envelope with red-and-blue stripes on the corners. Looking it over, he turned it to one side, then the other examining it.

"Cyril, this came for you, regular post. I haven't had anything sent like this in maybe forty years. It's for you. Who knew you would be here at this time with no return address? But it's from Canada."

Cyril approached Henry, looking bewildered. Ezek instantly looked over to his father, then both men hid their smiles. Cyril thought she caught them.

"No one. Okay, Tully, but she would never send anything here like this."

Cyril racked her brain when suddenly a shiver went up her spine as she looked at Ezek; he turned away.

Handing it over, Henry said, "Open it!"

Cyril held the envelope up to the light inside a small rectangle green piece of paper. Turning it over to see the handwriting, she gasped, looking straight at Ezek then back to Henry, both still trying to hide their smiles.

In old-fashioned cursive handwriting done with what might have been an old-style fountain pen was Cyril's name with Henry's address in her mother's writing. Ezek walked over, touching her arm, smiling; he said, "Breathe, sweetheart."

"How long have you had this?" Cyril, not looking up for an answer and not pausing, gently opened it.

Inside, she pulled out what was an old e-ticket from Disneyland. Small green with one perforated edge showing where it had been torn from its booklet. Then it described the latest and most exciting rides the ticket would afford. At the bottom of the ticket was a red *V* and eight numbers. Cyril was speechless.

Glancing back and forth at Henry and
Ezek, her heart swelled. Tears formed quickly in
her eyes when she said, "My mother is all right.
Everything is all right, everything."

"Look," Cyril said, pointing to the red *V*
and the numbers. "*V*, this is for Virginia. The
numbers, I think, could be a date. What's she up
to?" She stared straight at Henry for an answer.

Sven had a way of moving that she suddenly remembered she
had danced with him many times before. In his arms again, she
looked up and asked him point-blank, "Are we friends, or are you
just a teacher or an observer? What do you do?" It came out curious,
like a question she had no answer for. But he knew she would never
ask him a question she didn't already have the answer to. Was this
a game she was playing, or could this really be her searching for an
answer? What has she seen this evening? What wasn't she sharing?

Then she followed the large stardust particle as it hit the surface
of her forearm.

As the helicopter landed, she looked out the
open side door to get her bearings. The ocean to
the south, no, it was all around her. The sun was
rising to the east. *Could it be the Mediterranean?*
she asked herself. They were landing on top of
what appeared to be an island. These islands
must be volcanic small square buildings with
white roofs dappling the hilly surface. Large
prickly pear cactus covered the hillsides. Narrow
one-way roads climbed the hilly terrain.

"Take her inside," Sven ordered.

They were gentle with her. She noticed,
almost respectful. Pushing the chair to the side,
"Sit down," the man ordered. Cyril barely understood his words.

A man came in with a small glass box, setting it gently on the covered wooden table. "I'll be back with some water. Do you need anything else?" he asked before closing the door behind him. Cyril saw the other men from the helicopter waiting in the other room; some were collecting their things like they were getting ready to leave.

The rooms appeared as if they had recently been cleaned. The curtains made the rooms appear dark. The floors were mosaic tiles in a happy, colorful pattern in a small floral design. It seems someone spent a lot of time there. The smell in the room was that of rising yeast and warm bread. The furniture looked well used but loved.

Sven stood across the table, watching Cyril. Sven grabbed the back of his silk shirt, pulling it over his head, then laying it over the back of the chair in front of him. He stood there for a moment straightening his T-shirt as if he was searching his mind for something. Maybe even he wasn't sure he had done the right thing. Then he put both hands upon his forehead, combing his long fingers through his thick brown hair, stopping at the back of his head, elbows out.

Cyril had a hard time reading his expression. She sensed even he wasn't sure of his own thoughts. He sat down on the small wooden chair across from her, straddling the back of the chair.

Taking the glass box into his hands, he held it up and looked inside. Then he gently placed it back onto the tablecloth.

"Please just listen to me. This is important. I have to do this. It won't hurt you. I never wanted to hurt you, but this has to be done." He was saying it as if he was selling it to himself.

Furious and in a rage, she struggled to get out of the chair. "What are you saying? First, you trick me into thinking you have important information for me, so I come to Libya, then you leave Ezekiel behind. Who ordered you to do this? Who gave you this order? What are you going to do to me that won't *hurt* me? What are you talking about? Untie me!"

Cyril hoped her words were clear to wherever Ezek was.

She kept it to herself, but she knew Ezek can feel and hear everything that's happening to her. She never entirely understood it before, but her emotions were raw to him. She knew he can hear and feel her right this moment as a fast blue blur moved quickly behind Sven.

"Where am I? Tell me where I am. What island is this?"

"No one will find us here. I can't let you share what you know."

"What?" She shook her head in disbelief.

"It has been reported from the community that your team has substantiated evidence we are here. And you're going to share it with the world. Why all of a sudden do you think this is the right moment? Do you think the world is okay with that? Don't you understand the mass hysteria that's going to occur, or maybe they'll just think you're crazy? You have proven to the world you are a level-headed scientist. But this, this can't happen."

Cyril was struggling to get untied then stopped.

"I have studied this, and I do think the world is ready. My god, for over sixty years, they have infiltrated into our lives, our homes, our world. They happen to fit in nicely. It's a huge benefit to all of us. Do you think medicine, computers, all the scientific breakthroughs just happened overnight? That's what the world thinks, and that's not true. They need credit where credits are due. We would still be in the Dark Ages if it weren't for their technology. They know how to save our planet only because they couldn't save their planet in time.

"They're here to help us as well as themselves. It's time we take all their technology, not just the sprinkling of it so it doesn't come on so fast it would blow our minds. It would save all the damage we have already done here. Can't you understand the importance of all that?"

"I get it, but you're leaving out the fact that we're not all the same. Sure, our blood works the same for all Grays; but think about it, we will never all be equal whites against blacks. How long has that been going on? Do you think that if you put us into the mix then throw in the Grays that it's going to be one big happy family? Hell, that's a whole other color in itself."

"I never said the Grays should stay. I can't tell you how many I have sent off the planet.

"Is that what you want to hear? Yes, I have killed hundreds of Grays, knowing every day they harvest thousands of humans, and there's no way to prove it. It makes me crazy to think of all the people I know that are gone because of them. They took Ezek's mother. My parents are gone, no sign of them anywhere. Have they also been harvested? But it could also be someone's mother, father, daughter, son, friend, husband, wife. Humans come in all colors. All should be equal. Some are still struggling with that. Don't you get it? There's no room for the Grays here. How can you disagree with that? Tell me, how can you?" Sven laid a white cloth across the table. Then he took a small glass vial from the glass box on the table. Slowly and carefully, Sven tapped the glass vial's side, settling the contents to the bottom, then snapped the top of the vial in two, setting the lid back on the table. Slowly he sprinkled the black flakes along the surface of the white cloth. Shiny, like black glitter, melted into the fabric. Then like magic, it began to foam up like tiny sudsy bubbles form atop the surface.

Pantic came over her as she watched the black foam rise from the cloth.

"I was told this would take a few hours to settle in once it touches your skin. I'm sorry, but you won't remember anything after I put this on you. I do want you to know I do love you. I'm doing this for your own good. I was told this was the only way. Either that or kill you."

Sven took her face in his hands and kissed her forehead gently. "I'm sorry, I'm really sorry."

"You know you don't have to do this. You know that, don't you? Please think about it. You're going to erase everything in my mind. You're okay with that? Who convinced you that it was a good idea you're sending all of humanity back to the Dark Ages, and you think that's right? Please stop and let's talk about it, please.

"All the time we spent together, everything you taught me when I was little, how not to get lost, where the planets are, the black holes, the opening ports throughout the world. Who's who and why they're here. Now you want to take it all back. Why the hell did you tell me all this in the first place? Why couldn't you have picked someone else instead of me? Why me, tell me why? You could have picked any young person to teach, to brainwash. I thought you were my friend. Why now, why this?"

Cyril watched the black foam rise from the white cloth. "Why this way?"

Sven walked around behind her, adjusting her chair, inclining it to lay her flat. Then again, he gently leaned in and kissed her forehead. "Goodbye, my love," he whispered. "I do love you. I'm sorry."

Sven took one more look at her helpless, speechless, and still, as the cloth was placed gently across her eyes and forehead, pressing into her eyelids.

At first, it felt cool, almost relaxing. The black glitter sent beams of sharp, bright light across Cyril's eyelids; then like a flash of white light, she heard a voice say, "Do you think it was too much?"

He watched her lie there lifeless, checking her pulse every five minutes. He noticed it was faster than the last time. Her body started to move ever so slowly when her lips whispered the word out loud, "Ezek, help me!"

Almost eight hundred miles away, Ezek felt his pulse begin to race while the sand in the desert stirred. He looked up into the heavens and felt her warm whisper say, "Ezek, help me."

He dropped to his knees then looked to the heavens. He asked every star in the sky. Everyone he ever knew, every face he ever made contact with, even those that had passed on to pray for her to keep her soul safe. And to please not take her away now. Ezek had no idea what her condition was at that moment. He just needed to help her, and this was the only way he knew how. All he could do was go in the direction of her thoughts.

Cyril heard a voice whisper in her ear, "I love you."

Ezek also heard the voice in her ear until every thought was wiped clean, gone. For the first time in Ezek's life and hers, there was nothing. Not a wonder, not a soft voice, not even a whisper. No thought from any direction. He couldn't move. He couldn't stand. He couldn't even think. He had never experienced the void she was sending him, nor did he realize the void was hers. Ezek, for the first time, was lost; he had no direction. For that moment, he felt Cyril gone, void. He could only compare it to one other moment in his life—the moment his mother was harvested. The same moment she died. He felt the moment it happened. This moment was just like that. He dropped to his knees, looked into the heavens, closed his eyes, and prayed. Tears streamed down his face. He had no control over his emotions; this to him was death, death like his mother's death had felt. All he could do was go in the direction of her last thought.

Blinking her eyes over and over again, she adjusted her line of sight to Sven smiling down on her. "Hi, my love, where did you go? Can you tell me?" His arms held her tightly against his chest. Was this all some kind of act? He was responsible for her being scrubbed or erased. Her memory was gone, and it was his fault. He took the order to stop her from speaking at the summit. In a rage, she instantly composed herself and put her feet back on the ground. Survival training flashed in her mind, composure, plan of attack, all military thoughts then…

"Hawaii, I think I was in Hawaii swimming." Keeping the smile on her face, she kept what she saw to herself. Now she understood the way she felt when she first touched him.

When she turned and saw Ezek standing as if he was trying to say something to her, she just couldn't hear him. Did he see what she saw? Did he know what she knew? And if so, did he understand her silence, and would he go along with it? The music was soft as her dress floated like air in the cool breeze of the desert. She noticed people smiling at her, acknowledging her as she passed them on the dance floor. The large screen behind Sven showed earth at that very moment.

"Are you going to answer my question?" she said with a gentle flirting curiosity.

"Why do you need to ask me? Is there something wrong?"

She again tried to contain herself at the gall of the question. Now she knew why she had asked in the first place.

"Are we friends? Do you love me?" she asked again.

Trying to move out of the way before the stardust hit her elbow, she wanted the answer. How could hearing the words "I love you" be so haunting, hearing him say the last words, his last words to her? Blindfolded, feeling his warm breath against her skin, knowing she's about to be erased, "I love you."

The water in the canal was at high tide. The fog was like a veil; it softened everything, making all of Venice appear to be holy. It was quiet. Not even the birds were singing. The funeral procession of gondolas moved slowly under each awaiting archway. Family, friends, acquaintances stood atop each bridge, looking down, waiting to see them pass. Veiled in black, Cyril sat alone with the casket. The gondolier dressed only in a black robe and large veiled hat moved slowly on his route to the Isola di San Michele cemetery.

Looking down on her hand, she took the simple platinum band he had given her just three months before and moved it to her right ring finger. She thought about all their moments together. Fragments of their happiness were now starting to fade. Would the memories have stayed strong in her mind had he not been murdered? Would they have truly lived happily ever after as he had promised her?

"Let's leave the planet together," he would tell her.

"Let's leave the planet." Then he would make love to her, molding them together as one, not touching any surfaces like they were suspended lofting into the heavens.

Her heart was bleeding as the warm tears poured from her eyes, hiding her sorrow behind her veil for no one to share. The gondola stopped as she looked through her veil. The red brick walls enclosed the cemetery. The bell tower rang three times like a doorbell asking to be let inside. The gondola was steady against the stone stairs as the water gently lapped the side. She waited. Looking up, she saw Ezek's hand out waiting for her. He knew how hard it was for her. What had happened to her husband was out of his control. He also wanted to know who killed the man she loved. He too wanted to take away her pain. Right now, he had two essential things to do, comfort her, and see who was at the funeral. Who was her threat? Ezek held Cyril's hand while walking slowly.

Cyril thought first her parents, gone over Greenland, just vanished. With every step, she wondered, now her husband. Who else could they take from her? The long walk to the front row of pews left vacant for only her to sit. Ezek listened to her thoughts then sat next to her, releasing her hand. Everywhere she looked were flowers. Every color of long-stemmed roses cascaded over the casket.

Huge striking bouquets lined the outer sides of the pews. The altar showed a picture of Max smiling the day he was married again in his black suit. The casket was closed, a request he had written in his will shortly before they were married. Had her lifestyle and job taken him, did she want to face that reality? Could she have changed anything? It went over and over in her head.

It suddenly occurred to her—she needed to protect Ezek; he was all she had left. The ceremony was mostly in Italian, making it hard for Cyril to understand.

Max's relatives, friends, cooks, restaurant owners, and food critics came from all over the world. Some people she recognized from their wedding on that wet and rainy night, some she had never met. It had been a long day talking to people that, in her mind, couldn't change the outcome of the day.

After the wake, Cyril wandered the streets, walking by the little gelato shop where Max got his favorite *stracciatella*.

He said, "The chocolate they used made all the difference in the world. No one made it like they did."

Cyril wished for that moment they were open just one more time to bring it all back to her. Venice now seemed far away, like she was now a foreigner, a stranger in her husband's backyard. She traced their walks: the familiar shops and all the bridges where kisses were remembered. The Maleficio bell tower told her the day had ended and it was time to go back to her hotel. She stopped to sit at the fountain, listening to the water. She wanted to share her feelings with Ezek, hoping he was still awake. She always found it easier to write her most profound thoughts in text than to say them in person. She began her message, making it short, then she erased it. Then she tried again, only this time she left out the word "love." *No*, she thought and erased it again. She knew he's probably listening to her every thought, but this was different. She wanted it in writing. She really wanted him to see it and know it to be true. So she wrote it again, "I'm sorry. I love you, always will! Please stay." Cyril rethought what she wrote and erased the last five words then pushed send. Stunned, she stared at her board, unable to pull back. That's not what she wanted to share. And the words were gone now in his hands.

Collecting herself, she entered her hotel. The smell surrounded her; it's a combination of the waters of old-world Venice with a faint smell of Shalimar. It instantly relaxed her.

When she opened her door, she noticed room service had been there; two covered place settings were at the table. The door from the adjoining room was open. Ezek came to the doorway, walked over to her balcony doors, and opened them. Cyril stood there watching him, not saying a word. Ezek stood for the longest time, holding the doors open with each hand. His arms spread wide, his back to her. The noise from the passing boats came softly up into the room. Voices from the pier below echoed off the stone walls. Cyril sensed from Ezek that he was struggling. He couldn't fix what was happening to her; he couldn't take away her pain.

"I had dinner sent up for you. I thought you might be hungry. Where did you walk to?" He turned as he started to unbutton his shirt while walking toward his room. He stopped, turned, and said, "I got your text. Why are you sorry, and who do you love? You didn't finish it but sent it." Then he turned and walked into his room.

For a moment, Cyril wondered why he was asking because he was always in her mind every step of the way. He knew where she was at every moment. Was this his small talk? Was this him breaking the ice? Cyril was sure she was in his mind just as he was in hers. Was this his way to soften what Cyril needed to say to him? Cyril walked over to the balcony, and she felt the cool breeze coming up off the water. Kicking her shoes off, Cyril held the warm stone of the balcony edge. She was feeling something substantial in her hands—solid, stable, secure, all the things she needed right now.

Ezek turned and said, "I'm going to lie down. It's getting late." As he walked into his room, she noticed he left his door open. He stood in front of his bed while he unbuttoned his shirt. Cyril followed him in, walking up behind him. She stopped then put her arms around his waist. Her cheek lay flat against his warm back. He was solid, stable, and he had always made her feel secure, and now he was all she had left.

Ezek whispered down to her, "Breathe, sweetheart, do you want to lie down with me?"

He was asking. He was crossing the prominent line that had always been between them. Cyril saw the line in front of her. It was like they were both standing there looking down at their feet. The broad white line they had never crossed was before them. Passing in her mind as well as his was *they were both going to cross to the other side.* He turned slowly, putting his arms securely around her. As if she was weightless, he lifted her, laying her gently onto his bed. Their minds both acknowledged. Was she reading him the way he was reading her? Did they both need each other the same way right now? What would this be like making love to him knowing his every thought and him knowing her every thought? She wished her clothes were off before she had gotten into bed. She felt an urgency to feel his skin next to hers. The minute that thought crossed her mind, he began to unbutton her blouse. Then he stood back and slowly removed his clothes.

He looked at her before getting into bed and asked, thinking it to himself, *I can't get this wrong.*

Cyril whispered out loud, "You won't!"

Every button was a step closer; it wasn't like he had never seen her naked before.

His hands had touched every inch of her body at one time or another. This touch was different; it was curious.

Their touch was meant for pleasure and comfort, also for love most of all. It overwhelmed him once he realized what he was doing. His every touch intensified; he wanted to convey that he loved her now with his body. Every action he had ever taken with her was to protect her to keep her safe. Now it was to show her that he loved her.

Cyril took Ezek's face into her hands, pulling it toward her. Nose to nose, she said to him out loud, "*Stop!* I know you love me. I think as much as I love you. I have always loved you, always will, no matter what. But *stop*. Please stop thinking something will go wrong. Please make love to me the way I want to make love to you."

While he undressed her, Cyril felt like she was being untied, from her surroundings, from her past, from her present. Ezek lay next to her as she molded her body, fitting in as close as she could to him. His skin was everything she thought it would be. Smooth like velvet, then her fingers would tangle in the hair on his chest. His scent was familiar, but this time it stirred more than her imagination. She wanted him; then the thought crossed her mind: she wanted him inside of her. His hands wandered, his mouth kissing every part of her. His kisses were like saying, "Thank you," then asking for more.

Her hands startled him as she discovered something they had never experienced before. She got no advice from his thoughts; he just wanted her as she was. He wanted every bit of her just the way she was. He searched her mind and understood everything about what was happening was perfect for her right then and there. He felt like he had just unwrapped a gift; now it was his and no one else's. Cyril rolled over on top of him, her legs falling between his.

Her lips touched him as he entered her. How could something feel so perfect? The thought passed their minds. His lips sent his message; the softness then directness, the waiting of all the years before came to now. The rhythm was in sync; they were music together. How could anyone get enough? They both wondered at the same time.

Not wanting to stop, they discovered every spot that meant something. Then the thought of him climaxing crossed her mind; lingering was also the thought of how Max climaxed...

Ezek stopped. His hand went to move her hair out of her face; he looked straight at her. He was speechless. He saw a tear fall from her as his thumb caught it then wiped it away. He rolled her over and whispered in her ear, "It's okay, sweetheart." He made love to her with a passion she had never felt before. And when they climaxed, he knew it would erase all the other moments she had felt before.

The phone rang once, just once. Cyril rolled over at the annoyance, only to realize she wasn't sure where she was. A warm hand went around her waist, tucking her in tightly against his chest; it was like being in a cocoon. Cyril wondered, *Why only one ring?* Was that some kind of message, a signal? What did it mean?

Out loud, Ezek said, "It's Twyce. You didn't see him at the funeral. He's here. His room is just down the hall."

"What?" Cyril exclaimed, kind of shocked.

Ezek's arm held her from bolting out of bed. "He's coming. He's bringing us breakfast."

Questions swirled inside Cyril's head.

"*Stop it.* It's okay," he whispered softly inside her head. "He loves you. There's nothing you could do to change that with him. Why are you so concerned about what he thinks? It's okay."

Two short knocks on Ezek's door. Cyril froze, lying there naked, staring up at the ceiling, feeling vulnerable.

"Where are my clothes?" she whispered.

"I told him to go to your room. I'll let him in while you dress."

As he got out of bed, he leaned over to kiss her on the forehead. While he held her hand, Ezek noticed she wasn't willing to let him go.

He said, "I could ask him to come back later." His smile was agreeable.

"No, I'll get dressed and be right out."

Ezek put on his pants and shirt. He stood there, buttoning his shirt slowly while watching her.

"Go, go, answer the door. Go."

Two knocks no more. Ezek went into her room, closing his door behind him. Checking the room quickly, he went over to open her door where Twyce was waiting with a cart.

"Room service," he whispered as his neck stretched to look into the room. Twyce whispered, "You busy? I can come back later." He looked over his brother's shoulder to the adjoining closed door. Cyril opened the door only to have both their thoughts blocked out to her. Embracing each other, they stood there for a moment. The thoughts exchanged were from Twyce for only his brother to hear, *It's about time!*

Then back to Twyce, a message Cyril would probably never hear out loud, not even now, *I love her!*

As Twyce squeezed Ezek even harder, he whispered, "I know you always have."

"How long have I been gone?" Cyril looked out onto the dance floor, her head resting on Sven's chest.

"I didn't know you were gone, so a second, maybe two seconds. What you see has a lot of details which you equate as time; but to me, on this side of it, it's maybe a fraction of a second." Cyril glanced around Sven's arm, making eye contact with Ezek, tossing him a half smile. Ezek gave her the half smile back. He shared her flash of their moment in Venice; he remembered the way it all felt.

"Are you going to answer my question?" she asked again as she felt the stardust particle bounce off her eyelash onto her cheek.

Friends

Three computer screens wrapped around the top of Cyril's desk. On the corner sat a beautiful white cymbidium with a dash of purple in its throat. While sitting at her desk, Cyril saw the count across the top corner of her center computer screen, the date, and the number 904. Then the number quickly changed 1012.

She calculated in her head 110 in that short amount of time. NFE1 was busy today, she thought. Some days it may be two or three, but 110 in that short amount of time. The number changed again to 1024.

Three little knocks came from her office door while it opened quickly. Cindy went into the office while reading her board. Looking up to Cyril, she said, "I got it. I'm not sure what it means yet. I have people working on it. I still don't know where Sven is."

While reading her board, she sat on the sofa, holding a bottle of water. Then gazing out the window, she said to Cyril, "I thought you might want to know this. I'm not sure if they sent you the report. The Reds are here again. Hey, do you want to go get lunch later?"

"Again! Weren't they just here last month?"

"Yes, but now there are increasingly more sightings every day."

"Have they said what they want this time?"

"Same as last time. Yes, I told them again you're working on it, but they say you're not listening to them."

"Bullshit, haven't you told them what I'm up against?" She glanced over, 1105, as the numbers changed again.

"Do you know what the casualties are? If we have 1121 in custody right this minute, what is Sven doing?"

"Lunch sounds good. I need to get out of here." At the same time, Cyril closed down all her computers.

"I haven't been in contact with Sven in a few hours. Norie said earlier the holding facility in Arizona is full. But Sven's location is in Connecticut. He hasn't answered any of my messages."

Cyril looked over to Cindy and asked, "Is he working on something I don't know about?"

Cindy knew Sven requested to see the new facility in Connecticut, one of the biggest in the tristate region, located under a cemetery in a very inconspicuous area. Now only two states didn't have a holding facility. Cyril called her secretary in as Ezek walked in behind her. He sat down next to Cindy.

"So are you going with us?" Ezek, sounding excited, turned to Cindy and smiled, waiting for her answer.

"Of course, my bags are always packed. Where are we going?" Cindy looked over to Cyril.

Cyril told her secretary, "Send someone out to find Sven. Let me know where he is and what he's doing and with whom. I need to know before midnight. I don't want him to know I'm looking for him, okay? Thank you." After the door was closed, Cyril asked Cindy, "Have you ever been to Alaska? We're leaving early in the morning. I'll have a car come around and get you. I'm going to call Steam and see if he wants to go to lunch with us. Did you see him in the building?" Cyril looked over at Ezek.

"I love you," he said quickly before another stardust pierced her. "I love you. Did you hear me? I have always loved you." She did listen to him and wondered how many times he'd been saying it before she had returned. Looking up, she smiled, feeling his torment. Could she return the words she searched inside herself and couldn't answer back? "I heard you..." Then she gently laid her head on his chest, completing the dance. Slowly they moved to the rhythm of the music as the gold chiffon of her dress loft in the breeze.

From a distance, Ezek saw that she was relaxing and enjoying the moment, but how could she be so calm in the arms of the man who tried to destroy her? He realized she knew it was Sven who erased her memory.

The minute she heard his thought, she put this question in his head. *You have always known and haven't done anything or said anything. Why is that?*

Ezek heard her question and felt the tone of anger then responded, *I have waited for you to know the truth. I would never take that kind of revenge from you. All I could do was wait and never take my eyes off him. He is all yours to decide what you want to do with him. It's never been up to me.*

Her eyes were closed when she felt the cold piercing of stardust again.

The smell of baby powder was the first thing Cyril noticed. She felt wet then began to cry. She heard her mother talking to someone in the hallway, but the person wasn't answering her.

The light went on in her room. Then standing before her was a very tall Gray, maybe 6'3". For a moment, she thought the Gray was smiling at her. Cyril heard her mother say, "Acid, this is my child. Her name is Cyril. Your son's name is Yike." As Cyril's mom pointed to Cyril, Acid set Yike into the crib. While changing her diaper, Cyril struggled to see what went into her crib. Suddenly something had a hold of her foot.

Whatever it was, it wasn't cold or hot; it was just there.

Feeling the fresh dry diaper, Virginia sat Cyril up. Yike still had a grip on her foot. Both Yike and Cyril were the same size. Their skin was different. Cyril reached out to grab Yike. Her hand touched him gently as she wiped her hand over the surface of his skin. She heard him inside her head, a "cooing" noise ever so quietly. Cyril stopped and looked around the room to see where the noise was coming from. Then she touched him again. Inside her head again, the "cooing" noise. She threw her head back and giggled. This was funny! Not outside her head but inside her head came someone else's nose. Fascinating, she thought it only happened when she touched him. This new friend was different in shape and color from her other friends. Steam was one color. Yike was all different colors. Steam's noise was heard outside her head. Yike's noise was heard inside her head. Acid and Virginia sat in the room while they watched the two play and discover each other. It was clear they got along well. Cyril, looking outside her infant eyes, realized this was the moment her mother shared her friendship.

Violins were playing a soft relaxing tune when Cyril felt herself turn with the music. Acid, she thought, what a strange name. Her mother apparently had an ongoing relationship with Acid, and now she had shared it with her daughter. Was this her parents' conflict? Did her father not want her to have a relationship with the Grays? Did she grow up knowing Yike as a friend? Sven looked down at Cyril. "Are you okay?"

"Yes. I think so. Everything that's been happening this evening, it's a lot to take in."

That was Yike's hand she first saw this evening when the stardust first started. The feeling he left her with was to make sure she wasn't frightened. Was he her friend even now? The pieces were starting to come together.

The music changed, and so did the large screen on the stage. Now the beautiful twisting of lights following each other into a black hole. Stars, gases, supernovas, one at a time, sucked into the black hole.

Sven whispered, "Cyril, here comes…"

> Her eyes were closed in the distance. She heard cows, a sound that had always confronted her. Her leg swiped across the cold starched sheets. The morning sun pierced the lace in the curtains, shooting gold rays across the room. Before opening her eyes, she knew she was home. The sheets moved next to her, then a large hand lay gently across the small of her back, then a leg touched her. She's not only at home, but he's there too. For a moment, she stopped to evaluate her surroundings. Ezek's long hair moved, stirring his scent. She rolled over into him, burying her face into the hair on his chest. His arms were around her as he brought his body toward hers.
>
> She's home. For a moment, she remembered it all, the flowers that lined the patio. The view from every window, the quiet, the peace, the

way the floor felt under her feet; then she remembered it could all be gone in a heartbeat.

She heard a loud voice in her head. "Why did you do that when you were on such a roll? You went into that dark place. Stay out of there!" Ezek warned her while tightening his grip on her.

"Stop it. Stay out of my head." Cyril buried her head even deeper into him.

"I enjoy being in your head. It's like it gives me a heads-up, get it? I know what you're thinking." He tried to tickle her under the sheets. Instead, she wrapped her legs around him, twisting him on top of her while he looked down on her. She smiled.

"There was not even a bit of resistance from you." She said it almost as if she was protesting.

He kissed her lips gently and smiled. "Resist you now! No… I'm supposed to resist you. No, I'm not going to resist you, not this morning anyway." He tried to sound clever.

His hands found their way around her as she found her way around him, meeting in the middle. Yes, she was home. Making love to him was all she needed. It was a safe place, a comforting place like no other. He took her breath away as she looked forward to it.

Opening her eyes, she could smell the scent of Ezek's body lingering on her. Still feeling his hair brush along her cheek, she glanced around Sven. From a distance, she saw Ezek smile at her again. He was in her head, reading her every thought. It was that smile. She knew what that smile meant and smiled right back at him. Not only did he hear her, but he was back inside her thoughts; he also felt at home. She saw the comfort wash over him.

Feeling relaxed as they glided across the floor, whispering in her ear, he said, "For the record, I do love you. I see it's hard for you to say it back. I'm okay with that, but didn't you even miss me? You do remember who I am, don't you? You have had some flashes of our time together, haven't you? I haven't forgotten a single moment with you. Ask me anything."

Cyril took a deep breath to calm herself. Keeping her head on his chest, she whispered back, "Does anyone have an idea how long this dust stuff lasts? Are there any side effects after being subjected to it for long periods? When will it stop following me?" Of course, she knew who he was—she kept it to herself.

"I can't say I remember everything about us together. I know you're my friend, and you have been with me most of my life. That's about it. Oh, you taught me about black holes."

Sven released his breath as she recited some of their moments together, hoping the most tragic wouldn't pass her lips.

Was it guilt guiding him? she wondered. Then she felt him jerk her away from falling stardust only to collide into another.

"Close your eyes," she heard him say.

Her heart sank as the voice filled her memory. "Don't turn around till I tell you."

Holding her gently, he turned her slowly. She heard the crackle of an open fire in the distance; she smelled the smoke in the salty ocean air and forest floor.

"Okay, open your eyes."

Cyril saw a mound of cut fern leaves and a double sleeping bag lying over it.

"Max, it's beautiful. It looks comfortable too." It took her breath away.

"They say fern leaves mean new life and new beginnings. Do you think that's true?" he asked.

Max stood behind her, holding her in his arms. "I have one more thing for you." As he knelt on one knee while opening a tiny royal-blue ring box, Cyril turned.

"Cyril, I have known you now for almost a year. It's been a wild ride. I wouldn't change a thing."

Cyril, shocked, covered her mouth with both hands and listened.

"I wish I could have asked your parents. I know they would have approved. I think they would have liked me, even your dad. It took a lot of negotiating to get a yes out of your best friends. They said if you said yes, then it's all right with them. I'm not going to tell you what Ezek said, but he's okay with it.

"Cyril, will you marry me and make me the happiest man on the planet? I promise to do everything in my power to keep you happy and keep you safe for as long as I live."

Every moment flashed before her, the minute she first saw him. He was standing with his chef's coat partially open. He was talking to a customer. His hands were moving in the air, a gesture of something grand and happy; he glanced over at the same time she did, his arms still in the air. She remembered his first line to her: "Where do I know you? Did we go to school together?"

Her line back was "I don't know. Let's sit down and figure it out." Then she came clean and said, "No, I don't think so." After that, she had dinner there every time she was in Napa.

Till one day, he asked, "Are you free for dinner tomorrow? I'd like to fix you something special." He fixed it, all right. She met him at the restaurant the next day.

She discovered the restaurant was closed on a day it should have been open. When she went in, all the tables were dark except one next to the open window. Looking out the window was a sweeping view of the valley. A clean, crisp white linen tablecloth with a small bouquet of tiny white roses and baby's breath with one candlestick graced the table.

"I hope you like elk." Max came from the kitchen, holding two plates, looking extremely proud of himself.

"Elk! We're having elk? My father is the only one I know that knows how to cook elk properly. I would have to say that elk is on the top of my meat list, then venison, then Angus beef, in that order. I'm surprised. How did you know that was my favorite?"

"I have friends in high places who tell me things." Max smiled as he placed the plate in front of her, turning it, so her perfectly cooked elk was the first thing she saw.

Next to the elk was risotto with wild mushrooms and garlic; lying like they were resting were mustard greens. Cyril could smell the garlic. It brought a smile to her face. That night they talked till it dawned on them that the sun had been up for a while. They both knew they were in love.

It was easy after that they became inseparable, how both loved to cook, but he took it to a whole different level. He was known for his hunting, fishing, and camping skills; he knew how to survive in the most rugged terrain. The way he fixed elk or pheasant was world-renowned. What Max could do with a grain of rice was breathtaking. They traveled the world, her on business, him cooking at different friends' restaurants. Cooking everything he killed was what his dreams were made of. He loved what he did, but most of all, Max loved to watch someone eat and enjoy what

he'd prepared for them. To him, there was pleasure in that. Cyril savored every bite.

Max made the world seem small compared
to their relationship. Now nothing else mattered
to them.

"I know your job is important to you. I'll
never stand in the way of that only because I
understand your goals, but please give this a
chance."

"I travel a lot. Are you okay with that?"
Inside, Cyril was saying yes. But did he fully
understand when she said travel?

"Really! You asked the guys?" She shook her
head in disbelief.

"Of course, I did! You spend more time
with them than anybody." Cyril held her hand
out as he put the simple platinum band on her
finger. "I know how much you don't like to wear
jewelry, so I thought just a band would be okay."

Cyril held her left hand out, admiring the
platinum band when it occurred to her how the
moment was going to change her life. "Yes! Yes! I
will marry you!" She looked straight at him, hoping the moment would never change, hoping her
life as she knew it could be different, could be
almost normal. But her mind raced back to reality, the reality of what she was a part of.

The music had changed when she noticed Ezek had approached
them. Standing behind Sven, he tapped his shoulder and asked, "Can
I have this dance?" He smiled and looked at Cyril, paying no attention to Sven.

"Yes." Sven took a step back away from Cyril, opening his arms
to release her.

Keeping his eyes on her, Ezek said, "I saw that. You loved him.
We knew that. We saw how it changed you. You were happy, happy

like I have never seen you before. I understand now how love works. It consumes you."

She put her arms around him then stopped. "I need to take my shoes off." She reached down, unstrapping them.

"Give them to me. I'll hold them for you."

"You realize he's worried you'll remember what he's done. It's eating at him. I understand you'll need time to think about everything you've seen this evening. Please know this: soon you will be yourself again. Maybe not tonight. But soon."

"You felt my anger towards you. I'm just confused. I'm trying to put my life in order. I'm not mad at you." Cyril couldn't be mad. His pieces, his life was what put her life together.

"Do you see everything I see?" she asked as her cheek lay against his chest.

"Most of the time. But this stardust stuff is making it easier like it used to be."

"I had no idea you were always in my head."

"Will not always. I give you your privacy." He paused for a moment. "That is, I try to give you your privacy. Are you okay?" he asked with a tone of curiosity.

"I know how hard that was when he—" Ezek couldn't find the words. He couldn't say killed or murdered; it just couldn't come out of his mouth to her. He didn't want her to see it or feel it all over again. He just couldn't.

"Tell me how it happened. Tell me the truth."

"I guess I need to remind you we have an agreement we never lie to each other. It's just a waste of time only because we would know it was a lie. Do you really want to go there? It's always so painful for you."

"Yes, I've been racking my brain trying to figure out who I was married to. I was going to ask you earlier. Now, I know."

"So that's why you asked if we were married."

"You found me, didn't you?" Cyril looked up to him for his response.

"Yes, I found both of you. I promised you I would go back for Max. I had to dig him out of the sand. He had taken most of the blast trying to protect you. If it weren't for him, you would be dead. We never talked about it before, but the burning hair and skin that you smelled that day in the desert were yours, not his."

"Who was the blast from?"

"I guess I can tell you now, now that you're almost back. It was retaliation for the building in Germany. You knew what was inside of it."

"Yes, I knew I left the stones on the surface."

"Even after Sven told you not to, you left them anyway." She heard the frustrated tone in his voice. Almost sounding like a reprimand toward her. "I didn't want them to go after you or anyone else."

"But they went after the person you loved the most."

She could feel it radiating from Ezek, those words: "The person you love the most." It echoed inside her heart, giving even her pain.

Was this a moment when all her "I'm sorry" came together, only this time she really, really meant it? She wanted him to know she was sorry, sorry for all the pain she has caused him.

Cyril began to cry, trying to hide it from Ezek. He told her, "You forget. I feel your pain. I'm sorry I can't shield you from it."

"Just hold me, please. Just hold me." She closed her eyes. They danced like air across the surface.

Cyril felt like she wasn't touching the floor, making it easy to glide in his arms. Ezek remembered all the times they had danced together.

When they were little, she saw a video of a man doing what he called the twist. She showed it back to Ezek and asked, "Ezek, come on, do the twist with me." She moved her body in a pivoting back-and-forth motion. Ezek thought it was funny and went along with it, squatting down as low as he could go mimicking the man in the video. Then he told her, "No, this is how you're supposed to dance. Stand up straight in front of me. Hold still." Then he took her hand and bent over to touch her waist. After a few seconds, she stopped.

"I don't want to dance like my parents."

"But that's how you're supposed to do it," he said.

On the day of her wedding, he held her close, feeling the warmth of her body coming through her soaked wedding dress. She was stunning, dripping wet all in muddy white. He understood that this was the first time he would dance with her as a married woman. He did everything he could to stop his feelings from coming toward her. He could never let her know how internally it was destroying him. She was no longer his. He had always accepted her moments with other people. The minute it got personal, he would leave her to give her privacy, knowing she would always be back.

But he agreed to her feelings for Max and would never have denied her happiness. Even at the risk of his own. Seeing her happy always made him happy. For just that moment, he understood her all-consuming love for Max as he held her knowing he was going to have to let her go.

"Ezek, stop it! I'm right here." Cyril pressed her head into his chest, keeping her arms around him, giving him a short squeeze.

"What?" He looked down at her.

"I felt that!" Cyril was making herself clear.

"Felt what?" He denied where he had just been.

"I'm glad you're here."

Then in the middle of a gentle turn, everything was gone...

The plate in front of her was white china. Next to it was a tall crystal stemmed glass with the remnants of champagne at the bottom.

Cyril's eyes darted between the trees, following the moving shadows. Ezek read her thoughts then started to count the shadows. Looking over, she was sitting across from Henry. The table was at least one hundred feet long. Winery owners from the valley and other distinguished merchants and guests all feasted on the local harvest. Silvia, the winery owner, asked Henry, "Would you and your guests like a tour of the cellar?"

Cyril could see the expression on Henry's face; he was excited. "Yes, of course, we would enjoy that."

One by one, they went across the lawn through the trees to the side of the hill. They stopped in front of two impressively massive oak doors. Both were ornately decorated with huge iron hinges. As Silvia touched the doors, they creaked open with little effort.

Silvia explained, "The footprint of this cellar is a peace symbol, so remember that if you think you're lost." Massive barrels lay on their sides. Soft lights went on. The further you went in, the light followed you. Deep into the mountain, the temperature was cool and dry. The smell was that of fermenting wine and old oak barrels. Henry stopped and remarked, "I love this smell." Ezek sent Cyril a thought, *This place is huge. It goes on forever.* Then the lights flickered then went back on. Cyril looked over to Ezek and Steam; both kept walking.

Up ahead of them were Henry and Silvia, both chatting about the Crush and this year's crop when the lights flickered then went off. Everyone stood still for the moment. Silvia whispered, "Henry, where are you?" As she reached out to touch him, he was gone, vanished. Panic filled Silvia's voice as she tried to remain calm. Cyril could barely see inside the cavernous tunnel. She ran past them, trying to get to the double doors to the outside. People were running everywhere. Dim lights had just jumped back on, stealing the darkness. A secondary auxiliary power source hummed on in the distance, keeping the lights on. Cyril yelled as loud as she could, "Henry, where are you?"

Strangers were everywhere, fear surrounding them, but what was it? What could cause this type of hysteria? Then in the corner of her eye, she saw what most would think was a red laser light. Cyril knew better as she ran toward it. Two faint blue lights in the distance highlighted behind her, splitting and going in two different directions. The tiny red light moved quickly out of her sight so fast she knew she really saw it, and she knew it saw her. Behind her, the steady glow from the light of the red orb shone on her. As she watched, it intensified. She felt the power of the orbs move her hair, making everything around her red.

Ezek's voice came from behind her stern, and with authority, he said, "Don't touch her." Even she was afraid and froze; who was he talking to?

He said it again as she noticed the bright red glow from behind her widen, and no one was moving.

Everyone in her view had stopped.

Her thoughts were from Ezek. She knew not to move. She felt him tell her to stop breathing as she took in her breath and held it. Ezek walked around in a wide circle to the front of her then stopped. He towered over her as he warned the red glow, "Don't touch her." Was this a threatening game they were playing with him?

Her thoughts went to Ezek. *Where's Henry?* Then not able to hold her breath any longer, she fell to the ground as Ezek watched. The grass was warm and getting warmer. The red glow started to dim when she rolled over onto her back, now looking behind her. Two red orbs hovered now above her, collecting herself. She looked right at them and said, "Return them. Return all of them. Give them back to me. Give them all back to me." She would not negotiate with them, but Henry was gone.

Ezek's hand spread wide across her back as they moved gracefully across the floor. "Watch out!" he whispered, giving her a warning. "Here comes another one." His words stopped inside her head…

Light filled the room. The walls and floor were gone. Cyril was no longer in her bed, trying to sleep. She felt a pressure pushing her body into the void, starting at the top of her head as if it was x-raying her internally slowly and methodically. She felt the strain in her bones and skin, but she could not move overall; she was paralyzed and at the mercy of whatever was examining her.

Terrified, only able to move her eyes, she screamed inside, *Stop! I don't want to go!* No one heard her.

Her shoulders pressed harshly into the void, slowly reaching her chest. She knew it would stop her heart, and all of her would cease to exist.

Then out of nowhere, her scream was released. She felt her breath exit.

Hearing herself suddenly, the light was gone, the walls appeared, and she felt the floor suspending her. Not sure where she was, still unable to move, she waited until the hum in her head quieted.

Trying to remain calm, she knew hours were passing. Now lying still, she closed her eyes and waited for the blue light to cross her eyelids, sending Ezek her terror. Nothing, no blue lights, no message in her head from Ezek, nothing, as if she was utterly alone, not on the planet she waited. Then she noticed the air smelling like a bad air conditioner needing its filter changed. She knew that meant she was not on earth, and she was not alone. Like static electricity hitting and racing across the floor surface, Cyril heard the crackling noise it made. There was a current in the air.

Not cold or hot or even warm, something lay over her bare skin, touching every exposed part of her.

Her eyelids were sealed closed. She could feel her eyelashes lying flat stuck to her cheeks as she tried to open her eyes.

The hair on her head lay close to her scalp.

Then it occurred to her she was being hermetically sealed. Not able to move, she felt the vacuum begin to tighten and seal, taking every molecule inside and out of her.

Short breaths came from her nose. Her mouth was unable to open. Inside her nose, she felt something hard and small. She realized the air was coming from it like small oxygen tanks, making her breathing short and shallow.

Suddenly she felt herself go from there to somewhere chillingly cold. In the distance, she heard a faint wheezing sound like air escaping from something tight.

Then metal rolling over metal like a heavy door opening with glass rattling within the metal. The sound echoed, telling her the room was huge.

Then heavy footsteps walked harshly across a wet surface. They were suddenly coming toward her. Bright blue lights swirled across her sealed eyelids. Her exterior surface was sticky as whoever touched her tried to remove their hands to reposition them. Feeling their haste, they grabbed her and quickly walked out of the large room. She felt the walk of this person was confident and determined. Once out of the building and into the darkness, she felt fingertips rip across her face, exposing it to the fresh air. Pulling the pods from her nose, not breaking his stride, he whispered, "Sweetheart, you're safe now."

Curled naked in a fetal position, she could not speak. The wrapper containing her started to dry and crack against her skin.

As Ezek stepped up the stairs two at a time, he walked her to the back of the plane.

Kicking the door open, he yelled, "Get us out of here!" He laid her on the bed as his hands quickly took the dried, cracked pieces off her skin, throwing them to the floor as they shattered like glass. All she could do was listen. Powdery dust covered her. Ezek noticed small cuts everywhere on her body as if skin samples had been taken. As soon as they were in the air, seconds later, they were landing.

Wrapping her in a blanket, he took her into the dark, cold morning air. Cyril heard a hydraulic door open as they had approached it. Walking through, she heard the hollowness of a hallway. Her first impression was a basement of what smelled and sounded like it could be a hospital. The staff there was ready for her as they scanned her, quickly rolling her over to detect any abnormalities.

Cyril's eyes pried open. She heard the scanner *tick, tick, tick* in a constant beat, then a woman looked at Ezek. She smiled then shook her head no.

No words were exchanged; he smiled back as no was the answer he needed.

Then he picked her up and submerged her into a large stainless steel tub filled with what she thought was a warm bubble bath smelling of lavender.

The cuts on her skin were open to the warm water. Each cut was like a tiny needle stabbing her everywhere.

Gritting her teeth over the pain, Ezek stopped. "I'm sorry I have to get this stuff off you."

He swiped his hands coarsely over her entire body, dipping her hair, trying to remove all the dust. He picked her up out of the water then rolled her into a large towel when he noticed blood coming from every tiny cut. Wrapping her tightly, he laid her on a flat surface.

Slowly she entered a large MRI cylinder. The pounding to her was like a war drum. When the war drums ended, a team of nurses began to seal all her cuts as quickly as possible. Cyril could only lie there speechless.

Ezek wiped her hair from her face while pulling a black ribbon from his pocket. He tied her hair up in a ponytail. Then he whispered, for only her to hear, "We're leaving in just a minute, sweetheart."

The doctor outside the room was viewing a computer screen as she gave Ezek a cautious look through the glass. He caught her glance as she pointed to the screen in front of her. Leaving the room, he stood looking down onto the screen. Cyril could see panic over Ezek's face while he listened to every word the doctor said. Ezek's words broke apart as Cyril tried to listen to him, something about carrying something. She saw Ezek shake his head no then look back at Cyril. Cyril heard Ezek's thoughts, *She's carrying what?* Then the doctor asked him, "Do you know what that is? Do you have any idea what that could be?"

Ezek glanced over to Cyril. "I don't know. I don't have any idea," he said aloud to the doctor as the words slowly and methodically came from his mouth. He thought about it; he wasn't sure what part of her would have told him that, and if she knew, wouldn't she have told him? He said it again to himself, as if even though he didn't have the answer, *surely something like that she would have told me, she would have shared with me. Maybe she also doesn't know. Then again, perhaps it's her secret.* Ezek had no answers inside of him.

Then a wave of panic rolled over him. *Who put that inside of her? How long has it been there? Does she even know about it?*

The doctor pointed to one of her nurses. "Rinse her again! She still has dust on her. Rinse all of her, every part of her!"

Ezek understood the doctor's panic and made it clear to everyone in the room. "I'll do it. Don't touch her." Back in his arms, he put her into a different tub and scrubbed every inch of her body. When Ezek was finished, he wrapped her in a sheet then warmed her. The doctor said, "Let's do a sonogram."

Cyril lay still as Ezek opened the front of her sheet. His hand lay gently over her rib cage. The doctor rubbed the clear jell onto Cyril's skin then slowly watched the screen in front of her while moving the transducer over Cyril's ribs. Ezek looked at the sonogram. He too couldn't make out what she was carrying. "What's wrong?" Cyril's first words as she looked over to Ezek, blinking her eyes, not understanding why she couldn't hear his thoughts. "What aren't you telling me?"

"Whatever it is, it looks metallic," he said to her, as his right hand went to grab a handful of his hair, freezing the look on his face.

Feeling her bare feet on the dance floor, she stopped then put her right hand on the left side of her rib cage, still in Ezek's arms.

"What's inside of me!" she asked with a paranoid look on her face while staring back for an answer. "Was I carrying? Was I implanted? The words were difficult coming from her mouth. "What's happening to me?"

"They were checking your vitals and your blood. They were going to take you, only this time they were going to keep you."

"What, keep me, like take me with them forever?"

"Yes. Apparently, you have an agreement with the Grays that they were going to break."

"What happened for them to want to break it?"

"No one knows. I think it has to do with your parents." Cyril thought about it and wondered if there was a leak. What were her parents up to?

Ezek whispered down to her, "Here comes…"

Her heart was bursting. How could two people be so happy?

The door was already open. Max stopped to look in. Cyril's eyes caught the corner of the room. Waiting for her was a huge cut crystal vase with two dozen long-stemmed gladiolus in various colors. *Gladiolus*, she thought to herself, *a calling card*.

Max walked around the room. His finger traced the edge of the bedspread, noticing everything in the room. Max looked at the tailored black suit hanging from the door, pressed, not a wrinkle anywhere. Polished black leather shoes sat ready below the suit. On the dresser lay a black cloth bag; he wondered, *What's in here?*

"Cyril, who knew we would be here, and who knew you would be wearing that?"

Cyril took the card from the flowers as Max looked on. The card read, "I hope you have everything you need." Her thumb covered the *E* at the bottom of the note.

Her hand touched the arm of the suit. It was perfect, simple, straight, and for tomorrow's meeting. Max glanced over. "Is it always going to be like this? Wherever you go, someone gets there before us. They make sure you have whatever you need. I never see you call anyone to say where we're going. How does this happen?"

Cyril put her arms around him then kissed him gently. "Does it matter?"

Max kissed her back. "No, not really," as he took one button at a time in his finger, twisting it just so releasing it then on to the next. Cyril ignored it while kissing him.

She felt his lips still touching hers. Then again, her heart was torn. "I miss him," she said the words out loud.

Ezek saw her vision and whispered, "I know. We all do."

"It was different with him. He had to take me at face value. He wasn't capable of crawling into my head and having an advanced warning on my thoughts."

"I wouldn't say I crawl into your head. Don't put it like that. I see and feel your thoughts. I understand how you think." Ezek felt uncomfortable having to defend himself and compare himself to Max.

"I know there's no escaping you." Cyril wanted to take the words back but couldn't.

That was the difference. "He loved me without all the internal dialogue. I could never have been as close to him as I am to you, but we talked to each other. It forced me to find words to speak out loud. I can't tell you how many times I caught myself looking at him, wondering why he didn't understand. It was because I had taken for granted he couldn't read my mind like you do, understanding my every thought, but he couldn't, and I couldn't hear him like I am allowed to hear you. That is, when you let me." Cyril looked up and realized it was sarcasm, and she meant it to be so. "I don't think it's fair that you hear me all the time, and I just hear you when you want me to. I wanted Max to, without a doubt, understand that I loved him; but it meant words, very careful words, and actions. My god, how real words out loud make such a difference.

"I don't have that luxury with you. You always get the hard cold facts unedited. I miss talking out loud to him. There's a feeling I get when you close me out, when you shut yourself off to me. It's like you're not with me by choice. When Max and I were apart, it was different. I would long for him. I'd miss him."

"I heard you…" Ezek's eyes looked the other way.

"That's not what I meant. But now that you ask…how can I miss you when you're always there, there in my head?" Cyril pressed her cheek against his chest.

"Do you have any idea what it was like for me the moment your memory was wiped clean? For the first time, you were gone from me, *gone*. Do you have any idea what that was like for me, gone? At first, I had no idea what had happened. I'd never experienced it before. I thought you had died. That was the only thing that could have stopped your thoughts to me."

He pulled her away to look her in the eyes. "I thought you had died. Do you have any idea what that did to me?" Ezek had nothing to say after that as he told her, so in his thoughts, he could only stare into her to know she was before him alive and well, but alive.

"Teach me, teach me how to stop my thoughts to you. I want to know how to sort them like you do. You're capable of keeping your sarcasm to yourself. I'm not. You get what I'm thinking unedited.

"Sometimes not always, I wish I could stop what I'm thinking, but it's too late, and your feelings are hurt. I have never intentionally wanted to hurt you with my thoughts. Never. I guess maybe it's not my fault. If I've never been taught, then it's your fault for being there. No, that's not what I mean.

"Teach me, teach me how to control that. Well, if you're not going to teach me, then don't be hurt by what you see or hear."

"Okay, then let's try. Think about something... *No, not that!*" Ezek saw Cyril lying on her back as Max looked up at her from between her legs.

"Stop it. Think about something else," Ezek told her. "That's your privacy. You're showing me."

"I'm sorry. That was mean. Now how do I stop you from seeing it or thinking about it...how?" She stopped and looked at him for a moment, visualizing when they were little.

Standing at the bottom of the stairs in the old Victorian house looking up, she saw two figures sitting in the stairwell.

Ezek walked over then stood behind her, his hand holding the top of the doorjamb.

"Who's in there?" he asked while trying to pull the door open.

"What are you doing?" Cyril struggled to keep the door closed. Her thoughts went into his head.

"What do they want?"

Cyril listened for a moment, only getting bits and pieces of their conversation. Nothing was coming in clear. It was Yike and Sven.

"Why didn't you just say so!"

"Can you hear what they're saying to each other?" Cyril looked up. "Something about taking you after school."

"*What?* They want to do what?" Cyril's face looked distorted.

"That's what they're saying."

"Do you remember that day? Does everything go into your mind clearly? Can you see and hear me clearly?"

"Yes."

"Tell me how you do it. How do you block me? How can I block you?"

"I think about something else sometimes with you. It's hard, especially when you upset me, and I can't control it. I have to think about what you're thinking. I have to match it, so it's not my thought but yours. It's then the thought appears to be a blocked thought. It's simple to explain but very difficult to achieve. It takes practice. Stringing to you all these years makes it easy to hear you. I have noticed that the older we get, the harder it is to block you."

"So first, I have to know what you're thinking without you reading me. I don't want you to hear me, then I think about what you're thinking. That erases my thoughts to you. Right?"

"Yes...something like that."

"Okay, can I break your thought process and listen anyway? You know I hear you unconditionally as you do me?"

"No, I would never do that to you."

He watched the stardust float in the warm breeze then lay on her skin like confetti on New Year...

Looking out the window, Cyril turned to Ezek. "I've never been to Kodiak. What made you decide on this location?"

"Who would find us here?" He smiled.

"This is Steam, baby. He's glad to get them off the planet. Around three thousand of your little Gray friends are sleeping right now. They'll be traveling soon. We've had small shipments sent here for the past six months. No one seems to know what's being sent, but a small handful of deputies from the pertaining departments. No, Sven knows nothing about this plan." A small smirk showed in Ezek's eyes.

Cyril and Ezek just arrived at what appeared to be an abandoned warehouse out in the middle of nowhere. When Steam and Cindy walked out to greet them, Cindy held her board, reading it as fast as she could—then stopped in her tracks to answer back, hitting her board quickly. Frustrated, she looked up.

Steam's first words to Cyril, "Why do you always look like you're going to a funeral?"

Cyril, dressed in a casual black suit, responded, "I'm glad to see you too."

Ezek just shook his head, thinking they were still acting like childhood buddies, then shook Steam's hand and hugged Cindy. "How's it going? How long have you guys been here this morning?" Cindy looked at Steam and smiled. "Here, just a few minutes, but we got to the cabin last night. I heard you guys come in this morning. Where did you stay last night?"

"It's a long story." Cyril glanced over to Ezek and smiled.

Cyril and Cindy walked past both of them into the warehouse. You could hear a pin drop. It was so quiet inside. Caged in darkness were the Grays. Cyril knew they were asleep or what she referred to as asleep. Looking through the thick wired glass, she wondered, *No one would know if I eliminated them all right now.*

Steam walked up behind her, looking over her head into the warehouse.

Cyril looked straight ahead then asked, "How many spaceports have you set up?"

"So far, we have three. They're all taking off at different days and times."

"How many will be aboard each pod?" Cindy looked at Cyril with one eyebrow extended.

"We have to see how many wake up from this trip. We'll know then."

"We're trying to thin out as many facilities as possible. The Grays have noticed they're starting to come up missing just like us. Each pod will hold a thousand, maybe more."

Ezek looked over to Cyril and smiled, saying it out loud, "I like your idea."

Steam looked over. "I hate it when you guys do that. Just leave me out of the conversation when I'm standing right here."

"They do it to me all the time. They have whole conversations right in front of me, and I don't get to hear any part of it," Cindy said as she turned to walk away, looking through the glass doors.

"Tell them!"

"If I wanted them to know, I would tell them."

"Wow, don't get me in the middle of this." Steam began to walk backward.

"I just thought—no! I can't think like that." Cyril stopped her thoughts out loud.

Ezek read her thought and remarked, "I can. I can think like that all day long. Wait, I do think like that all day long. What am I thinking? We can all think like that. Hell, we're thinking that right now. Let's do it."

Cyril understood Ezek's hatred, having no patience for the Grays. Steam looked at both of them, almost like an acknowledgment. "They are very vulnerable right now. Besides, where would we put this many bodies if we did?" Cyril pulled from the inside of her blouse what appeared to be a small colorful scarf; holding it between two fingers, she waved it like a flag. Then she tucked it back in quickly.

Ezek saw the scarf. "Why not?" An exasperated glare came from him.

"Don't tempt me." Cyril realized it's not a game. Those were lives in there. Others cared about those lives. Just like she would if the table was turned.

His eyes scanned over the thousands of Grays lying still, almost appearing to be dead already.

She didn't understand why they hadn't found them yet. Then Cyril remembered the Block in Germany. The terrifying moment when she eliminated thousands of Grays at one time. Sven also wanted them dead but didn't want anyone to know who did it. How would he feel right now if she were to use the scarf? In one touch, the entire warehouse would be gone. Quieter-than-wind gone. She turned to Steam, and Ezek and Cindy looked down onto the floor and asked them, "Do you remember the Block in Germany I was traveling with Sven?" Her eyes darted as she looked up to Ezek for only one answer.

Ezek caught where she was going with the question, shaking his head. "No, no, it will only make things worse."

Steam leaned against the wall, staring out past the thick wired glass. "Are you sure about Sven?"

"No, I'm not. It was on that trip that is still crawling underneath my skin. Sven knew it was them or us. He wanted them gone, but he couldn't do it himself. Sven told me to bend it. He couldn't. He couldn't do it." She shook her head as if trying to shake the memory off.

"It was his job to do it, not mine. My stones are turquoise, and his are black. I was angry when I exposed them. He knew that. He knew what the repercussions would be toward me. And not toward him. He knew it all along."

The look on Cindy's face caused Cyril to ask, "What, what's he been up to? He's been off the radar for weeks now. I haven't seen any recent reports from him, and I have asked for them. I'm not sure who and where he's been spending his time."

Cyril, feeling threatened and frustrated, asked, "Who is he working with?"

Ezek leaned down. "How late are you staying this evening?"

I have to get this out before something else happens. I think I understand now, at least I think I do, about how you feel toward Sven. I'm adding it all up in my head. Looking up at him, she hesitated. "I can't trust anyone, can I? But for some crazy reason, I can trust you and Cindy and Steam."

"I know I have never done anything to make you not trust me. That is, I hope not."

Cyril smiled. "You know it's a process of quick thinking all this in-your-head business. You can hear me, so can your dad and brother. Who else?" she wondered for a moment.

"Sven, he's always tried to hear you; but when you're afraid of him, he hears nothing. When you were little, it was clear to him now it's not. I don't think he can hear you now, based on what I have seen this evening." Ezek eyes followed the arrow-shaped piece of stardust as it pierced her shoulder… She heard his thoughts as she looked into his eyes.

Outside her bedroom, the hallway was faintly lit. A short dark silhouette holding the doorknob remained still. Cyril clutched her pillow then heard her seven-year-old voice say, "Come in, Yike." Then the Gray silhouette partially closed the door behind it. Cyril jumped out of bed onto the floor, grabbing her friend Yike, hugging him tightly, "I missed you. Where have you been?"

"Look what I got for my birthday." She was excited and wanted to share. Cyril held up her new Sister Belle talking doll, arms stretched out, waiting for Yike to take it.

Cyril said, "Watch this," as she put her finger into the white ring and pulled the string coming from inside the doll's neck.

Suddenly the doll's voice said, "Can we go out and play?"

Yike jumped up, almost hitting the ceiling. On his way down, Yike gently grabbed the doll, staring into it. Cyril stood up, shocked, and watched.

Then Yike stared at the doll while slowly putting his long slender pointed finger into the ring while pulling the ring coming from the doll's neck, then releasing the string as the string pulled itself back in. The doll said, "I love you."

Cyril turned. Behind her was her new easy-bake oven. "Look, I can bake stuff. I have my own oven. Do you want some cake?" Glancing at her bedroom door, she saw another silhouette; this one was much taller. Ezek had been leaning against the doorjamb, watching and listening. He was not sure what he should do, hearing her message. "I'm playing," Cyril said in an exasperated tone.

Yike knew Ezek was there watching.

What hadn't occurred to any of them was they could all talk to each other without saying anything out loud.

Quietly they played as Ezek watched on.

Hearing their conversations, he gathered this Gray was her friend. Knowing it was not uncommon for her to talk to everything. He had seen her have long conversations with the cats and at times would read from her books to the dog. Strangely he got the impression the dog was actually listening.

It occurred to him if Cyril was never told to be afraid or to be cautious of someone or something, then she wouldn't.

Fear is something you learn; she'd never experienced that. She had nothing to compare it with. Fear was not part of her life. Yike was her friend; she had known him all her short life.

"That's not normal, is it?" Cyril said out loud to Ezek.

"What…you talking to strange things. I'm used to it." His smile beamed down on her, expecting every part of her and her life.

"Why didn't you ever tell me to be afraid, to be cautious, to watch out, to be careful?"

"It wasn't up to me."

"How long has it been going on? What a strange relationship."

"I agree. You're able to remain on both sides. In a way, this has kept you alive. There have been numerous times you could have been harvested. But no Gray will take that chance, knowing your relationship with Yike."

"To me, it seems like it's always been that way. It was a relationship you started as an infant. Your mother watched you sitting with a Gray in the stairwell one time, not saying a word. She knew you had the ability to string to them. She knew they came and played with you when her back was turned. Your relationship with the Grays is why I think our parents wanted me to string to you. Grays respect you and know you understand them. They are hoping you'll be their voice when the time is right. Only you will know when that is."

"This is all too much to take in. Tomorrow is Sunday. Thank god I don't have to work tomorrow, so I can stay out late and find out more about myself. Tully will be asleep when I get there. Do you know Tully? Of course, you do. What am I saying? You know all about my life."

There's that security thing again, knowing Ezek can hear her.

"I'm sorry, it's just hard to get used to. Having my guard down around someone. It's just hard to get used to." She shook her head in her own disbelief.

Cyril felt a cold piercing on top of her head as Ezek looked into her eyes, knowing she was leaving…

Cyril looked out the window at the city below, then over to Ezek. He's taking off his headset as the engine of the jet helicopter rested on the rooftop. Cyril unbuckled herself as her door opened. A man handed her a tablet; her eyes immediately caught the red capital letters across the screen. It read, "Virginia 3:00 p.m." Glancing at him, she asked excitedly, "Is she here?"

"Yes, she asked to be put on your schedule a few days ago. I'm sorry, I was asked not to tell you." The man smiled.

Cyril could hardly contain herself; she looked at Ezek to tell him when he said, "Yes, I know my father told me she would be here."

Cyril raced down the stairs down the hall into the conference room. There, her mother sat at the head of the conference table talking to Norie; she got up quickly to hug Cyril.

Virginia then whispered, "We're going to Greenland in the morning," saying it as if it was a secret. "They say it's ready for distribution."

Cyril smiled. "Mom, how are you? Where's Dad? Tell me how the test went and about your trip. Was it Africa? Is that where you were at?

"Greenland, huh, I've never been there. I thought Dad was with you? So if he's not with you, where is he?"

"No, I thought he was here with you." Virginia put the papers down then turned to look at her assistant.

"I talked to him just last night. I never thought to ask where he was. When we get back, we'll be at the Rock for a few days. Then we're off to China. It's their turn next."

Then Virginia waved her hand for Cyril to sit at her place at the table.

Cyril looked at all her colleagues as Ezek entered the room, taking a seat across the table from her mother.

Cyril stood at the end of the table and announced, "Let's get started. As you all can see, we have a special guest speaker today."

Cyril looked down to the far end of the table; there was Steam. He was also happy to see her mother.

"There is something so relaxing about dancing with you." Then Ezek noticed she was looking up at him as if she had just returned. Without saying it out loud, she felt suddenly uncomfortable. Putting the pieces together in her mind, just what was he capable of keeping from her? She thought that their thoughts were fluid and one, but now she knew that wasn't true.

She didn't know his every thought. She wasn't always in his mind.

He knew about the letter from her mother. He probably even knew her mother and father were not together that day. He knew her mother would be at the meeting. What else did he know that he's not sharing with her?

Ezek slowed while the music went on. Then he stopped. "Can we go somewhere and talk? I feel you're upset."

"What do you mean you can feel I'm upset? It's apparent to me I can't trust anyone. It's like for the first time in my life, I see the forest from the trees. It never occurred to me that you would keep thoughts from me, especially ones you know that are vitally important to me."

Still holding her hand as she turned to walk away, they both looked down to see the stardust falling onto the top of her hand…

The Smell

She could feel the brim of the straw hat across her forehead, keeping the sun from her eyes. In her hand was a fishing pole, her right index finger touching the line as she waited for a fish to strike. There was a calmness around Cyril. The water was still, the weather perfect.

"Tell me, Bernard, how would you write it? Who would be my beneficiary? I have no living relatives." Cyril glanced over to her longtime family friend and attorney.

"It just seems to me that you need something in writing. Who gets the company, who's in charge if something happens to you, or let's just say you're unable to make decisions for a while? All this must be considered," Bernard explained.

Bernard, a powerhouse of legal information worldwide. Now approaching early retirement, that day he wanted to show off his new fishing boat. Knowing how stressed out Cyril had been, he wanted to keep his word to her parents to keep an eye on her.

Still waiting for the fish to strike, Cyril leaned over and asked Bernard, "What do you recommend I do? I can't just leave things hanging if something happens to me."

"How long have you and Ezek been together?"

"I work with him. I've known him all my life."

"Do you trust him? Don't try and convince me that you are not together. I have my sources." Bernard rolled the ice in his drink with his finger as he glanced over the top of his sunglasses at her. Cyril smiled and gave Bernard a half look from below the brim of her hat.

"Yes, I trust him. I trust him with my life."

"He then is your family. He watches out for you and the company. I think he should be your beneficiary. Can you think of anyone else?"

"One thing I want you to put in writing is that if I am ever unable to make decisions or speak but am alive. I want to recuperate in private. I don't want to be a test subject, looked at under a microscope, or dissected with no privacy. I want my instructions carried out as if I'm there. The only people that will know I'm not giving orders will be Ezek and Steam, no one else. I would prefer to go home and not stay in a hospital. I hated it when I was stuck in the burn unit, unable to do anything. I felt like a lab rat. Just promise me that no one knows anything about my private life or my medical condition until I'm better. With everything that's happened to me in the last few years, I'm surprised I'm still alive. You know, it's almost like I'm always being watched and guarded at the same time."

"What are you putting in writing?" Ezek leaned down to hand Cyril a tall glass of iced tea.

"I don't think I'm prepared if something happens to me." She looked straight at Ezek.

"Nothing's going to happen to you, not today anyway, that I know of." He said it as if he's looking over his shoulder to see what's coming next, with a smirk and a smile on his face.

"I'm kidding. Okay, stop worrying."

"What are you going to do if you catch something?" Steam walked over to look into the water, holding his glass of tea.

"She's going to have Bernard write her will." Ezek shared with Steam.

"That's actually a good idea. The company has become very lucrative, with all the government contracts and the satellites we control, along with the patents and the new technology we share. There's a lot to be considered. With over two thousand employees worldwide, I think it's a good idea to keep it going to keep it safe. To keep you safe." Steam sat down in the shade, his pants rolled up, putting his bare feet up along the top rail.

Bernard looked over to Steam, then to Ezek, and asked, "Do you get along with each other?" while his finger rolled the ice in his glass.

Steam looked over to Ezek and held his glare as Ezek turned to stare back. Both men were thinking to themselves.

"I can't remember him not being around her," Steam said out loud to Ezek.

"The same," Ezek said back to Steam, nodding his head up and then down.

Cyril broke the conversation. "I can't remember not having both of you in my life ever. I'm not sure what I would do without both of you. How could this all be possible without the two of you? Bernard, I do need something in writing."

Cyril felt her right foot touch the grass off the dance floor. She turned to Ezek as he was walking behind her. She stopped and put her hand upon his chest to stop him while she looked up.

"I trusted you just then while on the boat with Steam and Bernard. I don't understand it one minute. I trust you, the next minute I don't. One minute I've got something inside of me, the next, I'm not sure." Cyril sounded exhausted and confused. "This is all too much for me. I don't know who she is. I don't know what's happening right here right now with us, you and me. What is it we do exactly?" Staring up at him, she felt the stardust hit the top of her head. For a split second, she wanted it all to stop. She wanted to be answered...

"I don't want you to go," he said out loud to her so even the neighbors, if they had any, could hear him. Showing his feelings and how he was worried about her was not like him. He believed in her, and he knew she could handle just about any situation. But things were changing this time; it was different. He never felt this much dread inside him, and that for the first time terrified him.

"I have to. I have to explain it to them. I want them to understand." She walked around the counter, putting the morning dishes into the sink.

"I'm going with you." Ezek grabbed his coat and gloves.

"Are you crazy? They'll kill you once they hear what I have to say."

"What makes you think they won't kill you?" Ezek stopped and waited for her answer.

"I'm going to see Yike. He'll listen. He'll know I'm there as a friend."

"It makes me..." Ezek stopped before he could say it out loud. His thoughts went through her head.

"I know they killed your mother. I'm reminded of that every day, just like they killed my husband. I understand the risk, but I don't think they'll harm me. I have to show them what's in their plasma. I want them to see it for themselves. I want Yike to see how it floats to the top. Then when it touches the air, it separates. They can't use our blood anymore. That's what's killing them. They'll never survive here. They have to move on or die here. They only use our blood to keep themselves alive. When they're on other planets with different atmospheric conditions, they're okay. But here, staying here, it's a lot of work for them to stay alive. Back in the 1930s and forties, they started traveling to other planets to find something more suitable for them. In trade, I'd like to know about the other planets they have to choose from. I think in our near future, we will also need another place to live like them. Their research could be helpful to humankind. I need, no, we need their information on where it's suitable to live. Who knows, maybe someday we'll be harvesting them on their planet to survive." Cyril looked around the room for her gloves.

"Does Yike know about the facility in Alaska and the pods? That's a few thousand we haven't gotten rid of yet. Why are you waiting? He reads your mind similar to how I do. How do you keep what you know from him when you're with him?"

"No, he knows nothing about Alaska or the pods. I just try to think about something else, something he's not interested in."

"You forget he does know about Germany and your turquoise stones. Don't think for a moment—"

Before Ezek could finish, Cyril interrupted, "Stop. I'm aware of all of this. I'm meeting him. Drop it," with a sharp stare.

Ezek took Cyril's arm as his eyes slowly opened to look at her. Washing over him was fear, fear of never seeing her alive again. Cyril pulled away then sat and laced up her thick black leather boots then stood and zipped up her coat again, all dressed in black. Her hair pulled back off her face.

"I'm not sure when I'll be back, but I will be back."

Ezek felt helpless but understood why she thought she must go. "Don't follow me. Don't send the orbs this time. I have to go alone. His red orbs know when I'm around before I even get there. Because of my blue orbs, they read what they're sending back to you. They can't go on this trip. Let them know that's important."

"Can I give you a distraction thought?"

"You are my distraction thought." Cyril smiled as she touched the buttons on the front of his shirt.

"They can hear your thoughts, so let me plant this to swirl inside your head. Marry me when you get back. Let me take care of you and love you the way you need to be loved. Please say yes. But give me your answer when you return."

For that moment, he stopped his thoughts going into her head. He didn't want her to know this would be the last time he would ever see her alive; his heart was bleeding inside. He knew, he just knew, her mind could not be changed.

Cyril looked closely into his eyes at the seriousness while reading nothing more coming from his thoughts.

"I have to go. Yike is waiting."

"He's in your head right now, isn't he?" Ezek looked into her to find him.

"Yes, I have to go," Cyril said slowly as if she was a prisoner of her own thoughts.

Ezek held out her long black leather gloves, holding them tight. Cyril reached for them, tugging at them until Ezek released them, releasing her. For that moment, he watched her walk away. His breath stopped. His arms felt like they were extended too far—reaching out for her. He felt he was falling. Unable to stop her, he took in every movement. The way her hand went to open the door, the way her hair moved when she turned her head to smile goodbye. The way her foot lifted from the ground the moment she was no longer touching the earth. The car moved slowly down the driveway away from him, taking all his breath away. He was helpless. She was off the planet again.

Up ahead in the sky appeared to be one very large cloud, cumulus nimbus, she thought. To the north of that cloud were three smaller clouds appearing to be moving slowly toward the east.

Cyril drove down the road, just past the county line in broad daylight. Her car's hood illuminated, making the car appear to be gone. Cyril felt paralyzed as she felt her surroundings being lifted. Then she heard her car door open, surrounded by darkness, feeling like only seconds had passed. There in the dark stood Yike holding the door open. The small vibrations had stopped. Thick moisture filled her surroundings while the stale orange smell in the air flooded her breath.

The lights went on slowly, almost like the sun rose, but in the opposite direction, down instead of up. First, she saw the top of their heads. Oblong in shape, their bodies different heights and sizes similar to most humans. Their colors were various shades of greenish grays, some darker, some lighter, some large, taller, wider—all different shapes and sizes. One startling image was that you could immediately tell which ones had reproduced and which ones didn't. When the light illuminated the inside of the craft, it seemed extremely larger on the inside than it appeared from the outside based on the clouds' size. Cyril was having a hard time wrapping her head around how that could be possible. Then a tickle came across her heart, almost like a flutter; could it be fear? Cyril grabbed her black satchel, throwing the strap over her shoulder, then looked out her windshield. The Grays were looking into the car, fascinated by their new passenger. Yike held his hand out, his long slender fingers pointed at each end, the tips curling at the ends waiting to touch her. Cyril stopped and said to herself, *Marry me. Let me love you.* The thought swirled inside her mind.

Getting out of the car, Cyril said to Yike, "Where are we going?"

His small mouth said nothing, but his words went quickly into her head. "We have arrived. This is one of our harvesting plants. I think that's what you call it. Does Ezekiel want to be yours? Do you want to be his? When did this happen?"

As Yike touched her, it was cold, almost slippery but dry with a suction. She felt he wasn't letting go of her hand as she felt his tug to get her out of her car.

Cyril felt an uncomfortable threat in the form of the way Yike's words and touch were delivered.

"You have known him as long as you have known me. It's time to be his." Hearing Yike say the possibility out loud to her made it real; it made her wish it was already done.

Yike stopped then let go of her hand and looked her in the eye; while changing the subject, he said, "I want you to tell me what's happening to my plasma and my platelets."

His first question was immediately drowned out by the fact he changed his thought.

This could only mean one thing: Cyril knew he had killed her husband; if not him, then someone from his group did. Now for him to change the subject, she felt a threat to Ezek and had to change her thought pattern.

"Where are we?" Cyril gripped the strap of her satchel, keeping one hand free. "What is this place?"

"Would it be easier for you to number the places we go? I'm going to take you to all the facilities we have on this planet. You brought your tester, and you're going to show me something about how it separated then floats." He had been reading her mind. Cyril stopped to clear her head. How could he have known that unless he had always been in her thoughts? Just how much did he know?

"Easter, I wish for Easter. I wish to belong to no one, not Ezek, no one. I wish it was Easter."

Pantic hit Cyril. The smell told her everything; as she walked through the glass doors, she saw hands dangling from the ceiling as the bodies were hoisted up. Thick moisture covered her like a blanket, causing her fabric to stick to her skin. The smell was metallic and sour like a slaughterhouse at noon.

Trying to keep her composure, she commented, "The smell is almost more than I can handle," as she casually walked to the edge to see the blood churning under the floor. Grays of all sizes stopped and watched as some had never seen a human alive standing up on two feet before; they weren't sure what to make of her. Yike gave some kind of hand gesture, and they all went back to work as new bodies were descending from the ceiling. The Grays arranged the bodies quickly as the faces all looked vacant, not needing any more help. Each round table in the facility held between ten and twelve bodies depending on the body sizes. The minute they were comfortably resting, the Grays went into what Yike called the powder room. Cyril noticed these human bodies were shorter in stature.

Most of the skin was lighter, almost transparent in color. The hair was predominantly straight black. She would refer to this location as East One. The draining room wasn't as big as the first and the only one Cyril had visited before. The first building went on forever; this building only held maybe one to two hundred tables, small in comparison to the other.

Following behind the workers up the ramp to the next floor, Yike said, "You can test here."

This powder room was different from the one Cyril had visited once before. This one was more primitive. It was almost like it was one of the best jobs on the planet to a Gray. They methodically cut the arms, legs, and head off each body; and they looked like they were enjoying it.

Again, Cyril had to say to herself, *Ezekiel wants*—Then she stopped. *Easter, I wish it were Easter.* Inside her mind, she saw herself in a pink-

and-white gingham dress, holding her mother's hand, walking in the garden looking for colored eggs. The day was cool, the sun was bright, and her Easter basket had seven beautifully colored eggs inside. *Easter*, she repeated to herself as the smell went up into her nose. Cyril looked over to Yike and asked, "Why is it different here how the bodies are prepared for drying?"

Yike remembered she had seen the other facility. There the bodies were just ground up, not cut, then dried.

Yike walked around the large table, looking over the working Grays' shoulders, as body parts were cut then pushed to the center of the table. They were moved quickly to be crushed then ground up to dry. Yike stopped and said, "This makes the workers feel better. So many of their own were killed by humans that look like this, like you. Cutting them up makes it almost go away." Yike turned his eyes from her.

The smell...the smell, looking at the empty expressions, the void in their eyes, the smell. Coming from the Grays, Cyril faintly heard kissing noises, some more rapid than others, like conversations between them.

Easter, what shall I fix, ham? No. Who will I invite? The smell.

Should I entertain in the dining room or maybe set the table up outside? I could make those deviled eggs Max used to make. I never had the heart to tell him they were just like my mother's. Easter, I'll color eggs like I used to. Then Cyril jumped, looking over to the other end of the room where an arm had fallen off the table. With a loud thud onto a metal surface, she got the feeling that they were all laughing.

To the far end of the room, Cyril followed Yike as heads turned and the Grays looked, watching her every step. Were they laughing? she wondered.

As they approached the wall before them, it slowly lit, showing small vials of blood, thousands of vials transparent, making the entire wall appear red. Strange symbols went down each vial. Could it be the location of where it was taken or maybe a date? Cyril couldn't make out its significance. Yike's long fingers wrapped around the vial.

Taking it out from the wall slowly and carefully, he held it up to the light. Moving through the crowd of Grays, Cyril noticed a very short Gray quickly approached them. Cyril couldn't hear their conversation, but she knew what they were about to do was not okay with this Gray. Suddenly she realized she was surrounded by Grays at all sides. Then she felt a small tug on her satchel; she clutched it now with both hands. Looking straight across at her eye level, she said to the Gray holding her strap, "No, you can't have it," as she delivered a threatening stare.

Yike was in deep conversation with the other Gray, now both holding the same vial in their long slender fingers. Their eyes fixed on the vial. Cyril saw the panic in both of their dark eyes. Cyril knew the vial was about to break. What was it about this vial that was so important? Out of all the vials he could have taken off the wall, this one meant something, something important.

"Stop it," Cyril said out loud to both of them when the entire room stopped then turned to look at her. Suddenly two very tall Grays brought what appeared to be a stainless steel surface over to Cyril. One Gray slapped his hand hard on the surface, showing Cyril it was steady as it floated suspended with no legs. "This is where you can test. Move it to wherever you want." The message went straight into her head as she looked at the tall Gray in the eye.

The short Gray let the vial lose as Yike handed it over to Cyril. Glancing back at the Gray still holding her strap, she tugged it out of its reach and put it upon the stainless steel surface. Pulling out a small centrifuge and tiny vials, she began her tests. Again, Yike's hand motion set the other Grays to work, cutting the body parts off, pushing them onto the rapidly moving center.

Cyril watched the blood exposed to air separate and change colors. This blood was tainted. Cyril thought of her parents and how hard they had worked to—

Her thought stopped. *Easter! Springtime, everything is new and beautiful, Easter!* Her parents were quickly washed from her thoughts as images of past Easters flashed in her memory like a storm.

"Step over here." Yike pointed to the floor. All the Grays stood with their arms next to their bodies with their heads down when he did. Yike explained, "Don't move." A clear glass liquid formed over them, molding them into a glass-like dome.

"This next facility you can call Mongolia. I like this word 'Mongolia.' Do you remember it? Mongolia!" Yike repeated into Cyril's head.

"This is the very biggest harvesting plant on your planet." Cyril was struck by how they had gone from one place to another so quickly. Feeling something wet running from her nose, she wiped it with her wrist. Blood was running from her nose.

"You can't move me that fast," she said in a panic, putting her hand out to show Yike she was bleeding. Yike's hand touched the back of Cyril's neck. Ice cold, her bleeding stopped almost instantly. He sent her the thought *You're okay now.*

Yike's long slender arms and fingers went out to display the vastness of the facility. Clutching her satchel, Cyril was stunned at how she could not see the end of the room in any direction. The tables were all the same size as the others she had seen. The people on the tables were predominantly red, some darker than others in skin color. Most had no facial hair. The majority had a dark blue spot or spots somewhere on their skin. When Cyril went over to examine it, Yike said in her head, "Birthmark, not to worry. Just birthmark."

"But it's blue!" Cyril almost touched it, thinking it might be something else. *Mongolia,* she repeated to herself. "So does this mean we're between Russia and northern China?"

"Yes." Yike nodded.

This facility was like the rest. The large round holes were on the floor. You could hear the dripping below echoing off the ceiling while churning beneath them. *The smell,* she repeated to herself, *that smell...*

They checked the blood in that harvesting facility. The results were the same; the blood platelets did float then separate just like all the others. Then Yike again asked her to stand where he pointed. She knew this time what was going to happen.

"Please don't go so fast. I don't think I can handle it when you move me so fast. Please slow down!"

Again, the liquid glass contained them; and before she knew it, she was standing at a table where most people had dark skin. Yike touched her shoulder, taking her thought away. Cyril wiped her nose, checking for more blood when suddenly Yike's fingers went around the back of her neck. Again, like ice, it made her shiver; but no blood appeared. "This is the smallest harvesting facility," Yike explained while his fingers unfurled. The Grays turned to look at her and Yike. Cyril heard the kissing-like sound the Grays were making, and she knew they were talking about her.

Yike turned to explain, "They were told we were coming. You are alive, and that disturbs them. Stay close to me." His hand went to touch his side like patting himself.

One Gray, just a little taller than Yike, came over to Cyril. Cyril did not look him in the eye, but she could see the transparent hair on his skin stand up on end the closer he got to her. She felt a conversation was happening right before her. She sensed it wasn't going very well when she saw Yike take a step back. When he did, his hand went in front of her, pulling her back behind him at the same time. Before she knew it, the liquid glass encased them.

Suddenly the smell of fried food was everywhere. Yike had already put his hand on the back of her neck, causing her to shiver again. She noticed these bodies were tanned, not black, not white.

"What happened back there? Why did we have to leave so quickly? I got the feeling he was threatening us."

"I don't have a very good relationship with him. That was my brother."

"*Wow*, who would have thought... You have a brother! What's his name? Do you have a sister also?" It had never occurred to Cyril he might have siblings.

"His name is Bloom. I have twenty-one siblings so far. Four are male, three are female, and fourteen haven't decided yet what they want to be. I'm the baby."

"Awww, you're the baby, really? You never told me you had siblings."

Yike's head tilted to one side, letting her know he found no humor in the conversation or no value to it. So Cyril went back to business.

"What should I call this facility?"

"How about the South? We are below the equator now."

For as far as she could see, the tables were full. The stench coming from the corpses were warm, almost like they were spoiling right in front of her.

"The temperature is wrong here. It needs to be cooler, at least forty degrees or colder."

Cyril followed Yike up the ramp to where the vials hung behind the glass. As he randomly took one by one off the wall, Cyril checked each one. This time Yike watched as the blood did not separate or float.

"So this is good. This is okay. This won't kill us?"

"Yes, that's correct. This blood so far has not been contaminated, at least for now." Cyril could not understand how this blood was so clean. How did the vaccine not have made it south? Doesn't anyone here get a flu shot? Were they using old flu vaccines? Were they just not getting shots at all? Why was it different? Not one vial was bad, not one. Her thoughts had escaped her. Then memories of beautifully painted Easter eggs filled her vision. *Easter, I love Easter!*

"This was a good trip, my friend. Again, I have learned something new. You have helped me. I understand the information you want. I'm not able to give that to you right now. I need more time. We will meet again, my friend. I have kept you too long this time. Ezekiel is waiting for you."

For that moment, Cyril's panic was gone; her fear had subsided. She felt the trade was evident in his tone.

When her eyes blinked, she was looking at her car. Six Grays were walking around it, wiping their fingerprints and lick marks off its surface. She kind of gave them a smile. To them, it was her way of saying, "It's all right."

But apparently, it wasn't all right. Yike made a strikingly sharp movement with his left hand, and the room was cleared immediately.

"We are in a position for you to return home. I will put you on your property."

Yike stood in front of her. His eyes this time had just a little more yellow streaks in them; his head went down. She felt his smile as he opened the door to her car. Clutching her satchel and throwing it to the other seat, she felt him say thank you. Watching him close the door, she smiled goodbye.

Once it was closed, she was parked in her driveway.

Cyril felt the cool grass under her feet. She stopped then turned, holding up her hand as Ezek moved right into it. Her hand on his chest, he put his hand over hers, clutching it.

"My god, what was that?" She wiped her nose to check to see if she was bleeding again.

"I think you're tired. I'm taking a helicopter into Las Vegas for the night. Go with me?" He stared into her for an answer.

Cyril did everything she could not to smile. *What an invitation*, she thought. She collected herself and tried to calm her excitement. Then it occurred to her she couldn't hide anything internally from him, including her last thoughts. *Damn...*

"Technically, I just met you, and you're asking me to spend the night with you." She smirked. "You are rather forward. Do you always come onto women so quickly?"

Ezek was caught off guard; he didn't know how to respond to her. He wanted her back; he wanted his life back, his life with her. But who was she now? How was he supposed to talk to her, like a complete stranger? Like someone he'd just met for the first time? That's crazy, he thought. Where's his Cyril? Didn't the stardust make any difference at all?

"I didn't bring a change of clothes." She shook her head as if saying no.

Ezek, wetting his lips, smiled with a small huff. He was trying to remain patient with her. "If you had checked your car before you left, you would have found that Tully always makes sure you're prepared for anything. Like spending the night with me."

"Yes. I told her it was too far for you to drive back after the party. That I would make sure you had a place to stay. I have two adjoining rooms at the Cosmopolitan. We can leave whenever you wish."

"What is it with you guys and helicopters?"

"It's just a quicker way to get around."

"Las Vegas, huh." Cyril didn't like the idea. "Vegas," she repeated to herself out loud.

"I just thought it's not that far. Is there somewhere else you'd like to go instead?" He politely clutched his hands and waited for her answer. He was willing to take her anywhere in the world she wanted to go.

"Can we get out of the desert?" Cyril looked up, letting him know in her own way she was willing to go with him.

"Of course, I'll see if the Rock is ready for visitors. Do you remember the Rock?"

Ezek took his phone out, touching it once to make a call.

Cyril walked to the table to sit down. The Rock...the Rock? The word didn't seem familiar to her, but nothing did at this point.

"Are you guys leaving?" Steam got up and took the chair next to her.

"Yes, I'm tired. This has been a hell of a night. It's hard to take it all in. Who is this crazy person you work with? Yeah, remind me it's me. Really, I find that hard to believe that this is me. Do you have any idea how long this dust stuff lasts?"

"No, Cindy researched it. Once you experience the dust, she said it's like tearing open your memory so it can all come back in. Tonight were some of the pieces that let it flow in. In the next few days, that's when hopefully you'll see the other pieces come together. But no one knows for sure." Cyril looked down the path at the end of the row of trees. A car slowly approached the end of the walkway. The driver got out and waited, giving Ezek a nod. Ezek came over and put his hand out toward Steam to shake his hand.

"Thank you for your help this evening. We're spending the night at the Rock. We'll stay there for a few days maybe." Ezek's eyebrow went up, knowing his answer was probably wrong. "Things change. We'll see how it goes tonight."

Steam got up from his chair and walked away from Cyril, letting Ezek know to follow him.

"What's up?" Ezek looked Steam in the eye like it had to be important.

"You know they've been watching her all night."

"Yes, I think there are four of them."

"Really, I only saw two." Both confirmed the counts as they both walked back to where Cyril was sitting.

Cyril looked up at both of them while putting her glass down. "Really, you guys! There are six of them. This is the first time I've been out by myself in a very long time. I think they're seeing how I'm doing. I first noticed their red orbs earlier this evening. Does that mean Yike is around here somewhere?"

Ezek gave her a half smirk. "I see you're catching on. Yes, he probably is. Only you'll know. Let me know when he's in your head."

"I'll be right back. I want to say good night to my friends." Barefoot Cyril tiptoed through the cool grass then over the little bridge to her table. Cindy wasn't there. She was dancing with Norie.

Mimsie smiled. "So it worked. It was his stuff."

"Yes, thank you for everything, including your patience with me. I have a small idea of who I am. I apparently have a long way back to myself... Well, you understand. Well, anyway, I was just leaving. See you all back at work. Please tell Cindy and Norie good night."

Ezek waited on the other side of the bridge. He caught every shadow and looked every person in the eye, and after a quick scan, he said to Cyril as she approached him, "You have twelve visitors."

Cyril smiled. "There's one you didn't count."

Looking up at Ezek, she saw the moment his hand went to grab his beard. She watched him as his hand glided down, then up to grab it again as they walked toward the waiting limousine. What she saw was him worried. It happened again as if he was soothing himself.

Walking toward the car with him, she asked, "Are you petting yourself?" She said it with a fair amount of disgust while trying to change his thought.

"Yes, I believe I am." He nodded with a smirk across his face, looking up, almost proud of himself.

Then it occurred to her; she had never seen him with this much facial hair. He was always clean-shaven, maybe a mustache once in a while but a full outright beard. And his hair had always been long but never this long. He could hear her thoughts as he opened the car door. Inside, the driver was a woman. Her hair was short but wild flaming red going in every direction.

Her skin illuminated white; she turned and smiled, almost like she was flirting with him. "Where shall I take you, sir?" Her English accent was faint, but Cyril picked up on it quickly.

"To the landing field, please."

As Ezek put up the window between them, he straightened his coat while trying to get comfortable; he needed to find the right words. He couldn't keep it to himself any longer. He thought maybe Tully might have picked up on it, but to him, it was his own private battle as he tried to explain to Cyril. "I need to share this with you."

Cyril heard a seriousness in his tone that caught her attention.

"The moment your mind went blank was a moment I had never experienced before. It overwhelmed me not having your thoughts in my head. I have to confess it changed me. I know it's scary to think, but it stopped everything. Nothing would ever be the same after that. I wasn't able to think about how I looked; it just didn't matter anymore. I was more concerned about you. I felt like I had failed you. Had I gotten into the helicopter first then helped you, we both would have gone together. I have played every scenario in my head. So many different ways it could have unfolded. But the fact that it happened the way it did, I have to tell you I am sincerely sorry I was not there to prevent it. I'm sorry, Cyril, really I am." As he reached out to touch her, he noticed her hands slowly pulled away.

Cyril studied the look on his face; it was painful and hard to look at. She had the overwhelming feeling to put her arms around him and tell him everything was okay. Something was stopping her. She was unable to show him comfort as she searched inside herself to figure out why. This man was genuinely distraught over what had happened to her, and he felt responsible.

Ezek's fingers threaded through his hair, pulling his hair back, tying it with a black ribbon he had just pulled from his pocket. He was right. He didn't know her or who she had become. That's not how his Cyril would have reacted. The car stopped, and the door opened. Before her was a fleet of helicopters all different sizes, white, orange, and blue with *FIIC* across the side in big letters.

"Would you like to take the controls this evening?" Ezek walked to the pilot's door, opened it, and waited for her answer.

Surprised, she said, "Hell no, I'm not flying this thing." Her face puckered, leaning back, shocked as she walked to the other side of the craft. Ezek dashed around to open the door, moving the seat belts out of her way.

His hand went out as he watched her decide if she would take his help. She looked at his hand, trying to figure out where this was going, where they were going; the idea of how it all felt so right, so normal, so the way it was supposed to be, frightened her.

There was that moment of "It's okay. It's all right. You're safe." There was that safe thing again. Being safe just didn't fit right, as if it wasn't tight enough. Or then again, it was too tight, safe. What is that really? Would there ever be a moment when she didn't have to look over her shoulder to see what was coming next? She had tried to relax; it was part of her rehabilitation. They told her she needed to find a place inside herself to slow her breathing and think about beautiful things and moments in her life that made her happy. Moments in her life. *Can anyone tell me what that is?* She would ask them. Tonight she saw some of those moments most, causing her to look in the sky for what was next. Happy times in her life it had occurred to her; they all included him. He was there during all of it.

When she looked out from his eyes, she experienced him feeling the overwhelming burden of protecting her. He felt responsible for all the bad things that had happened to her. In her mind, this was out of his control. But he didn't see it like that. All he knew was if he could do it all over again, he would have done it differently. How could she take his guilt away? She did have moments when she felt safe. Like when he was carrying her out of the hangar that cold night after she had been abducted by rogue Grays. Or the time she returned after two long weeks with Yike. The look on Ezek's face to know she's alive.

Or the time she found herself sitting under a tree in Bonn while she watched Ezek drive up, four hours after the summit was over. She was all right then. Cyril, in some cases, hadn't been physically harmed. But emotionally, it had taken a toll on her and Ezek. Fear and all that she had seen that evening was comfortably falling back into the crevices of her memory. Callusing over the person she really was or was becoming again. Then she remembered lying on the bed of ferns, hearing the fire crackle in the background, Max's warm arms around her. That was safe. Could all the moments in her life be like that? Why not? Did being safe have to come after every tragedy or disaster or abduction? How do you wear being safe like a comfortable suit that fits you right in every way?

She wants that...

She wants that safe thing...whatever it is.

The Rock

Cyril had only stardust memories of being in a helicopter, so to her, this was an adventure. The jet engine began to hum as it started. Ezek fastened her seat belt then adjusted her headset. "That's to protect your hearing. I know you can hear me without the headset on." He smiled over to her while he flipped the toggles on the ceiling, adjusting the instrument panel. "Are you ready?" he asked before they lifted off the planet.

The trip was quiet while viewing the sprinkling of city lights in the darkness.

Saying it out loud, breaking the silence over the headsets, she asked, "Do you remember Venice?"

She caught him off guard, his first thought as he closed his eyes and felt the moment; it was the way she became his. Quickly he shelved the thought and got flashes of all the other times they had been there. Keeping his thoughts to himself, he asked, "Which time? The first summit we ever went to was in Venice. We all met up one summer when we were in college. Your parents even showed up. It was for three days, but we were all family again. I still have the pictures."

Cyril wanted to get right to the point. "You're going to make me be specific, really? You're a stranger to me, and I'm in your helicopter. You're taking me somewhere. I don't know where the Rock is. I don't even know what that is…but I'm going there with you. The only memory I have of Venice is *that memory*," she said out loud with force.

If he could have stopped the helicopter in midflight to express his point, he would have, but they were moving forward too fast. "I'm sorry, of course, I do. That's not something you forget." Ezek looked ahead, checking the instrument panel, trying to remain calm. Feeling vulnerable, he asked, "Tell me what you remember. I saw parts of your memory while it was happening to you tonight. It was different watching you remember. You were afraid while you were in the moment, but when it was really happening, you were all in. I'm sorry, that probably wasn't a very good way to put it. That moment changed my life."

"I was afraid, you're right. You sensed that?"

"Of course. It was the other way around while it was really happening. I was terrified, not you. Terrified of making a mistake, terrified of losing you, terrified of crossing the line."

"So let me get this straight: we never before ever did anything like that before, really?" Looking him up and down, she expressed it again, "Really?" She couldn't imagine why not, why it would have taken them so long to get to that point, knowing in all the small memories how she felt about him. For just that moment, her thoughts were not her own; everything she was thinking he was hearing. How the hell was she supposed to get used to that? *Just own it*, she said to herself, *own it...*

"No! We never did. Never. Nothing like that." That was his Cyril he just heard; she was in there somewhere. He knew it.

The moment was silent as they both looked out into the darkness. Cyril had a moment to put the pieces of her life in order. *What order?* she thought. She had no order to her life. She didn't know what came first, second, or third, the chicken or the egg. Then she asked out loud, "Do you ever look at someone and wonder what kind of life they have? You know, the ordinary day-to-day stuff. Put yourself into their life, look outside their eyes. Their family, their friends. The issues of how different everyone's life is. Their secrets, their untold moments that they deal with. Then I look at what little I know about my life. Sure, it's different, just like everybody is different. Talk about friends in high places. I suppose not everyone has friends like Yike or Acid, but what a difference it's made in my life. It frightens me just thinking about it. But after all the weirdness is as different as it is, you make it bearable. You make it easier to cope with, you understand? I don't have to explain it to you. Hell, I don't even understand it at this point. But it so neatly fits into my life as I know it now."

"Wait, hold on, I never said I understood it. For as long as I have known you, I still don't really understand it. I just know this is your life, and I've watched you cope. That's probably been the hardest part. I wouldn't change anything." He shook his head, smiling at her. "I'm fortunate to be a part of your life."

Cyril looked out into the darkness at the twinkling lights. Then on to the light on the instrument panel, trying to understand it all.

"So I know how to fly one of these?"

"Yes, you do or that you used to. We learned together. It was on our bucket list."

"We have a bucket list?" Cyril turned to look at him.

"Yes, we started it when we were little. Let's see, oh, that's right, you wanted to go horseback riding, and your dad said no. You said you were putting it on your list of things you were going to do. All the things you were told *no* to went on that list."

"What have I crossed off so far?"

"Well, one of mine was to go skydiving. You couldn't find a reason to jump out of a perfectly good plane. But when I told you I was getting it off my list, we did it together. You said you couldn't let me die without you. Your landing was perfect. I got a fractured ankle. I was in a cast for almost two months. We saw the northern lights one cold November when we met my dad in Iceland. On summer break, you swam with dolphins. We invited Twyce, Cindy, and Steam. That was on your list. Oh, you also rode an elephant and a camel. We went on safari, Twyce met up with us. You two took pictures while I watched out for wildlife. I have your list. You have a lot of things you still haven't done yet."

Silence came over them as Cyril tried to find the moments. Ezek smiled as he looked ahead, thinking about his past with her.

Then in his head, he heard her say, *You intimidated me this evening when I first met you. It wasn't until I heard your voice I knew who you were. But you're very intimidating at first glance.*

"I had no idea you saw me like that. It was never my intention. I never mean to frighten you. Just know that okay."

Needing to change the subject, he looked out. "We'll be landing soon. See the water? That's Lake Tahoe. Up on the left just a few lights up ahead, we'll be landing there."

Tall trees surrounded them, stirring the fragrant pine smell. This wasn't the coast, a scent Cyril now had in her memory, or the forest floor. The mountains are a sharp contrast in altitude from below sea level of the desert floor. The familiar pine scent became a comfort to the strange surroundings.

The Rock was one of the older buildings in the Tahoe area. Two-story shale shingles layered the exterior, with a rustic flair to the way shingles were put on. Some shingles were cut to look like the lake's waves cresting along the walls, creating a hard cold surface. Upon the second floor, the shingles were cut to show the stars and the moon, and on the east side was the sun. With all the fires that had gone through the area in the past, this house remained with its armored gray stone surface.

"Do you think they followed us?" Cyril asked as she unbuckled herself as if she had done it a million times before. All the lights went off as Ezek powered down the helicopter. A loud winding down till the props had stopped.

Ezek grabbed their bags then commented, "Of course they did. If you're here, so are they."

Cyril carefully got out of the helicopter and noticed the blue lights under her seat. She stopped and saw what she thought might be a leaf on the floor.

The blue orb's light stayed on the small object. Taking it into her fingers, she examined it. Then she asked, "Is this your helicopter, one you fly all the time?" She thought for a moment, *If this is the only one he flies, then he's the person I'm looking for.*

"Hold on, what's this all about? I just take what's available. I don't have one assigned to me if that's what you're asking. Why?"

"Do you know who flew in this last?"

"I can find out. Are you upset that it wasn't cleaned first? You're not going to get on someone for not cleaning it, are you? Really. What's this about? What did you find? Show me."

Cyril's hand went out. In her palm were two old sunflower shells. "I want to know who left them here. Even if I have to do a DNA test, I want to know whose they are."

"*Wow*, okay, what's this all about? Hold on, you saw this in the back seat the time you were taken and missed the summit in Bonn."

"Yes, when the window was open, three shells came back into the car. They were from the person in the front seat. They had just spit them out the window. I don't think they knew they flew back into the back seat."

"Yes, I saw that also tonight. Who do you think they belong to?"

"I don't know. Let's find out."

"I'm the only one that has flown this copter in three months. But I'll have its logbook copied and sent over. Okay?"

Cyril looked around the forest surrounding them, shadows everywhere. Lights from a small cabin off in the distance showed her the way down the driveway. Realizing they were probably being watched, she said aloud so any unsuspecting Grays could hear her, "Do you think they're here right now watching us?"

"Probably," he also said aloud while walking up the center of the stairs in front of the Rock.

Ezek stopped then turned. "Come on, they won't bother you, not tonight anyway."

Shocked, Cyril quickly went up the stairs. "How do you know that for sure? Did they say they weren't coming this evening? Do you talk to them?" She raced up behind him.

"Stop. They're not going to bother you." He tried to say it convincingly, words even he didn't believe. But he knew Cyril needed to rest; he didn't want her to worry.

Cyril stopped once inside; she saw the beautiful knotty pine paneling the red plaid carpeting. Mounts that adorned all the walls came from all over the world. The elephant's trunk went up to reach toward the ceiling, and its tusks swung toward her. Next to it was a kudu; its spiral black horns brought back a moment. Cyril stood and stared.

Ezek stood next to her and said, "That's your kudu. Remember your first trip to South Africa your dad took us?" Cyril didn't remember, but there was something about the horns that caught her off guard.

"Okay, let me show you your room." For just that moment, he understood this was all new to her. A place she knew like the back of her hand was uncharted in her mind. His memories flooded back to him; all included Cyril. While walking down the hall, he said, "You shot your first bear up here. He was standing behind me. It snuck up on me while we walked back from the lake. I'll never forget, you turned then pointed the gun straight at me and fired the shot. I thought for a fraction of a second I was dead. It all happened so fast. You just turned and shot, didn't aim or say anything. The bear's paw was in the air to swipe me, and you killed it. I'd like to say again thank you for that. You saved my life." As Ezek went to set their bags down, he looked up, now arms out in a bowing motion. "That was the first time you saved my life. It wasn't the last." He smiled up at her. "This is your room. It's always been your room. Unless, of course, you'd like to look around and pick another room?"

The room was beautiful. On the bedspread and drapes were colorful embroidered chrysanthemums on the light green silk background. Large windows covered the east wall looking toward the lake. The carpet again was plaid, this time in a delicate white-and-green pattern. The light on the dressing table was a candle. Cyril stared and tried to remember it all but nothing. Dark shadows danced across her walls in the flickering candlelight while all her childhood monsters remained forgotten and quiet inside her closet. A small jewelry box sat next to the candle. When she opened it, the music went on; it was "Thank Heaven for Little Girls." Inside a delicate gold box chain with a locket closed tight. Cyril pushed her fingernail in between it to open. The heart shape inside was a picture of a newborn child's face all scrunched up, eyes squinty. Cyril closed it, knowing it had to be her as a child. Also were pearl earrings and a key with a black ribbon tied to it.

Ezek glanced in to see her expression. She listened to the music, reciting the words to the song aloud until the music came to a sudden stop. Putting her hand on the lid, she closed the box. Turning toward Ezek, she asked, "Where's your room?" Kicking her shoes off, Cyril's right eyebrow went up to one side.

"Here's the thing." Ezek's head went to one side before answering. "My room is always next to yours, wherever that happens to be."

"How about a tour so I know where everything is?" She noticed the lights were on when they got there, so she had to ask, "Does someone live here?"

"No, not in the house. The caretaker's house is just down the driveway. You must have seen it when we landed. We should have everything we need here. If you need anything, let me know."

Cyril walked across the hall then opened the next door, only to look in and find it was the linen closet. She asked, "Where's the bathroom?"

Cyril walked alone around the house. One room she knew had to be her parents' room with pictures everywhere. Her parents' wedding photo. Cyril stopped to hold one of the pictures. It was her and Ezek as they were growing up. For just that moment...

Ezek was sitting across the table from Cyril. She heard her mother ask, "What's it like to become a teenager, Ezek?" Cyril was in the moment feeling the same shock she had back then. "Oh my god, it's his birthday. I forgot it's his birthday... Oh my god..."

Her mother placed a carrot cake covered with cream cheese frosting and thirteen candles in front of Ezek, his favorite cake, as he looked over the fire-laden surface, inhaling his breath, then stopped when he heard Cyril yell, "Make a wish! Close your eyes first. You have to close your eyes first..." She came up behind him, hands out to cover his eyes.

He closed his eyes while Cyril stood behind him, her hands securely over each eye, making sure he can't peek.

She whispered in his ear, "Don't say it out loud. Keep it to yourself."

So he thought about it for a second, trying to keep his thoughts to himself.

"Did you make a wish?" Smiling uncontrollably, Cyril put both hands down on his shoulders and leaned in to help him blow out his candles.

There was that moment caught in the picture. Cyril's past was captured in the photo. The smoke rising off the candles, some still lit, her hands steady, leaning in, their faces cheek to cheek as they blew the birthday candles out. Both were smiling from ear to ear. You could see they were close, maybe even best friends.

One picture in a frame made with popsicle sticks was with Steam and Cyril on a playground walking in the Halloween parade. Steam was a robot with lights lit up on his chest while Cyril walked behind him, striking the ground with her bullwhip. She was wearing a giant sombrero in her cowgirl outfit. Her chaps were made from an old sheepskin her dad found in the garage. Cyril thought it was perfect; she wore them almost every day till Christmas. Also among the pictures were the hunting trips to South Africa. Cyril, Ezek, and their guide, Mpho, a very slender man with a huge smile missing both his center front teeth. Mpho stood behind the kudu while Cyril gripped the tip of the spiral black horns. Taken recently in a simple black frame were Cindy, Steam, Ezek, and Cyril. They all stood together in front of one of their satellites that were about to be launched into orbit the following week—so many pictures in beautiful frames of her life on top of the dresser. No moments were sticking; only to see them would not be enough to keep them in her memory.

The next room was for a young person. A massive mobile at least six feet across planets and stars with moving black holes hung from the ceiling to the floor like a chandelier. The mobile was so big you had to walk around it. Each planet was hand-painted, then a clear line going through its center to connect it to the ceiling. Some had fuzzy fabric to represent gasses or other cloudy elements found in space. One by one, Cyril saw the placement of each planet, now identifying them.

She understood this was a road map of her galaxies, like seeing her own backyard. Saturn was easy to identify with its rings with its familiar moons, Mimas and others. Then Jupiter with its many moons like Callisto, Megaclite, Harpalyke, Io, and Europa, just remembering a few along with odd-shaped rocks circling in their orbits. For a moment, Cyril sat in the chair next to the window and wondered, could this be the room she grew up in? There was nothing in the room that seemed familiar to her.

The next room had a huge carved mahogany four-poster bed. Along the walls were antlers from every kind of animal in the world. The wallpaper looked like fresh green leaves were placed neatly everywhere. Large windows went along one side of the room. Leaning in the far corner of the room was a powder-blue Blueridge acoustic guitar. Next to it was a chair covered with sheet music. Cyril leaned on the side of the bed. Something was very comfortable about the surroundings.

"This is it!" she said out loud to herself. "I'm taking this room," she said even louder for anyone to hear.

She heard Ezek coming up the stairs down the hall, then he leaned against the doorjamb.

"Okay." He nodded while trying to hide a smirk. "I'll be in the room next to you. So you find this room the most comfortable, huh?"

Catching his look, she asked, "Wait, is this your room?" Cyril felt almost shy.

"Yes, you can sleep here if you want. I don't mind." For just that moment, Ezek felt something warm hit his heart. She made a choice to pick his room. All he could do was smile and keep it to himself.

"Wait! Have I slept here before?" She felt the underlying current coming from him.

With a cautious smile, he said in a matter-of-fact tone, "Yes, many times."

"With you?" Cyril caught the corner of Ezek's smile while he tried to keep it hidden.

This was all so very forward, she thought. *I don't know this man, and here I am in a house alone with him, whoever he is.*

About that moment, Ezek came toward her, took her hands, and explained, "Please know this: I am your friend. Don't ever think otherwise. I am not a stranger to you, and please know I will never harm you."

"You were in my head just then, weren't you?" She looked into his eyes.

"Yes, do you need anything? I'm going to bed." Ezek turned to walk away, going into his room adjacent to hers.

She said out loud so he could hear her from the other room, "So IF I GET SCARED, CAN I COME IN AND SLEEP WITH YOU?"

There was a moment just long enough she knew he was thinking about what she had just said. The pause said everything. She thought she felt a smile on his face.

"Yes, of course. Good night, Cyril."

Cyril thought about the thirteen Grays outside the Rock. The thought of her being taken while she was asleep crossed her mind. How would that happen? Would she just disappear and end up somewhere else? Would it be a stranger, a Gray she didn't know? Would she go through the part where she would be paralyzed and could only move her eyes?

"STOP IT! No one's coming for you tonight. Good night, Cyril!" Ezek yelled from his room.

"HOW DO YOU KNOW THAT FOR SURE?" Cyril yelled back.

Ezek thought about how he would answer her. He didn't know; he had no idea if they would come while they were sleeping. He had always missed the moment she was taken. He could be with her twenty-four hours a day, seven days a week, and nothing helped. When they wanted her, she went, and there was nothing he could do about it.

"They know you're tired and need your rest. Don't worry about it. Good night, Cyril."

Looking around Ezek's room, it was like being in a hotel room; there were no memories here. Looking up at the canopy of the four-poster bed, out of nowhere, Cyril flashed a moment one night while downstairs alone.

Cyril reached over to turn the stereo off. Still having the last tune humming in her head, something stayed with her in the song's words. (Riding into the danger zone, heading into twilight, spreading out her wings tonight.) All the lights were off except the one in the downstairs hall. She decided to sleep in Ezek's room. She thought if he would be coming in late, she'd be there when he got home. It was easy to fall asleep in his bed; his scent engulfed her, creating a peaceful slumber.

It happened all at once; the lights in the house all came on at the same time. The televisions in the house all went on simultaneously, all five of them with different volumes and different channels. Then all four radios, the stereo CD player, the fans in all the bathrooms, the microwave, and the oven started to cook. The alarm system went off, sending a blaring horn into the neighborhood. Three alarm clocks went off with different sounds. One beeped, the other chimed, and the one in Ezek's room was the sound of revealing a horn so loud it sent Cyril flying. Her eyes were peeled back as she sat in attention while she tried to figure out what was happening around her. The noise from everything created chaos. She got up and started to turn the alarm clock off; it remained on. She went over to the light switch, putting the switch down, and the light remained on; she went out into the hallway trying to turn anything off. Nothing went off. Everything in the house stayed on; no matter how many times she flipped the switch, nothing worked. Even the volume on the televisions wouldn't go down. Nothing stopped the chaos. She remembered the breaker to the house was out on the south-side corner. Thinking she might need a flashlight, she saw all the lights on the patio were also on, even the lights down the driveway. But strangely, no other lights on the hill or at the caretaker's house at the end of the driveway.

Flipping the breakers off, still, everything was brightly lit. She went back inside and called Ezek. When he picked up the call, he said, "I'm on Highway 89 right now. I'm almost there. What's going on? Are you okay?"

"All the power is surging in the house. Nothing will go off. Everything is on."

"It's okay. Stay inside where it's warm. I'll be there in a few minutes. Talk to me while I drive."

"Okay…how was the meeting?"

"It all worked out just like you said it would. If you see a messages from Ms. Walker, it was from nothing I did."

"I love it when you put it like that. You're always so innocent."

"You know me better than that," he said in a serious tone.

"I know, but it's fun messing with you. And just what does this Ms. Walker want?"

"Her father is the CEO of a small company we did business with a few years ago."

"You're not answering me. What does she want?"

"Me. She was very persistent after the meeting."

"Is that why you're so late getting back?"

"Well…yes."

"Hold on. I just figured out what you're doing. You're keeping my mind occupied. You're so clever. So what's outside you don't want me to see? Oh, holy shit, they're here messing with me. They know I'm alone."

"I never said that!"

"Yes, but you're thinking about it. Why else would this be happening?"

"You know all the lights along the lake are off except where you're at. I can see the glow in the darkness from this distance. I'm almost there."

Cyril went to the front door and opened it wide. The lights along the driveway were lit halfway down. Way off in the distance, she saw one lone light cutting through the trees, then up the driveway as it winded toward the house. Ezek sat in the car for a moment, watching, waiting. Then the minute the car door opened and his foot touched the ground, all the lights went off, leaving Cyril standing in the dark.

"Magic!" she yelled to him.

His long legs took two stairs at a time to get to her. "I'm here to rescue you from the darkness." Lifting her, he carried her into the Rock.

She looked up at the canopy back in her moment, trying to stay calm. *I'm not alone. He's in the other room. I'm not alone*, Cyril said over and over to herself while trying to wash the memory away.

"Cyril, I'm right here. Go to sleep!" Ezek yelled from his room.

That morning in the tree outside Ezek's window, one lone bird was talking to no one. No answer came from another bird as Cyril lay between the warm sheets listening. The bird chattered on, still no response. Ever so quietly, she got out of bed and opened the door to the closet. She touched the fabric of his shirts, all ironed with crisp starch collars and French cuffs. His suits were all tailored with fabric that felt nice to touch, and all hung neatly, not touching each other. His leather shoes were polished and ready to go. Tall boots looked like they had seen the highest mountains. Large hat boxes lined the top row, giving her no clue to what was inside.

Feeling like an intruder, she turned and left the room, closing the door quietly behind her. As quietly as she could, Cyril tiptoed out of the bedroom. Just a few steps down the hall, a door was slightly open.

Glancing in, she stopped. There lying asleep on his back was Ezek. Leaning against the doorjamb, she remained still as she watched his chest rise then fall. His long black hair spread wide across the pillow, his tanned skin a sharp contrast to the bright white sheets. His thick beard almost covered his lips, his mouth closed. The room was almost completely dark; a small slit of morning sunlight escaped into the room and illuminated him. Cyril smiled and thought how at peace he seemed. How very handsome he appeared. His breath seemed shallow and relaxed.

Then out of nowhere, "Good morning. Are you okay?" Ezek said aloud while his eyes remained shut.

She saw his lips move; startled, she raced back to her room. While lying back in her bed, she realized he was in her head. She answered him, "I'm fine. Just wide awake."

"Do you know what you would normally do at this time in the morning because you always get up at 6:00 a.m., no matter what? Well, if you're not going to work, you would crawl into bed with me if we weren't already in bed together."

"Do I smell bacon?" She quickly wanted to change the subject.

Then just as quickly, he answered her, "It's Anna. She'll cook something then leave. If you happen to see a short man with white hair in the yard, that's her husband, Allen."

He felt her awkwardness for that moment; she wanted to retreat. "Will she come upstairs?"

"No, she won't. I'm going to take a shower now. I think I'll shave my beard off." It occurred to him he was asking her permission. Permission to shave his face. He paused for a moment, giving her the chance to either say okay or "No, don't I like your beard." But she said nothing. Even hearing her thoughts wasn't one way or the other.

She heard him get up and walk into his bathroom. She wondered, would he look like the man she saw during the stardust last night? His hands were cool and wet, wiping over her skin while she was dying in the desert, the same man who changed her opinion on how she felt before leaving Venice. The same man who never told her he loved her but had always tried to show her he did.

Instead of putting his words straight into her head, she heard him yell it out loud over the noise of the water for even Anna downstairs to hear.

"YES, I'M THE SAME GUY! IT'S ME!"

Cyril went downstairs following the scent of bacon. On the table was an everything bagel covered with cream cheese and sun-dried tomatoes sprinkled with salted sunflower seeds. A pot of tea was steeping with a crocheted cozy over it to keep it warm. Fresh cut and peeled cantaloupe and strawberries lay across a crystal platter. A pile of almost-crispy bacon lay on another platter.

Two huge sprays of gladiolus flanked both sides of the French doors leading out to the lake. Cyril stared for a moment touching the flowers, admiring their beauty and how significant they were. Cyril decided to sit outside to have breakfast and wait for Ezek. The smell from the pine trees with the morning air was intoxicating. Cyril took her half bagel and walked across the lawn toward the lake. Between her toes, the cool, moist grass felt familiar. At the edge of the grass was a grove of elderly pine trees. Just beyond that were boulders leading to a small sandy beach. Her foot touched the cold clear water. Dashing it back out of the water, she walked further on to the wooden pier extended out more than thirty yards; the floating wood moved to the wake of the passing speedboat.

Cyril knew Ezek had finished in the shower; she turned to walk back to the house when she stopped. The words in her head were exact, like a whisper talking directly to her.

I will be here at your noon. As you would say, it's important we talk. I have things you need to know.

Standing in the middle of the lawn, Ezek watched Cyril suddenly look up into the sky then turn and quickly look around her. She stopped then looked over to Ezek. Her heart skipped a beat. Was it the message, or was it Ezek's new appearance? Staring intensely, she reached the table to sit, taking her tea to her lips, almost feeling like she's guilty of something. Ezek leaned in, both hands spread wide across the table; his hair fell forward with a threatening look on his face.

"YOU'RE GOING WHERE?" he said aloud so even the passing boat driver could hear him.

"So I guess you heard that?" Cyril leaned back, trying not to respond to his threatening tone.

His head went back and forth. "No, not really. He has a way of scrambling things when he knows I'm listening."

"I told him I would listen. He's very clear. He said he needed to tell me something."

"Why aren't you ever afraid?" Ezek stood up straight, shaking his head back and forth, his fingers threading through his hair like a giant comb. *His clean-shaven face*, she thought, *he's handsome with or without a beard.*

"What gives you the impression I'm not scared shitless? I'm terrified, but Yike's my friend. He won't hurt me. That is, I get the impression he won't. He needs me to listen. There's something he needs me to understand. He said he's been watching me and thinks I'm not well. He's not sure why you haven't cured me. That concerns him." Hearing Ezek's rhetoric in her head, Cyril yelled, "STOP IT! I TOLD HIM I'M COMING!"

Ezek walked up to Cyril, taking the chair next to her; sorting through his thoughts, he pulled himself together. Then with a gentle voice, he asked, "And if I asked you not to go, would you, would you please not go… Please?"

He kept his eyes on her as he opened his heart; he needed her to stay. The last time she left the planet, she was gone for two weeks, twelve hours, eighteen minutes, thirty-seven seconds, and twenty-one nanoseconds. He knew when she was gone. Something happens when she's out of his atmosphere.

Getting out of her chair, she repeated, "I'm meeting him, at my noon by the water. He's concerned I might not be well enough to travel. He wants to check to see what's wrong with me. I agreed. I know what's wrong with me. I have no past. I'm not sure who he is. I can only go by what you tell me and what I have seen with the stardust. He said he's just going to check me. He said he's been checking me for as long as he has known me. He's my friend. I've grown up with him, but most of all, I'm his friend. Apparently, in his world, that's huge. It just doesn't happen that way. I've got to get ready to go." Cyril pulled her hair free, shaking it out as she walked by Ezek. "I'm going to take a shower."

He followed behind her, looking at the way her hair fell onto her back. Into the house, keeping his distance, he arrived at the bathroom door as she slammed in his face. Face-to-face with only the door, he waited. Then he began to pace up the hallway back then forth, then back again. He leaned against the wall then heard the water shut off. He knew she's drying off, and then she smeared that smelly lotion on her hands, wiping it all over her skin; he repeated it to himself, all over her skin, as he imagined it all, her skin. Now she's putting that clear stuff in her hair. Her fingers moved quickly through her hair, then twisting it into a knot stabbing with a lacquered stick.

Ezek can't stand it any longer; he can't let her go. He leaned against the doorjamb, trying to sound casual but failed. "I'm coming in…"

"No, you're not!"

"I'm coming in!"

"No, you're not! I'm not dressed yet."

The door opened before she finished her sentence. Cyril quickly swiped the towel around her.

"What is so important that I can't have my privacy? I need to get ready. What do you want?" Cyril turned her back to him to look into the mirror.

"You're going, aren't you? Can I go with you?"

Cyril turned while glaring at Ezek; she saw the terror across his face.

She didn't have the heart to say what she was going to say aloud. Her words went into his head anyway, something she wished she could have prevented; his eyes went down as he left the bathroom. She knew he'd heard her thoughts.

"How do I stop my thoughts directly into you? How does that work? I didn't mean what I just thought. I'm sorry." She took his arm, stopping him. "I'm sorry, I have to go see him. It'll be okay. Really it'll be okay. Trust me."

The sun was directly above the Rock. Cyril noticed no one in the house, not a sound of Ezek anywhere; she took a sip of tea then decided to go looking for him. He's not in his room, but his bed was made. She searched the house calling out to him; he's nowhere to be found. No one was answering her. Then for just that moment, she remembered being told that when you're taken, everything and everyone around is paralyzed, unable to move or respond; so could Ezek be paralyzed somewhere? *Is Yike here now?*

Cyril ran out onto the patio across the grass through the trees then stopped at the boulders just before the water. Ezek saw her from inside her father's office. Unable to move or answer her, all he can do was move his eyes. He had felt this feeling before, and there's nothing he can do about it, paralyzed and unable to stop her. He remembered the first time it happened to him the first night sleeping in his new home.

Cyril came into his room and pulled herself up onto his bed. She gently put her little cold three-year-old hands on both sides of his face, startling him awake.

"Are you all right?" Cyril's big green eyes almost glowed in the dark, looking into him.

"Yes, what was that?" Ezek felt the moment when he could finally move his arms.

"I didn't want you to be scared. They're gone now." Cyril dropped off the side of his bed quickly and peeked outside his door. Cyril closed the door, cutting off the light from the hall.

She stood at his bed and explained, "When they come, I can't move either. They visit my mom. But they're gone now." Patting him on the cheek, she told him, "It's okay. Now go back to sleep."

Ezek leaned over to watch her walk out of his room. Her little hand clutched her long nightgown, dragging her black-and-white panda across the floor. Like a little soldier after a hard battle. She left the door slightly ajar. He had to wonder, *What am I up against?*

The air had a static electric feel. Cyril saw the hairs on her arms stand up on end. When she looked over in the shade of the tree was Yike. Like a chameleon, he blended into the surroundings.

This moment was far different than Cyril had anticipated. She could move; though she didn't try, she could hear him in her head. Now at the moment, she was terrified. This was real; it was really happening to her.

Quickly she said to Ezek, "I'm here now. It's nothing like I thought it would be..."

"I want to check you for travel. Be still." Then she suddenly found herself in front of him, standing in the shade. She watched four red orbs race behind him as her blue orbs stayed at a distance over by the boulders. She noticed the calmness of the water. It was almost like glass; even the water wasn't permitted to move. Yike's slender arms went toward her as his fingers unfurled. One second he's holding her hands, then next he's wrapped his fingers around her head. The point of his fingers dug deep into her hair. Then he asked her, "Why hasn't Ezekiel cured you? Why have you remained this way for so long? This is not conducive to who you are."

Shocked, Yike took his hands from her head as he looked deep into her eyes. "I'm not here to scare you. You are ill. Who brought this illness to you? This illness was given to you against your will. You don't know me." He felt her fear. Yike was confused within her thoughts.

Of course, she knew him; how could she not? Yike repeated, "Who brought this?" He knew someone had done this deliberately to her. He had to help his friend.

Cyril studied his face; blotches of grays and browns covered his face and head. He seemed older now. Scars marked his skin; some you could see cut more deeply than others. All were telling his story of survival. He didn't move with the swiftness like in her stardust moments.

Suddenly, she felt pressure across her skin as she could no longer feel the ground under her feet. Cyril's eyes opened as she looked around, unable to move. She felt nothing holding her, but the feeling of being controlled was overwhelming.

Inside her, she heard, "I'm sorry. I must heal you if he won't."

The faint stale smell of citrus surrounded her. Only now, she was unable to open her eyes. She was somewhere else. She heard quiet kissing noises in the distance. She remembered it was a noise often made when the Grays were talking to each other. Analyzing the noise surrounding her, she concluded, she was being watched by thirty, maybe forty Grays, all discussing what was happening to her. Some opinions were angry that she was even aboard; others she felt wanted to chop her up, but Yike made it clear, "This contact needs our help. She is my friend. We will help her."

The very pointed tip of Yike's index finger penetrated Cyril's temple. She felt a slight pain then felt her warm blood race down through her scalp.

She saw herself sitting up in a crib when Yike's mother, Acid, a tall slender Gray with wide white sides, came into her room, setting Yike in his infancy next to her. Then flashes of her life were like strobes of light sticking inside her. She saw her and Yike enunciating words repeatedly while she tried to explain what it all meant and why. Then she was about six years old. It was Thanksgiving night after everyone had gone to sleep. She had invited Yike to try the food. Cyril remembered the look on Yike's face when he first tried the cranberry sauce. Cyril told him, "I only like the cranberry sauce with the rings." Her little finger pointed to the side of the gelatin. "See the rings on the side." He was intrigued by its color and texture. Transparent but cloudy. The irises of his eyes were a black purple with bright yellow spikes, his eyes closed. She had never seen his eyes closed as he sucked up all that remained in the bowl. He made it clear to her then he would not be eating any more white meat from things that flew in the air or birds as she called them. Many nights she, Steam, and Yike traveled together, observing other Grays and chasing orbs. Tucked away in her thoughts, she saw Ezek observing her staying out of her way. Her relationship with Yike was her own;

it was something she didn't share with him. She realized Ezek hated it but respected her relationship with other things. She began to feel the conflict of the two very different lives. She needed to study Yike's life and understand him; it was essential to her and for all of humanity. This was an opportunity she couldn't pass up. Besides, he was kind and interesting and like no one else anywhere.

Her life's moments all started to fall into place. Yike stood waiting for his friend's memory to return. For a moment, Yike thought he had stopped her heart. Worried, he placed his long pointed fingers across her chest. He felt the faint rhythm of her heartbeat slowly as it began to get stronger. Cyril took in a gasping breath as her eyes opened. Yike's thoughts were cluttered with questions coming from Cyril as he quickly tried to answer her.

It had never occurred to Yike how she should feel about him. Reading her thoughts, he surmised she should hate him, even want him dead. It's what you do when you're confronted with a Harvester. In her mind, he had taken both her parents, murdered her husband, and harvested Ezek's and Steam's mothers; and because Henry had disappeared, that was probably Yike's fault. Swirling into Yike's thoughts, he was confronted with her conflict and hatred. He saw her thought process, survival of the fittest. For that moment, Yike felt her emotions; he felt her thoughts when she realized her parents were off the planet, no sign of them over Greenland. He felt her pain physically in his chest when she was told her husband of three months was dead.

Yike's hand went to where Cyril's heart was pounding; he rested it gently on her chest while spreading his fingers wide. He physically felt her sorrow when Ezek first came to live with her. It was like his pain became her pain. His mother was gone; his father never explained how she died, just that if she knew how to fly, she might still be alive. He remembered seeing her as a child holding Steam crying in each other's arms over his mother's death. Yike had to stop her pain. But her memory couldn't be stopped. It was still loading her life as she once knew it. It was coming fast and filling in all her life's time.

It occurred to him that she had always taken a risk being in his company. He thought about when she came to share her findings.

She helped him, spending her days teaching them how to check the bodies before harvesting them.

The flu shot everyone got each year had an element in it that was killing the Grays. The advertising each year reported that you must get a flu shot or die of the flu. But that was only part of it. What was really happening was you must get a flu shot so it would kill all the Grays using their blood. Wasn't the flu just a part of the overall harvesting process to begin with? It had always been their flu, an illness no one could escape, thanks to the Grays. But there it was again. The Quiet War no one talked about. She didn't need to share that with him; the element added to the flu shot was working. No one needed to know if they were harvesting humans. Their blood was like poison to a Gray now. *Here they give us the flu to kill us, then we try to stamp it out with a vaccine to kill them. What a weapon our blood has become.*

Cyril's head was spinning fast; she felt like she was spinning in the rope swing that hung in the big oak tree. Steam would wind it up, twisting it round and round; then when he let it go, this was her unwinding. It was happening so fast she had to close her eyes. Cyril sat up, and both her hands went to cover her face as she began to rub her eyes.

"What are you doing to me? What is happening to me?" As she looked around, she saw a crowd of Grays watching her. Yike's hand made a striking movement when all the Grays became quiet and turned, now their backs to her. Realizing where she was at, she asked, "Why am I here?"

"We don't have a lot of time. I need you to know this: I did not take your parents. Your mother worked on the flu shot to kill Grays. She has done her job well. You should be proud. Your father and mother don't think the same. Your father is alive. I did not kill Max, but I will find out who did it since you need this answer. I did not kill Ezekiel's mom. I did not take Steam's mother. I could not save her. She got her illness from the area she grew up in, so did others in her village. The element is in the soil. They have all died. Her cells could not be reversed. I tried, and in my trying, that I think is why you think I harvested her. *I did not!* She was already dying. I don't have Henry. He is, in fact, alive, and I think with your mom if what I'm hearing is correct.

"This is important. We are leaving. Time is running out here. We have found three planets that will sustain us. The black holes called Sagittarius A and V616 Monocerotis. You don't have to worry about them. When we traveled, we noticed strange energy that is hard to detect or see. It's not as big as the other black holes you and I have studied, but it's equally as dangerous. In time, its 'event horizon' will decrease with everything it consumes, which then will force Earth into it. Nothing will escape. But that is not what concerns me. It's when it takes your sun. I have prepared this for you to show your colleagues. It explains where this black hole is. My calculations are defined, but as you have always told me, it's best to check each other's work. I agree. I hope I am wrong for your sake. I have one thing to ask." Yike's hand motioned. All the Grays left the area.

The lights in the craft slowly dimmed. In the distance, it sounded like air was escaping from a vent behind her. They were alone now, just the two of them. Cyril got up off the suspended surface to walk around. Once her feet were on the floor surface, she felt more comfortable, less of an undercurrent of motion.

"I have to walk around. I don't feel very good." Cyril's head felt like she had a sinus cold clogged and ready to pop. Uneasy in her steps, Yike took her arm to steady her.

Yike walked with her around the inside of the craft while she examined the lights, his long arm to one side, holding her arm gently. "I have to ask you…"

"Yes, of course, what is it?" While trying to steady herself, Cyril stopped to look up into his big black-purple, yellow eyes. He stalled for a moment as if he was trying to find the most convincing group of words.

"Will you go with us?"

His long fingers unfurled and hung straight down, almost appearing to be relaxed, but it felt more like a surrender.

"Remember when you were little, your mother once told you, 'Tell them you want to go.' You laughed and said, 'No way.' I would like you to go with us. I will give you time to calculate then an answer."

"Yike, you know I'm not wanted here. I would never fit in or survive how you live. But I thank you for your information. I can't imagine you not being here. Not being a part of my life."

"You can have more time to calculate before answering. No need to answer quickly. Think about it. I will make sure we get you everything you need, your favorite stuff to eat. I will even provide air that is fresh. Go with us!" A faint kissing sound came from him.

"I can't. Please understand. I can't." Cyril's head was spinning, her eyes feeling dry with the pressure, wiping her nose to check for blood. The metallic taste and smell was overwhelming.

"I will still study you. I will be back. We have so many on this planet that we get sustaining information from. You are the only one that will know we are gone. We won't be able to collect everyone before we leave. We have found some don't want to go, so do what you want with them. They have made their choice. Is there anything more you need?" Yike's hands went up to her scalp, examining her one last time.

"Still, please." Yike stopped while his hands clutched her head. Cyril stopped while Yike studied her.

"I have taken your dream state from Ezekiel and let you remember everything. You must go back now. Someone is waiting." Yike's hands went down her face, wiping the blood from her temples. One of his fingers wrapped a lock of her hair around it, then stopped slowly, placing it behind her ear.

"You have to go now." His large black-purple, yellow eyes closed again for the second time.

"I'm not sure what's happening here, but I feel I miss you. I have remorse over you going away." Could for that moment seeing his eyes closed be Yike's emotion? Was it difficult for him also? She felt sorrow come from him; it felt heavy upon her heart.

Messages had gone out to all those in Cyril's closest circle. It was a short text. "CLP" was all he sent: "Cyril left the planet." Ezek had sent this message out quite a few times, leaving everyone in a holding pattern.

Cindy in Anomalies 1 had her team ready to scan her the minute she arrived…if she arrived.

Steam had his team of doctors and their equipment ready in case she needed medical help. Every satellite the company had was on alert, checking the skies for any sign of movement. But Yike was good at that; he knew how to avoid detection. He learned from the best.

Ezek sat on the patio; his long legs stretched out in front of him, ankles crossed, his eyes closed while his harmonica slid slowly over his lips. The song was the blues, a slow lazy song that he made up as he went along. The music was filled with heartbreak and loneliness. Day after day, night after night waiting, waiting for any sign of her. He had to think about all the things they would do when she got back. He wondered if she would bring something back with her. What would she learn? How might it change her? How might it change all of them?

Would there be a message? Would they understand it? Would she be able to decipher it for them?

All the trips were different, every single one of them.

Once she came back, the first thing Ezek noticed was the color of her eyes was different. That lasted almost eight months, then the color returned.

One time when she came back, she didn't talk for over a week. She had been sitting on her patio when Ezek heard her first word. She said "waffles." Tully made her waffles. Would she have tiny cuts all over her skin or dust? Would it be hard to get it off her skin like last time? Or would she walk around asking everyone if they smelled blood? Then she always grabbed her shirt or collar and put her nose on it to sniff. Then she would reply, "No, it's just me. I smell like blood. I can't get the smell out of my clothes."

That went on for over four months. Cyril's close associates' and friends' reply was "I think I smell cinnamon rolls, do you want one?"

Cindy would hear her comment about the smell of blood, holding up her arm to smell it, thinking it was on her skin.

"No, I smell apple pie. It smells good, doesn't it?" Cindy knew why she smelled blood to her; it was like reliving a nightmare. Cindy made a point to bring in things that smelled strong, like apple pie, lavender, lemons, or big bouquets of daphne or lilacs. For just a moment, the smell of the blood churning under her feet was gone. Seeing the bodies lie there helpless above a vast ocean of blood, knowing the smell was penetrating her skin made it hard for Cyril to escape the memory. Then the crushing body parts sent the odor everywhere, even into Cyril. Ezek made a point of mastering scratch pumpkin pie. He saw how the expression on her face would change when she got home. It could easily change all her thoughts.

It was seven in the morning. Everything about the day was perfect. Ezek had been lying on the grass in the shade when a text came across his board.

It was Henry. Shocked, Ezek sat up to read it. The words were coming fast. First, he acknowledged Ezek's text to him.

"CLP AGAIN," he wrote in capital letters. Then he went on about "Green, you heard me GREEN."

He replied, "GREEN ORBS never seen or heard of them before. Any idea? When is she coming back?" Henry already knew the answer to that.

Ezek answered, "Don't know. Green, are you sure?"

Henry quickly responded, "Saw five of them. I'm in Iceland."

"Iceland. Who are you with?" Ezek was hoping the answer was Cyril's parents. He recalled one time long ago his father telling Cyril, "I would know if she were gone. I feel she's still here. I love your mother," referring to Virginia Cyril's mom.

"Just left Iceland heading to Greenland, finishing up. I will be in the US in three days. Where are you?"

"At the Rock, come visit, alone here."

"See you soon. Love you, Dad." *That's it!* Ezek thought. *That's all! Who's he with? Is he alone?* he wondered.

Ezek lay back down as the sun was shining in his eyes when he heard a voice in his head so clear he thought she was standing in front of him. The first voice in six days, eighteen hours, twenty-three minutes, eight seconds, and three nanoseconds. He lay still, not wanting to miss a word, knowing it would not be repeated. He was surprised it was coming over so clearly, knowing how Yike always scrambled her thoughts to him.

Going home. Love you all. Her voice sounded strong.

Ezek waited to hear if there was more. Nothing. He released his breath pools, filled his eyes as he tried to compose himself. He felt for a moment relief as if a weight had been suddenly lifted from him.

He closed his eyes, and for a moment, she was right where he wanted her in his head. He said back to her, *I'm waiting for you. Did you hear me? I'm waiting for you.*

Then as quickly as she came, she was gone. Ezek's thoughts were empty, his mind confused as he listened. Nothing. His thought to her, *Don't go.* Ezek began to send a text to Steam, Cindy, Sven, Cyril's parents, Henry, Twyce, Bernard—all were to get the same message. Before writing it, he stopped. She wasn't back yet. He didn't have his arms around her. He couldn't look her in the eye. He waited; he lay back down to close his eyes.

Cyril lay on the suspended surface; her mind was racing as her memory crammed into every crevasse inside her. Like being shocked, her eyes went wide open when she heard, *I'm waiting for you. Did you hear me? I'm waiting for you.* Then a pause. *Don't go.*

Looking up inside the craft, the lights all meaning something flickered as she felt a strange tightness come over her body. Behind Yike, the Grays slowly entered the room, and all eyes were on her. Turning her head, she glanced over to Yike. Then she smiled. His voice inside her head was clear. She knew the other Grays could all hear what he was saying to her.

"You have shown me that when people, your people, believe in something, it becomes a force and energy. Like love, it is all-consuming energy. You have taught me a lot. You have shared your values and taught me how to be safe here. You will remain my friend. This holds everything you need to find your way to other planets you can sustain your life on. All the mathematical equations for your safe travel are in this chip. This information is suitable for your planet and your safety. I will see you soon. Others are waiting for you. But know this to be true: you are loved."

Fly

Darkness suddenly surrounded Cyril. Then she felt like she was suspended in midair. The surface she had been lying on was gone. An unbearable tightness was surrounding her skin. The pressure made her head feel like it was going to crack wide open. Then she smelled metallic salty similar to blood as if she had a bloody nose; unable to wipe her nose or move at all, she felt something pouring down the side of her face, missing her mouth. Cyril gripped the chip Yike had given her, holding on to it as tightly as she could. It occurred to her what was happening. She had felt this feeling before she was on her way home. This was her traveling home, a feeling like no other.

Ezek walked to the water. The pier was just ahead. He went to the middle of the pier and sat down, putting his feet into the water.

Then it happened.

He felt it; she was in his atmosphere. He knew what the text should say now as he wrote it. "Almost here. At the Rock."

Behind him, he heard, "Are you waiting for me?" Standing next to a tree, she walked out of the shade into the sunlight.

He stood, not knowing her condition; just knowing she was here in front of him was enough.

He approached her slowly as the sun cast its light on the blood dripping down the side of her face. He asked, "Are you okay?"

Cyril smiled as her left hand went up to wipe the blood from her nose. "I'm fine, just a little overpressured." Catching her breath, her eyes closed as if she was trying to balance herself.

"I'm fine." Her head tilted to one side.

As she stood there with all the confidence in the world, her legs swayed to one side. As her eyes rolled to the back of her head, she passed out.

Ezek dashed over, catching her before she hit the pier. He laid her gently down, placing her legs out straight. Overhead he heard an approaching helicopter as he touched his board to give them his location.

Clutching the chip Yike had given her, Ezek tried prying it from her fingers. She had a death grip on it, so he let it go. He took her arms, resting them over her chest.

In the distance, he could hear people coming running toward him. Car doors slamming, people in the distance talking running through the yard. He counted four helicopters all landing around him.

Cindy was the first to arrive. Her team quickly scanned Cyril as she lay there, appearing to be dead. Cindy's first impression was that of shock when she approached. Then she saw the blood down Cyril's nose and the sides of her temples. Ezek smiled. Cindy's heart skipped a beat, and she read him, "She's alive."

Cindy's team scanned her for almost twenty minutes.

Steam and his team approached with a gurney. One of Steam's nurses quickly swabbed Cyril's skin, then small samples of her saliva and hair were taken and put into vials for testing.

Ezek wrapped Cyril in a thin cloth, covering her like a cocoon. He put his hand on her face, feeling her skin; he concluded her body temperature was 96.5 degrees with a heart rate of 52. Ezek placed Cyril gently onto the gurney while following her into the Rock.

From a distance, Ezek gave Steam a thumbs-up while they both smiled.

Cyril opened one eye, and she could hear the beeps coming from the instruments in the room. The smells were comforting to her, then she heard whispering. Over by the window were Steam and Ezek. They were in deep conversation.

"I told you before not to touch her when she first arrives. We're never sure if she's been contaminated with something unknown. You run the risk of spreading whatever it is she brings back. Let me see your hands and arms."

A nurse came quickly, taking sample swabs, placing them into vials.

"I've been using that stuff you gave me on my skin as you asked. Isn't that supposed to prevent any contamination? See, look, no spots." Ezek held both arms out for inspection.

"It's just to protect your skin from her. You don't know where she's been or what she's been doing."

"I don't think Yike would let her get sick. He's very concerned about her health. She said he was going to check her to see what was wrong with her. Even he noticed it." Cyril heard their whispers, not making out what they were saying exactly. She found it strange; she couldn't hear Ezek's thoughts. Then Ezek said inside her, *Hello, sweetheart.* He turned and smiled.

Steam saw the smile come over his face. He knew what that meant. He had seen it enough times before he turned to Cyril then said out loud, "Hey, kid, you're back. You okay? Looks like you had a rough trip."

Cyril's hand went out to touch Ezek as he walked over to her slowly. Scooting a chair over to the side of her bed, he sat down. Emotions filled him as she began to flood his mind with questions. Ezek read her thought, then looking over to Steam, tears filled his eyes; he had waited for this moment.

"Where is she?" she said it out loud for everyone in the room to hear.

The room went silent.

Steam caught Ezek's look. As Steam smiled, he also knew what that question could only mean.

Cyril could only be asking that question if her memory was back.

Ezek held her hand. "She's coming," he said, unable to contain himself.

"Does she know who I am?"

"Of course she does. I tell her every day you're on a very long trip. She has your pictures. She knows all about you."

Far off in the distance, the front door slammed. Small feet ran through the house. Toys, bells, squeaky things, things of less importance were dropped along the way.

Ezek dashed past the nurse out the door heading down the hallway. Then a little voice said, "Is Mommy in her room?"

Cyril's bedroom door swung open wide when the nurse stopped her from entering. All eyes went to Cindy as she gave the nurse two short nods. The nurse waved her hand over to Cyril.

Cyril's arms went wide open as Azalya bolted herself into her mother's arms.

"He said you were coming. He told me you were here. Are you going to stay this time?"

Azalya's big bright light-green eyes looked into Cyril, seeking her answer. Everyone stopped quickly, glancing over at each other. Everyone had the same "not guilty" look on their faces, as if saying, "It's not me she's talking about!"

"Who told you Mommy was coming?"

"Yike—he knows everything! He just left. Yike wants me to tell you not to worry, and he's cleaning it up for you." Azalya giggled, putting both hands up to cover her mouth.

"Mommy, don't worry." Her little hands held Cyril's face. "It's all right. It's okay. Yike said so. Don't worry, Mommy, he said he's going to clean things up for you." She puckered her face, not understanding the message.

Cyril moved Azalya's thick black hair out of her face. She looked into her eyes and saw Ezek's eyes as clear as if he were standing right there. "Daddy didn't fix my hair this morning. Where is Daddy?" Azalya looked over to Anna.

Anna put both hands out as if to say, "I don't know."

Cyril looked over to Steam. "He was just in the hallway, wasn't he?"

Azalya was excited to share her message. "Sven, he'll be back soon. He said he has something to add to the strings in my room."

Trying to comprehend what was happening, Cyril had to clarify. "So Sven was with Yike? And Yike's going to clean things up. Did Yike say what it was he was cleaning?" A panicked look flashed across

Cyril's face. "And Sven went with him, but he'll be back soon to add to your strings? Do I have that right?" She tried to put the pieces of the message together. Cyril squeezed her for a moment, wishing all the time she was gone would come back to her.

When suddenly she saw, Ezek was wiping the perspiration dripping from Cyril's forehead. In a calm, commanding voice, she heard him say, "Slow, one two three… Breathe slow." He said it out loud, calming her.

"Push, now push *harder*. Push," he repeated. Then the sound of her first cry as Cyril looked into Ezek's eyes. "She's here!" Ezek whispered, feeling the umbilical cord. The pulsing had just come to a stop. He clamped it in two spots then cut in between the clamps. Then he laid her across Cyril's chest, moving her gently; he kept his hand on her back, feeling the warmth from her new little body, the same warmth from Cyril's body. "She's beautiful." His words broke as one lone tear fell from his right eye. He couldn't contain his emotion; his hand stayed steady on her back. It was the moment Ezek delivered his daughter and let Cyril know they had a girl.

In the corner of Cyril's left eye, she saw a blue haze flash quickly across the room toward the door.

Azalya said, "Your friends are here, Mommy. There they go." She pointed across the room, laughing in a happy giggle.

Cyril followed the blue haze to the door. Then she asked, "Where is Ezek?" A haunting empty feeling washed over her. Then panic as she noticed the hairs on her arms were standing straight up.

"Where is he?" she repeated. "Find him!"

Azalya lay on top of the covers, trying to kick her shoes off.

Azalya noticed her mother clutching something in the palm of her hand. "Is that for me? Did you bring me something?"

"No, that's for Ez... No, that's for Daddy." Cyril handed the small chip from Yike over to Steam. He moved in quickly, holding a cloth out to lay the chip on.

Cyril's mind felt Ezek's energy was gone, no thoughts from him at all. He left no message to her. Her mind heard no goodbyes. Panic set in as she looked around the room helpless Ezek was gone. She could no longer hear him. Studying how she felt, fear consumed her. "I can't hear him!" she said aloud, sitting straight up in her bed, repeating it louder. "I can't hear him. Doesn't anyone understand what that means?"

Her first thought was he's dead.

Then the thought was quickly erased from her mind as if the thought was taken from her and replaced with *He's just gone. He's not dead…just gone.*

Three small knocks on the door, as Atwood stuck his head inside the room. "No sign of him anywhere," he reported.

Ezek's eyes remained closed while lying across a cold flat metal surface; next to him, he heard what sounded like fish breaking the water surface gasping for air. No, Ezek changed his thought when he heard small feet shuffling across the floor next to him. A crowd, maybe twenty or thirty bodies, were moving about, touching each other. Then a tiny gust of air moved around him. He realized he was not permitted to open his eyes. So he lay still and listened very carefully, leaving his breathing shallow to avoid missing a sound. *Kissing, it sounds like kissing,* he convinced himself.

All the moments after Cyril had returned flooded back to him.

He recalled her stories of what it was like when she was with Yike. Then he hoped it was Yike who had taken him and not some other Gray. He had always tried to pay close attention to the details of her events, but the emotions of her just returning clouded what she had gone through. It would have been vital information for him right now, realizing he had no advantages. It didn't matter how tall he was or how strong or intelligent he was; none of that mattered right now. He was at the mercy of his enemy, whoever it was paralyzing him. Shuffling noises came from the floor's surface again. The kissing noises stopped suddenly, and the air became still but surprisingly clean like orange blossoms. Unable to sit up, he waited. Then inside his head, he heard a voice say, "Sorry if that scared you." He felt a hand take him by the shoulder to help him sit up.

Now permitted to open his eyes, he asked, "Where am I? No, of course, I know where I'm at. Yike, why am I here?"

"You know who I am?" The voice in his head sounded startled.

"You're Cyril's friend," Ezek stated; understanding the importance of their friendship, he thought he needed to acknowledge he knew and respect it.

"Yes." Yike turned his head to give Ezek his full attention. "I want you to understand she is important to me. I watched her during her illness, and you made no effort to cure her. Why not?" The yellow in Yike's purple eyes expanded.

The question came to Ezek in the tone of a threat; to Yike, this was unacceptable.

"I had no way to cure her. I tried every way I could. Nothing worked. I want her back. I needed her back, you of all—" Ezek stopped; no words could describe him or what was happening right at that moment.

"You sent her away. You left it up to strangers. You wanted others to cure her when you had the power to do it yourself. You said one time out in the desert. You whispered it in her ear. She could barely hear you. Your words were 'You're not dying.' You didn't believe what you said to her when you said it, but you prayed for it to be true. You told her you were praying in the only way you knew how. You sent your words to everyone you had ever met or came in contact with, and I even heard your message. For as far and as wide as your heart went out, you did not want her to die. You even sacrificed your soul for her to live, showing your true love for her. That in itself is the only thing that saved her that day. Her injuries were severe, and you had no way to save her, and you knew that. She really was dying. Do you recall that night in the hangar when you came to get her? You ripped her out of the bag so she could breathe. How did you know where to find her? It was reported to me that she was being taken for study by rogue Grays. I didn't get there in time, but you did. How did you know where to find her?

"This all proves to me you alone could have cured her. She has tried to explain to me what love means. I have found it to be very complex. And I have observed many relationships here that express this feeling you referred to as love. You both have that, and it has saved you both many times. This can only work if you have it and are willing to give it to someone, I have discovered. Your love for your mother has been sad on your soul. Your understanding of her is wrong and not my fault. I need you to see this clearly. You mean a lot to my friend, so I owe this to her, for you." Yike gently placed his hand on top of Ezek's head. Ezek leaned back, not wanting to be touched when Yike told him, "Be still."

Ezek heard his father tell him, "If your mother had known how to fly, she would still be here." The seven-year-old Ezek didn't understand these words as his father repeated them anytime someone asked how his mother died. During a moment of his father's remorse, he remembered hearing she was harvested.

Yike interrupted his thought, almost yelling it like a protest of his innocence. "I did not take your mother! I did not harvest her! I did not!" Adjusting his hand on Ezek's head, he told him, "You said to Cyril she must see it with her own eyes to believe it in her memory. Watch this and know it to be true."

Ezek's mother had just walked out the sliding glass doors to the outside cafe. She decided to sit at the table without the umbrella, giving her full sunshine. She swept her hand under her skirt to sit. She placed her gloves and purse on a chair next to her. Her eyes squinted as she looked up to the sun, feeling the warmth across her skin. Reaching into her purse, she pulled out a folded white piece of paper and read it for the fifth time. She was confident of what it was telling her; the language was simple and clear. She folded the paper neatly and put it back into her purse.

A waiter stopped at her table. "Are you ready to order?" the gentle voice asked.

"Yes, please, just iced tea, no sugar. Thank you."

"Did you want lemon with that?"

"No." She smiled and shook her head with her eyes closed.

She was thinking about what she had just read, making it her secret. She took out her lipstick and a small pearl compact Henry got her on their last trip to Paris. First, she checked her eyes; they're clear and bright, with no mascara smudges.

Then she put her lipstick on ever so carefully, staying within the lines.

Then she wiped the corners of her mouth. *Perfect*, she admired herself. Looking back at herself, she studied her features for a moment.

Putting the compact and lipstick back into her purse, she removed her tortoiseshell comb and gave her long auburn hair three quick swipes. Taking her right hand, she fluffed her hair, feeling its silkiness upon her palm. She got up from her chair, taking her purse, snapping the closure tightly, securing the strap in the crux of her left arm.

Then her right hand smoothed the wrinkles across the front of her skirt.

With all the confidence of someone going somewhere, she walked forward, sat on the edge, and then pushed herself off.

Falling 40 stories, approximately 404 feet at a speed of almost 95 miles an hour, 6 seconds later, she was hard to recognize.

Yike took his hand from Ezek's head. "I have brought you pain. With it comes the truth. She could not fly because she didn't want to. It is that simple. Did you hear her last thoughts? She loved her boys and her husband and wanted her beauty to be in your minds forever. Never to change, so she stopped her illness and left you only to remember her kindness and beauty.

"I have cured my friend. I ask that you take care of her. I will still study her and you in the future. But for now, you are to care for her while I am gone. If you ask, for me, I will hear you as I hear her."

Cindy's team quickly scanned the room. Then down the hallway. Cindy came in with a look on her face Cyril had seen before. Shaking her head, she said, "They were here. He's gone."

Cyril realized the tables were turned. For the first time, he was gone, not her. Ezek had never been to the other side; he had only heard about it from her or others.

Anna came over to Azalya. "Mommy has to rest now. Let's go back to the house and wait for Daddy to get home." Cyril sent Anna a sharp look. As Anna took Azalya's hand, they walked out of the room with no protest from Azalya.

Westlund came into the room, handing Steam a tablet. "We found this in the office."

Steam quickly swiped his fingers across the screen. He was reading Ezek's last message from Henry. He was shocked to see the words about green orbs. "Henry will be here in a few days," he said out loud to himself.

Steam held Ezek's board in one hand and walked to the side of Cyril's bed. "I've been waiting for the right time to tell you this now that you're back."

"What is it? Not more bad news, I hope. I don't think I can take it anymore."

"In late spring, a coalition of scientists are meeting in Geneva. They have formally invited you as the keynote speaker. They understand each time you have tried to speak you're detained or unable to attend. None of it has ever been your fault. They have put together a security plan to guard your safety. The minute you acknowledge you're going to attend, security will be enforced, and your travel accommodations will be at the highest scrutiny. But we have one problem. We have no idea what you're going to say this time. So you'll have the floor for twenty minutes. With the highest level of security to protect you this time and their backing, it's apparent they want to know what your findings are. I know this isn't a good time for you to think about it, but let me just put it out there. So if you plan to attend, we need to prepare what you're going to say and who's going with you."

"Ezek will go with me. What do you think they want from me?"

"It's more what you want from them, Cyril. You have always wanted the world to know the Grays are here and always have been. Only this time, you're going to prove it to them. With real proof."

Steam turned around behind him to see who was at the door. "What is it?" Steam asked Atwood.

"Cyril, you have a guest! It's Twyce. He'd like to come up. Is that okay?"

"Yes, of course. Oh shit, what am I going to tell him?"

One by one, the room emptied. Bernard came over and held Cyril's hand. "Have someone call me when he gets back." The smile wasn't very reassuring. But Cyril agreed.

Steam gathered his things then looked at Cyril's chart. "Stay in bed. That kind of travel is hard on your muscle tissue. You need to get used to this atmosphere. Gravity is your enemy right now. If you get another bloody nose, call me. I see no signs of internal bleeding. You're not carrying anything strange either." One eyebrow went up with a smirk on his face. "So far as I can tell, you should be all right. Just get some rest. He'll be back soon. Don't worry about him."

Cyril's hand went up. "Wait, before you go, could you do a test for me?"

"Sure, what is it?"

"Over on my dresser is a small plastic bag with two sunflower shells. Could you see if you can get a DNA sample off them? It's very important to me. I don't want anyone to know. Tell only me what you find. Only me, no one else."

"Sure, what's up? What's this about? Can you tell me at least?" He shook his head.

"I'll explain once the results are back. How long do you think it will take?"

"Is tomorrow okay? I'll have someone work on it tonight."

"That'll be fine. Thank you."

The nurses collected all the samples in the room and were given instructions from Cindy. Cindy stood in the doorway with a half smile while Steam stood behind her as they walked out and closed the door behind him.

The room was silent, no voices; only the instruments monitoring her vitals were heard. The curtains were wide open, letting in the glaring afternoon sunlight. In the distance, long-striding footsteps came quickly up the stairs two at a time, then swiftly down the hallway. Someone was in a hurry.

Then the door flew open, hitting the wall. As Twyce entered the room, he stopped abruptly. Cyril's first thought when seeing him was that his appearance said he was in a hurry and wasn't concerned about what people thought. His tie was a powder-blue stripe that accentuated the watery blue in his eyes. It looked like the tie was trying to escape sticking awkwardly out from his half-unbuttoned brown suede vest. His tweed jacket said he had come from somewhere cold, and his shoes said he had been somewhere it had been raining. Twyce's long auburn hair was pulled back in a braid with a brown leather strap like an afterthought. He stood there and smiled while quickly taking off his jacket and throwing it over the chair. For a moment, you could see in his expression he was hoping his brother would be in the room, already knowing it not to be true.

"He's gone, isn't he?" Anguish distorted his face as he held back his fear. Walking up to her bed, he leaned in, putting his arms around her, holding her tightly just longer than a greeting. He was holding on to hope.

She whispered in his ear, "He'll be home soon, I promise you." She closed her eyes and wished it to be true. His scent was similar to his brother's as his long braid fell over his shoulder.

He recoiled, holding her away at arm's distance. "How do you know that? How can you even say that? Do you know where he is?"

"Yes, I think I do." She tried to say it with confidence.

"I can't hear him! Do you have any idea what that feels like? Please tell me he's alive." An avalanche of tears ran down his cheeks. "I can't hear him." He was shaking his head now, crying uncontrollably. He repeated, "I can't hear him!" as he gasped for breath.

"Please listen, listen to me. Ezek is alive. I feel it in my soul. Stop, listen." She took his face into her hands. "He is alive. Please believe me."

"How can you be so sure? I can hear you, everything you're thinking. I can hear my dad, but I can't hear him. Never, do you understand, never in my life have I not been able to hear him no matter where he is." As Twyce wiped his eyes, trying to contain himself, he looked Cyril eye to eye.

Exhausted, he lay on her bed above the blankets. He put his head on the pillow with her. His breaths were short, as if he was trying to breathe in all the way but couldn't. She can't stop her thoughts to him. *God, I love the way these men smell. God, I miss him.*

"It's going to be okay, trust me."

Hearing Twyce catch two short breaths again, Cyril remembered Ezek telling her about the moment he couldn't hear her. He said it felt like she had died; the moment could only be compared to when his mother was harvested.

They lay there quietly in the security of each other's company. Twyce whispered, "Can I take my shoes off?"

Cyril whispered back, "Yes."

After an hour or so had passed, Cyril took the pulse oximeter off her finger and rubbed Twyce's arm. His breathing was shallow; he was so quiet she thought he had fallen asleep.

"Come on, let's go get something to eat." As she tried to get up out of bed, she melted onto the floor.

Twyce caught her before she landed. "Hold on, sister. I don't think you're ready to travel. Just tell me what you want, and I'll get it for you." Cyril grabbed her robe as Twyce helped her put it on.

"Please help me downstairs," she insisted.

"Ooookay." He reluctantly took her arm.

Strange, this feeling like being in Ezek's arms, she said only to herself.

"Really! Is this the way he holds you?" Twyce looked down and smiled.

"Oh shit, I'm sorry, I forget you're in my head like your brother."

"How am I supposed to get used to this? I forget you and your dad both do that. Didn't we just talk about that a little while ago?" She was shaking her head while slowly struggling to get to the end of the hallway to make it down the stairs.

Once down the stairs and into the kitchen, he helped her get comfortable on the barstool.

"You know my dad's on his way here. He texted a few days ago asking if I could meet him here. I hope it was okay."

"You never have to ask. Of course, it is." She shook her head at the thought.

Twyce stood in front of her. The watery blue in his beautiful eyes were bloodshot and tired. He appeared to be unraveled. He leaned in and asked, "What can I get for you?" as he draped the white towel over his forearm.

Then she said to Ezek, "Please hear me. Twyce and I are waiting for you. I'm waiting for you. Please come home."

Twyce looked at her. "Did you hear him?"

"No, but he might be able to hear me. Don't stop talking to him. There will be a moment when your messages will get to him."

"You're so optimistic at this point all I can do is believe you." He smiled, turned, then opened the refrigerator door.

Flickering flames danced across the ceiling in Cyril's room. Startled, she lay and watched, trying to figure it all out. Someone was on the patio. Slowly she managed to get her robe on then her slippers. Carefully she made her way down the hallway. Keeping the lights off, she tiptoed as quietly as she could. Into the den, she stood at the glass door where she noticed Twyce lying back in the chair with his feet up on the edge of the firepit. Knowing it had to be cold out there, Cyril grabbed the blanket off the sofa. Wondering if he was asleep, she tried to be quiet. Twyce turned as she had just woken him; he smiled.

"Are you okay?" she whispered.

"Come sit with me." He looked up at the stars. "Tell me where you think he is right now. Do you think they're above us just hanging out? Or do you think they went somewhere far away where he can't hear me? Is that how it works?" Twyce patted the seat next to his, showing Cyril where he wanted her to sit.

"Tell me how it works. Help me understand. I don't understand any of this. All I know is I can't hear him." Both his hands went to cover his face while he tried to breathe, gasping for breath. She realized he was crying uncontrollably. His hands wiped his face while he tried to calm himself. The flames snapped and crackled as they rose to the heavens. Cyril looked into the fire and had to take his thoughts away.

"Do you remember the last time you and I made a fire? Do you remember where we were?"

Twyce, still looking up at the stars, thought about it for a moment. "Yes, I do. We were alone, you and I," he said slowly as if he was going back there to see the moment.

"We had just stopped to make camp. Australia, yes, we were in Australia deep in the outback. It had been so hot all day, who would have thought the night would get so cold? Ezek, if I remember right, left early that morning with our guide, Luke, while you and I went to take pictures all day. The night came on quickly. You said we needed to show them where we were, so you collected branches and twigs to start a fire. Now that I think about it, it was pretty hilarious we got down to the last match when you boldly questioned me about my Boy Scout skills. With only one match left and only the jeep lights to shine on us, you said we need to turn them off, or we'd be stuck out there forever. Right about then, we heard the dingoes. I was terrified while you, as usual, stayed calm. You said, 'Come on, they're just dogs.' I said, 'Yeah, just wild, crazy, hungry dogs. We're fresh meat just sitting there waiting for them.' My brother, of course, was nowhere to be found. It was after the full moon came up. It was like seeing the full sun at night for the first time. It was huge, like you could reach out and grab it. To this day, I have no idea how he knew where to find us. But he drove right up with everything we needed, including more matches. Actually, now that I think about it, he started the fire that night. He took care of everything. Once he got there, everything was okay. Everything was all right." Twyce's fingers threaded through his thick auburn locks clutching the top of his head.

"He cooked quail on the barbie. We had a feast that night thanks to him and Luke. Even the dingoes were gone."

Twyce covered his face again then took in a deep breath. When it occurred to Cyril, he was sobbing and out of breath.

"It's always okay once he's there." Twyce turned to Cyril, waiting for her to agree.

"Have you ever noticed that? He makes everything all right. No matter how bad it is at that moment, he can make it right. How the hell does he do that?" His hands wiped the tears from his face when he turned to Cyril for an answer.

Cyril heard Henry in her head. Twyce looked over to her and asked, "You heard him?"

"Yes, he's here." She smiled and stood up to go toward the door.

They both saw the white Land Rover come quickly up the driveway. Cyril noticed another passenger, small in stature, with dark hair. Then it occurred to her Henry was answering her question. "Yes, it's your mother." Twyce and Cyril went down the stairs as the car approached. Cyril noticed down the driveway Azalya and Anna were walking hand in hand toward the house. Twyce went to the passenger door, opening it for Virginia as he took her hand to help her out of the car. Henry quickly came around to assist when Cyril noticed the frailty in her mother. She asked Henry as he passed her, "Is she all right?"

Henry answered Cyril; in her head, she heard, *She's tired. We need to get her inside to rest.*

Suddenly Henry stopped then put his arms around Cyril then gave her the three kisses, then held her again for a very long time when she heard him say, "You're back! You're really here! Your memory is intact. Oh, how I have missed our debates. Welcome back, sweetheart."

Sweetheart, he said, as Cyril melted in his arms. Henry heard her in his head. *Ezek is the only one that calls me that. I miss him.* She collected herself while she held him tightly.

Twyce heard his father and took Virginia's arm while hugging her. He said, "Slow down. Let me help you."

Twyce said to his father, "Yes, her memory's back, all of it. Wait till Ezek's hears this. Even her dreams, all her dreams, all of them are back, all of them!" He shook his head in amazement.

Slowly they made their way up the stairs. Like Mount Everest, Cyril noticed the struggle. Azalya ran up and grabbed Virginia's leg.

"Grandma, where's Grandpa Mikie? He's not with you?" Azalya's arms went up to Henry. She pulled on his teal *thawb*. "Hold me, Grandpa."

Henry took her into his arms. "How's my girl? I missed you. You're getting so big." Henry's arms went tightly around her.

Virginia stopped in the middle of the stairs. "What, honey, what did you say?"

Twyce gave his father a cautious look then read him; a shocked look came over Henry's face. "Come in the house. I'll explain."

Cyril took her mother's arm as Twyce went into the kitchen.

"I'll make you some tea." Twyce turned to Anna. "Get her a blanket, please," he whispered.

"It's good to be home, Twyce. Please tell your father where Ezek is. He's been so worried. He can't hear him. What's going on? Why is he so quiet? That's not like him."

She turned to smile as Cyril's expression changed.

Catching Cyril's expression, Virginia's voice changed, and panic consumed her. "WHERE IS HE?" She demanded an answer.

Henry sat down, feeling the dread, knowing he wasn't ready; he couldn't prepare himself for what he was about to hear. For a moment, he wanted it all to stay the same, just him and Virginia, his son and her daughter and their granddaughter; but that one piece was missing Ezek.

Cyril went and sat next to Henry. "He'll be home soon, don't worry." Twyce came over with two cups of tea, sitting one on the credenza.

"She keeps telling me that I have to believe her. Ezek always said I should believe her…so I do. He'll be home soon just like she said." He said it in an almost convincing way. He wanted to believe, to believe in her.

"You know where he is?" Henry moved his hair over his shoulder and waited for her answer.

"Yes, I think I do. Ezek is safe. He's with my friend. He'll be home soon." What Henry heard was as close to a prayer as he could ever imagine. She had put her prayer out to all those that could hear her. For as far and as wide as her thoughts and energy could go. She believed he would return. In her soul, she knew it to be true.

"I thought your father was here. Have you heard from him?"

"No, I thought he was with you. Where have you been? The e-ticket you sent me at Henry's—my god, that's today. Your flight over Greenland, what happened? I thought you both had died. Mom, what's going on? Henry, what's going on? Someone tell me what's happening?"

Cyril noticed Henry gave her two short nods. Then for only her to hear, he said, "Not now. Where is Ezek?"

"Hold on." Cyril heard a chime come from the other room. She dashed into her father's office to retrieve her board. A message came from Steam. It read, "Call me; I have your results." Cyril went to close the door to the office then called. Steam picked up immediately.

The first thing he said was "Before I tell you, tell me what this is about."

"Okay, but you have to keep it to yourself."

"Not a problem. Cross my heart." When she heard him say that it was like her childhood was right there in front of her, she knew for him to say that he would die first before it ever passed his lips. It was something they both understood. For that moment, Cyril realized that was part of her past. So she began to explain.

Shut

Sitting on the suspended surface, Ezek looked at the enormity of the inside of the craft. He had no idea it was that large, seeming to appear hollow inside.

"So what happens now? How did they just wipe her memory away? With Cyril, they used black crystal." Yike walked over to the body lying still. "Ezekiel, you have waited all this time to let her have her revenge, knowing, watching, waiting for her. I need to do it for her. I don't want her to hold regret. That is the only reason I want to do it for her. If she ever feels she has made a mistake, it will be my fault, not hers." Yike turned to Ezek. Yike looked at the body lying still and began to tell Ezek, "While it was happening to her, she watched him prepare the cloth as the black crystal foam was rising. She pleaded to keep her memory. Her first thoughts were angry: 'I'm going to kill him if I can get out of here.' Then it changed to 'I'll wipe his mind so even he doesn't know who he is,' then it went to 'I'll lock him inside of himself so he can't get out and no one can hear him.' In her mind, it was how she thought she would feel if her memory was erased. She was hoping her memory was still there. She could no longer be heard. She had no access to it, and she was right. It has always been there. He just blocked it from her. Now we both know how she needs to control things, especially her own memory."

Ezek couldn't help but think about all the ways he could have prevented it from happening to her. He felt responsible. He knew he couldn't take her revenge, but Yike could. He knew he had to stop thinking about the things he couldn't control or change. He thought about the first time he couldn't move in his bed, a moment just like this one. He was lying still; he thought the figure came from his closet until he saw the clear glass evaporate toward the ceiling. The tall figure stood at the end of his bed. Only his eyes could move. He watched the figure walk around to the side of his bed. In its arm, it was holding something like it was connected to its hip. The tall figure watched him helpless, not able to move as he looked it in the eyes.

He listened, thinking it might talk to him, but no noise came from it as it just stared.

Frightened, he remembered his father telling him one universal voice that speaks the loudest is a smile. So Ezek smiled. It was a sincere smile when he noticed it smiled back. Its mouth never moved; the smile came from its eyes. The tall figure walked out of the bedroom into the hallway. He heard it go into the kitchen. When he heard the tone of Virginia's voice, he knew everything was all right. He knew Mikel wasn't home yet and wondered what would have happened if he had been home. Would this visit be all right with him? Wasn't it the dad's job to protect them?

Ezek thought about the morning his life changed forever. He stood at the front door with his bags. His father had already explained to him, Mikel was not his new dad, that he would always be his father; but for right now, this was his new home. He remembered how Mikel said he always wanted a son. He even overheard him say to Virginia one time, "I love him like a son." Mikel terrified him; at first, there was a strictness in the house.

Once, Cyril explained to him what the rules were. He remembered as her little voice came into his head. He had no idea just how smart and aware she was.

She told him, "It's easy. Do as you're told when you're told to do it. Don't waste time. Don't hesitate. Don't sass back, and remember you're not boss yet. Play by their rules until you're in a position to create your own rules. Get all the education you can, then no matter who it is, you'll be able to outsmart them. But for now, pay attention." For a moment, he felt her warm little hand in his leading the way.

Then like she was standing behind him, he heard her say, *Please hear me. Twyce and I are waiting for you. I'm waiting for you. Please come home.*

Yike looked over. "You heard her."

"Yes." A smile slowly came over his face.

"As for Sven." Yike walked around to the other side of the body lying in front of him. He touched the shoulder, helping him to sit up. Ezek's eyes stayed fixed. It was Sven. Sven gripped the sides of the cold suspended surface as he got his bearings then rubbed his eyes.

"Yike, why am I here?" he asked with a commanding voice while he was startled to see Ezek standing there witnessing what was about to happen to him.

Hearing his voice, Yike stopped as his eyes closed. Slowly the yellow became brighter and brighter as they shut.

Ezek took one step back, feeling the overwhelming sense of emotion radiating off Yike. Not able to take his eyes off Yike, he braced himself. Ezek watched as Yike's fingers relaxed and got longer and longer. Yike stood still when suddenly Ezek noticed the room was gradually lit and filled with the sound of kissing. The noise approached from the darkness into the light from all around them. Twenty then maybe forty came into the area.

The Grays kept their distance. The kissing noise became louder and louder. As far as Ezek could see, Grays had surrounded them.

Softly in Ezek's head, he heard, *Sven, I have had time to think about what you have done. Cyril has taught me to think before I react. You are someone she has always trusted, and you betrayed my friend and me. I sent you to care for her and teach her about our surroundings so she would always be safe. It has never mattered if we were detected or not. It was always going to happen eventually. Now who believes it and who doesn't is another issue. Sven, you cannot be trusted, so I will not let you return to this planet.* Yike's eyes opened as the bright yellow subsided; only spiked deep purple appeared.

"What do you mean?" Panic flooded his voice. "You'll stay here with us."

Ezek rubbed his lips and chin, taking in what was happening in front of him.

When Yike turned to Ezek, he said, "I heard that. I agree. She will miss him, but I cannot risk who he might be influenced by again."

Ezek walked over to Yike; looking around the room, he felt anger from the Grays but not toward him. Yike looked Ezek in the eyes. "I put her into your hands. I will study her as I always have so expect me."

Twyce walked over to the gallery wall in the den. "The gladiolus are beautiful. My brother must have gotten those for you." He turned then smiled as he touched the first peach flower. On the wall was a huge print of Mobula rays, thousands of them swimming in the warm waters in the Sea of Cortez. Mixed in with thousands of rays was a small body in a bright-red wetsuit swimming with them in the distance.

"Your parents sent me a nice thank-you note when they got this. I packed it well. I was worried the glass might get broken in shipping. You know I never thought we would get your mom in a wetsuit."

"Yeah, me either. Mom still can't believe it's her." As he stared at the photo, he remembered the weekend.

Cyril was stacking the breakfast dishes on top of each other. Taking her cup of coffee to her lips, she said, "I still can't figure out how you did that. Even my dad got in the water that day. It was amazing how you could reach out and touch them. They were everywhere. Your brother had a hard time with that. It was funny."

"We all need to do that again. That was a good trip. Now that I think about it, that's when I noticed your relationship with my brother had changed."

"What do you mean changed?"

"I don't know. I guess it was the way he would look at you. It was different."

"We weren't even out of college then!"

"Yeah, I know, but it was different. I noticed something was changing about you two."

"Hey, help me walk down to get Azalya."

"She didn't stay here last night?"

"No, Steam doesn't think I'm ready. Come with me."

"You should call the doc first and see if you're ready then."

"What! Call and ask if I'm ready to spend time with my own child?"

"Yes. I don't think you're up to it either. Call the doc. Just see what he says." Cyril texted Steam. "Am I out of quarantine so I can spend time with my daughter?"

Steam immediately texted back, "Sorry, not yet. Short visits, ten to fifteen minutes only. You still need to adjust to this gravity and give it two more days. Your sea legs should be gone by then. All tests should be back by then also. We are currently on standby. We need to know the minute he returns. See you soon."

"I'm going to call Anna to see if she'll bring her up."

The house was dark as Cyril tiptoed quietly to avoid waking anyone. Once in the kitchen, she looked out onto the patio and saw a dark figure looking toward the Sierras.

"How long have you been out here?"

Twyce turned startled, his hands in his pockets, tears running down both cheeks. Wiping his face, he smiled at her. "I wanted to see the sun come up and bring me a new day, hopefully, a good day."

Cyril saw the sun outline the tops of the mountains. As she put her arm around his, they both stood there and watched the new day begin. "Would you like coffee or tea this morning? Anna will be here soon. Azalya is going to stay for a while today. I'm hoping when Ezek gets back, it doesn't freak her out. It could happen in front of her or you or me. I just wish it would happen."

"I finished the puzzle. That took us what…four days, not bad. Do you want to finish watching *Gone with the Wind* tonight?"

"Yeah, that sounds good. I'll make popcorn. Does your dad like popcorn?"

"Yeah, he does. Do you want to play chess later?" Twyce walked around the kitchen island.

Cyril started to sauté onions and garlic. On the counter, Twyce saw the pile of chopped celery and potatoes and grated carrots. Cyril threw everything into the pot and began to stir them about with a wooden spoon while adding water to the pot.

"Are you making soup?"

"Yes, Ezek's favorite," she said as she stirred everything together.

"What do you mean he eats everything?"

"Yes, he does, but he loves clam chowder. That is my clam chowder! He said one time it's comfort food for him. It's like warm and fuzzy. It makes him feel like he's home."

"Oh my god, he told me about your clam chowder. He said it's better than Mom's. And hers was really good."

Twyce looked up to the ceiling and apologized to his mother. "Sorry, Mom, but that's what he said, so it must be good. Can I watch you make it, see what your trick is?"

"Yes, of course." Cyril chopped the rest of the potatoes. "Hay, grab the sour cream out of the fridge."

Twyce went to the fridge holding the large container of sour cream. He said, "So this is the secret ingredient. No wonder my brother loves it."

Looking out onto the patio, Cyril noticed Henry coming from the lake, drying himself off. "Twyce, your dad's been swimming. He's probably freezing. I know I would be. Get him another towel."

Twyce raced over to his dad with a throw from the sofa. "Aren't you cold?"

Henry sat at the patio table, covering his shoulders. "I wonder if your brother is okay."

"I think he's fine. I'm not sure what he's doing, but I think he's fine. When we see Cyril freak out, then something changed. She's making chowder for lunch."

"I think your brother told me about her chowder. I look forward to it." Henry twisted then tied his hair behind him in a knot.

Cyril heard short scoots coming from the hallway. Dropping everything, she dashed over only to find her mother gasping for breath, leaning against the wall. "What's wrong? Are you okay? What's happened to you? Are you sick?"

"I'm not sure. I'd like to have my blood analyzed as soon as possible."

"I'll call Steam. He'll send someone over. What do you think it might be?"

"I'm not sure. I have a scarf in a sealed plastic bag in my suit-case. I'd also like to have that tested."

"Where did the scarf come from? Do you suspect someone?"

"Cyril, don't ask. Let's just get it tested, okay."

Henry came from the patio. "Why are you up? Lay down here on the sofa. Twyce, get a blanket. I thought you were going to stay in bed?"

"I have to find out what this stuff is before it gets worse."

Cyril asked Henry so only he could hear. "Where did Mom get the scarf? Who gave it to her?" Henry looked over to Cyril and thought about it. He was there when she opened the package. It was sent by a special courier and anniversary gift from her father. Cyril saw Henry, remember-ing the moment as he shared it with her. Her mother was surprised her husband of thirty-five years remembered the day. She saw the scarf in a shop while in Canada. Henry recalled her saying, "It's the Barreau. How beautiful." Henry watched her wrap it around her neck. He too thought it was lovely; the colors were soft, and they accentuated her skin. Then she was instantly repelled by it. She laid it across her dresser and wouldn't touch it. The next thing Henry knew, it's in a plastic bag.

"Your mommy is waiting for you in your room." Twyce took Azalya's hand.

"Uncle Twyce, can we take Mommy to the water? Mr. Allen has floaties for me. Can we please? Mommy likes the water, doesn't she?"

"We'll ask her, okay? She might be tired. Let's go ask."

"Is Daddy back? Can he go with us?"

"Daddy's not back yet, but he'll be home soon."

Azalya went into her room when she stopped cold and stared at the strings hanging from her ceiling. Her hand went out to touch the strings while Cyril and Twyce looked on. More curious about the strings than her mother, Cyril studied her then looked at Twyce, trying to figure out what Azalya had noticed.

"What is it, Azalya? What are you looking at?" Cyril studied the planets. She too had to memorize all of them; this was a road map of her backyard and galaxies.

Azalya slowly walked around the mobile while pointing up toward earth, then her little finger moved slightly to the right, and up she stopped.

In a voice that caused both of them to stop, Azalya slowly said, "What's that?"

"What's what? What are you looking at?" Suddenly Cyril realized Azalya knew every string with every planet, every moon, every black hole, every cloud of gas in every galaxy. Cyril was impressed.

"That, Mommy, what is that?" Azalya walked around the wide hanging mobile to view it from a different angle.

"That's new. That's what Sven wanted me to see. Oh no, it's too close. He must have that wrong. It's too close to us. We're in the right spot. That's how you show an invisible black hole. He showed me what they looked like before he left. Azalya threw her head back to laugh. "How do you show something that's invisible? Like that!" Her hand went out and pointed to the red and gray puff suspended on the string. "He must have that wrong. It's too close to us. I'll ask him where it should go next time I see him."

Cyril motioned with her hand as Azalya went into her arms. Holding her tight, she asked, "How are you today? I missed you!"

"I'm okay. I ate too many waffles. Anna makes good waffles. Are you staying for a while?"

"Yes, I hope for a very long time. Is that okay?"

"Yes, you can have waffles with me, Uncle Twyce. You like waffles, don't you?"

Twyce went around to the window to sit on the floor while he looked up at the mobile. Then he said out loud, "Fascinating. Yes, I love waffles. I like bacon with my waffles." He said it like he was talking to a child.

Then suddenly, Cyril heard inside her head, *Let's hope that's wrong because if it's right, we're all in trouble.*

Cyril looked at Twyce, hearing him when Azalya turned to Twyce, and said, "Why are we in trouble, Uncle Twyce?"

It occurred to both of them she was in their heads, and Cyril had no control over it. Twyce stared at Cyril, trying to keep his mind blank.

The shock of it all was running ahead of them. There was nothing they could do to pull it back in…

Ezek found himself lying on the suspended surface. "My friend is upset. She fears you might be dead. Your brother is there to console her. Be still. I want you to see this."

Yike's hand went to the left side of Ezek's head. Suddenly like watching a movie, he saw Twyce crying uncontrollably while lying on Cyril's bed.

Then he saw Azalya pointing at her mobile with Twyce and Cyril. He heard conversation drift in and out of his head. "Daddy, where are you? Come home." Then "I know you're not dead... You're not dead because Cyril said so, and like you have always said, 'Listen to her. She's never wrong... Listen to her.' Well, brother, I'm listening, come home!" Over and over, the warm and fuzzy feeling of love surrounded him as he heard the soft voice say, "I love you... I love you... See you soon... I love you."

Suddenly the room was quiet; and the Grays parted while watching Yike's mother, Acid, walk into the room. She stopped next to Ezek as he smiled at her.

His childhood flooded back to him. He recalled Acid's smile when he learned to listen to her in his head. She would talk to him, telling him in a soothing sound, "It's all right. I'm not here to harm you. You know my son Yike. He's Cyril's friend. Please don't be afraid."

Acid looked at Ezek, her eyes a dark purple, hardly any yellow at all. You would almost swear she was smiling at him. His first reaction was he was glad to see her, a Gray he knew. His smile was his exchange, and in her eyes, he saw it too. In his head, she told him, *My friend Virginia is dying. This will give her time. Please hold her for me, hold her tight. She must drink this, all of it.*

Acid handed Ezek a tiny blue metal container with a glass stopper on top. She set it into the palm of his hand. She took his hand, closing his fingers, around the container to secure it. Both her hands closed around his. She was letting him know to hold tight.

"I will take care of the person that contaminated her. Please tell her she was right. She will understand." Acid's long slender arms came up; her fingers unrolled like fern fronds to touch his forehead. Ezek stayed still, keeping his eyes wide open. Then her fingers entwined in his hair as she studied it for a moment, moving her hand to see the colors and shine.

"I don't think I will see you again. Thank you for our relationship and all we have shared." Acid turned and walked back into the crowd of Grays disappearing.

Yike stepped next to Ezek, putting his hand on his shoulder.

"You must go now. My friend is hiding her stress. I can't let that overwhelm her. You must go now." Yike's hand made a striking motion as the room cleared. Ezek watched clear glass mold around him as he felt the pressure begin. Now lying still, he recalled Cyril telling him how the travel back always scared her. The quickness of it and the pressure always made her head feel like it was going to crack. Often her nose would bleed, and her eyes would dry. Suddenly he felt something warm down his face and then went quickly into his ears and then down his neck. Then as soon as it happened, it was gone.

Cyril heard the clock on the mantel strike at 3:30, one strike representing the half hour. As her arm went up to uncover herself, she couldn't move; nothing moved. Frozen in time, not even her heart could skip a beat. She knew what this all represented; that is, her thoughts hoped so. Her eyes glanced down to see the hair on her arm stand straight up on end. The moment was quick, and then it was gone. Screaming as loud as she could, "HE'S HERE... SEND THE TEXT."

Feeling the carpet under his hands, he found himself lying on his back, on the stairs. His eyes remained sealed shut. The smell of cake cooking in the air was sweet; it reminded him of birthdays and happy times, of family and being surrounded by loved ones. His head went back on to the top stair; and he said to anyone listening, glad to be home, "Sweetheart, I'm home," while he laughed inside, relieved and exhausted. He heard a bell drop to the floor, and two little feet ran in his direction from a distance. Then he heard a door open as Cyril flew out, landing on top of him. Holding him, she repeated over and over again, "Are you all right?" She noticed his eyes were shut. Twyce ran with his board, pressing it three times, then dropping it to the floor. Cyril was looking over to Twyce. "He looks like he's okay? Are you okay? Talk to me. Open your eyes. Look at me! LOOK AT ME!" she yelled while holding his face in her hands. Ezek lay there feeling the weight of his arms in the gravity that now engulfed him. A weakness he had no control over kept him at its mercy. Inside Cyril's head, she heard him say, *I'm okay. I think...I think I'm okay. Water, I need water.*

"Water, I need water!" Cyril yelled while she wiped the blood from his face, checking his body, touching him everywhere. She put her arms around him. Ezek buried his face in her hair. She heard him take in a deep breath. She listened to his thoughts.

The smell of her hair was home... He knew he was home. Unable to lift his arms or open his eyes, he could only take in her scent. Then in the distance, she heard a helicopter landing in the yard, then another, then another, then another. As he lay there, the house ran with chaos; Cindy's team checked his vitals while taking samples. Steam had him lifted and taken into his room. The nurse carefully cut Ezek's clothes from his body. Every part of him had a sample taken. Steam pried his eyes open as he noticed his pupils were dilated, causing his eyes to appear black. When Steam flashed his penlight across Ezek's eyes, he saw the pupils didn't quickly close. They remained open and black.

A nurse brought over a pair of very dark sunglasses. "Wear these. Don't take them off until I tell you. Understand?"

Cyril got into his bed. She put her fingers through his hair and noticed on his left temple a streak of white hair dominated this hairline, and across his chest, white hair covered his heart.

When his eyes opened again, he found Cyril lying in a fetal position on top of his sheets tucked in next to him. Twyce was asleep in the chair next to his bed. Azalya's toys lay next to his pillow. Tucked under his arm was a black-and-white teddy bear. The curtains were partly open, and the sound of beeping told him he was alive.

Twyce sat up in the chair and stared, then smiled, then whispered, "She said not to worry. I had a hard time believing her like you said she was right." Cyril stirred then turned over, putting her hand on his chest, looking up to him.

"You're back. Please don't ever do that again, please."

Ezek kept it to himself. He knew now she had experienced his worst nightmare. He could not respond out loud. His words could not leave his mouth. When she came back, he remembered one time she couldn't speak for over a week, but her first word was "waffles." She sensed his struggle and smiled, curled up next to him, and whispered into his ear, "I missed you. I know you can't speak out loud, so just tell me what you want them to know." Cindy and Steam entered the room.

In her head, he asked her, *Where's your mom? Please tell me she's here? I need her to drink this, all of it now!* as he slowly unfurled his fingers like they had been frozen shut.

"Please bring your mother here!" Twyce and Cyril heard the urgency in his voice. Twyce repeated out loud what he had just said. Steam motioned for the nurse to find her and bring her.

"What is this?" Cyril thought for a moment Ezek might be handing her the small blue container, but he made it clear no one should touch it. So Cyril backed away.

"You're going to give this to my mother and not even tell me what it is?"

In her head, she heard him say, *I don't know what it is, but Acid said your mother is dying and that she needs to drink all of this now. I don't think she means to harm her but to help her.*

Virginia struggled to enter the room, taking the chair next to Ezek's bed. "What is it, son? I'm so glad you're back."

Twyce looked at his brother then repeated out loud to Virginia. "Mom"—Twyce looked at her—"this is what my brother can't say out loud to you. I have a message from Acid for you. She said she knows you're dying, and she wants you to drink all of this. She also wants you to know you are right! She said you would understand. She said you were deliberately contaminated and that she knows who did it and they will be taken care of. She wants me to hold you."

Ezek twisted open the small blue container, handing it to Virginia.

Henry stood at the door, watching it all unfold. When he said abruptly, "You don't know what it is, and you're drinking it. You trust her?"

As Virginia nodded her head yes, she swallowed the contents gulping twice, then she turned and asked, "Water, can I have some water?" Ezek's arms went out, leaning toward her. Twyce said, "Mom, I have to hold you. Acid needs me to hold you." Virginia leaned into Ezek's arms as he embraced her, holding her tight. Twyce said aloud, "Acid wants you to know you are loved." Henry watched as both his sons helped the woman he loved. Trying to contain himself, he wiped the tears from his eyes, still not knowing what she was drinking. Ezek noticed Virginia relax almost to the point that it frightened him. Twyce asked her, "Mom, Ezek wants to know if you're all right."

Virginia pulled away from his grip, still close enough to look him in the eyes. "I'm fine now." She smiled then whispered, gasping for breath, "I know why my daughter loves you. I love you too. Thank you. Thank you for this message."

Henry went to hold Virginia. "I'll take you to your room."

Ezek, still unable to speak out loud, asked Cyril, *How long was I gone?*

Cyril asked Steam, "He wants to know how long he was gone."

Steam brought up his tablet to answer him. "Based on the test we ran, you've been gone nine days, three hours, forty-nine minutes, fourteen seconds, six nanoseconds to be exact."

He explained, "It's easier to calculate your distance in time based on the structure of your molecules or cells when you return. Something very abstract happens to them. The combination of our atmosphere and gravity the moment it hits you after being with Yike. It changes your surface skin temporarily. But all your tests show you're normal. You have a slight B deficiency, but we can take care of that, not to worry. It happens to Cyril also when she returns. Let me know if you get cramps in your legs. It's all part of it, okay? You're going to be fine, but don't get out of bed. Your body is not ready to walk in gravity, so give it a few days. Just like I always tell Cyril, gravity is your enemy right now." He smiled.

Ezek took the teddy bear from under his arm and put the question in Cyril's head, *Is Azalya here?* She heard fear in the question. He had no idea when Azalya put the bear under his arm. He knew that it was a tall sacrifice for her to give up her bear, sensing his daughter's fear.

"She put Teddy there to comfort you. She's in the kitchen with Anna making you a cake." Cyril felt his fear, the fear that had consumed his daughter. She read him; he needed her fear to stop, a fear all too familiar to him, a fear now familiar to Cyril. Cyril looked at Twyce as Twyce repeated this time out loud. "Please, bring her here where she is?" Twyce stood, understanding his brother's emotion. Knowing only that, Azalya could probably hear him like she could hear her mother, uncle, and grandpa.

"Are you hungry?" Cyril went to straighten the blankets covering him.

Yes, I'm starving.

"I'll be right back." Cyril thought about how this was Ezek's first trip on her way to the kitchen, that is, that she knew about. Every trip was different. You never knew if you were coming back or not or how it might change you or the world. The change was always something terrifying for her, but on one trip, when she came back, Cindy asked a startling question.

It was the way Cyril answered her that caught Cindy off guard. But it was Cindy's response that changed everything. She asked while storming out of the conference room, "That doesn't even sound like you." Then she stopped, turned, and looked Cyril in the eye, maybe for that moment trying to see if Cyril was really in there somewhere. In a defiant tone, she said, "How do I know that this is you? How can I be certain that the person that left is the same person that returned? Everything that you have said to me so far is so off the mark to the way you think. Who are you? Where's my friend? What did you do to her?" What test could she give him to make sure it was really him? Steam took all the blood tests that were already happening, but what else could make her sure?

Cyril brought back hot clam chowder. Twyce helped him sit up when he heard him say, *Where's Dad?* Henry stood at the door and answered him. No words were exchanged out loud.

Green, you said? Ezek looked him in the eye.

Yes, green, we'll talk about it later when you get your strength back. Henry moved out of Cyril's way. *This girl was on a mission to feed you! She made her famous clam chowder. She must have known you were coming.* Henry watched her as she sat on the edge of his bed.

Ezek smiled as he watched her wipe the bottom of the spoon before putting it toward his mouth. In her head, she heard him, *This is different, you feeding me instead of me feeding you.* For that moment, they both recalled all the times it had happened before. Twyce watched the exchange then commented aloud, "Man, you guys have been through a lot together." He witnessed the tenderness between them as they both at one time or another fed each other when they were either sick or injured.

Cyril asked, *What's this about green orbs? Let's get Cindy in here. She'll know about them.*

Cyril's hand went gently across Ezek's forehead. *Tell me what it was like for you. What happened?* Cyril grabbed the blanket at the end of the bed to cover herself.

You're right, no matter how you think it's going to be, it never is. All the times you tried to explain that to me... I was listening, but once you're there, you feel it, you smell it, the coldness in your hand. I can't describe it. It wasn't anything like I thought it was going to be. Acid was there. Ezek held up his hand to stare into his palm, remembering the moment.

Wow, I haven't seen her in years. How is she?

She said she thought she was never going to see me again, he said while looking bewildered. *She appeared like she was aging right in front of me. Her sides were no longer white. I remembered that about her. She seemed taller than I remember. She's much taller than Yike, and he's pretty tall for a Gray.*

How did she know that about Mom? And what did she mean about Mom being right? You're doing it already. I can feel it, stop it... Cyril was frustrated, almost sounding mad.

Stop what?

You're deliberately blocking me. What happened up there that you're leaving out? Tell me.

Trying every way he could to keep it from her, he suddenly heard Twyce in his head, *If you don't tell her, I will,* as Twyce walked into the room and sat down in the chair next to the bed, giving Ezek a cold stare.

Suddenly leaning against the doorjamb was Henry. Then Henry's head turned as he watched Azalya run up the hallway into Ezek's room. "Daddy, where did you say Grandpa was?" A surprised look came over Azalya's face.

I didn't say where he was.

"Yes, you did!" As Azalya struggled to get up onto his bed. "Is he with Acid? Is that where he went? Are they together with Yike? When is he coming home?" All questions Cyril would have asked if she had known where her father was. But now Azalya knew.

Cyril pulled herself back to get a good look at him. "What! Is that what you're trying not to tell me? Why is my dad there? He doesn't like them… He's probably freaking out, being the control freak that he is." Cyril dropped flat against the pillow next to Ezek. At the same time, she glared up to the canopy, Azalya snuggling to get in between them.

Henry walked up to the end of the bed holding his arms out wide, grabbing both bedposts.

"Answer her!"

There was an evil look in his eyes, one any normal person would have feared. Henry knew what was in Ezek's head. Even he was trying to figure out how he would break it to Virginia.

Ezek inside him said to Cyril, *What's Mom going to do? How is she going to take this news? Why can't I keep it just a little longer?* Then everyone in the room looked at Azalya.

Steam came in quickly. Cindy was right behind him; they both looked like they were in a hurry. "What's going on?" Steam stopped as he looked at Ezek's pulse from the monitor. Cyril looked over the same time Steam did. Ezek never had high blood pressure. Both Steam and Cyril looked at each other, noticing the change.

"I'm not sure what's happening here, but everyone needs to leave the room. Yes, Cyril, you too."

"I'm not going anywhere until I get an answer."

Hearing a noise in the hallway, Cindy turned. She said loud enough for everyone in the room to hear, "Hi, Mom," as she moved out of Virginia's way.

Everyone in the room remained silent—even Azalya.

"Everyone's just leaving. Ezek's blood pressure is just a little high." Steam knew what was going on; he knew about the DNA report results from the sunflower shells Cyril had requested. Now he knew why it was so secret. Earlier, Cindy told Steam how Sven and Mikel had been off the radar for weeks. Cindy had concluded after searching for so long then to not find them only meant they were not on this planet.

"What's going on? What aren't you telling me?" Virginia stopped to catch her breath.

Henry went to put his arm around Virginia when her arm went down quickly. Stepping away, Henry stood behind her.

"Azalya, sweetheart. Tell Grandma what they're all talking about."

Suddenly it felt like all the air went out of the room, and everyone stopped as Ezek told his daughter so Cyril and Twyce and Henry could hear, *We don't want to upset Grandma. So please just tell her we were talking about Acid. Please, sweetheart.* Ezek smiled over to her.

Looking over to Virginia, Azalya smiled. "I know Acid. She's Yike's mommy. You know her too, Daddy?"

Out of breath from standing too long, Virginia's hand went down the side of Azalya's hair while looking into her eyes.

Taking a deep breath, she said, "Okay, if you're not going to tell me, I'm going to take a nap. When I wake up, we'll all…and I mean all of us." Her finger pointed to everyone in the room.

"We'll all have dinner downstairs and discuss this. Ezek, you can tell us about your trip, okay? Have I made myself clear?" Her glare went across the room. Like small children, they all nodded yes, even Henry. Virginia struggled to turn and walk out of the room.

"Let me help you." Henry went to take her arm.

The conversation between Ezek and Cyril was fast and furious, but only the two could hear.

Steam looked at both of them, holding his arms out to try to separate what they were saying with no luck. Finally, he said it out loud at both of them. "STOP IT…STOP IT, BOTH OF YOU!" He couldn't hear them, but he knew they were still in a heated conversation.

"Cyril, you have to leave, *now!*" Steam said as he watched Ezek's blood pressure spike. Cyril's eyes glanced over to the monitor; she turned and left the room.

Cindy gave Steam a harsh look and followed Cyril out of the room, down the hall, then down the stairs. Cyril stopped at the stairs and sat down.

Cindy looked at her, putting her hand on her shoulder, sitting next to her. "Hey, I was coming to tell you about your dad and Sven."

"Hold on, Dad and Sven? Tell me what you know."

"Finally, a moment to catch up now that you're back. Can I just give it all to you? I've been holding so much classified information you need to know about."

"Let's go into my dad's office. We'll have privacy there."

Closing the door behind her, they both sat on the suede sofa, looking out to the lake. "First, how are you, my trusted old friend?" They exchanged warm smiles.

Cindy stopped, holding her hand up. "You realize when we're in this position, we have to be sure."

Cyril closed her eyes for a second and took in a deep breath. "You're right. You and I can be sure, but how do I know if that person upstairs is really Ezek?" Cindy saw panic cover Cyril's face.

"Let's worry about us first. How about just to be sure we both write it down. Then exchange it like we always have." Cindy got up from the sofa and went to the desk. Taking one sticky note and two pens, she tore the paper in half, handing Cyril one half with a pen.

"Do you think this is ridiculous?" Cyril asked before writing anything down.

Cindy gave her a cautious look, almost like a warning. Then she began to explain as if she might be talking to a stranger.

"When one of us has left the planet, this is something we have always done to be sure it's us. We have done this for as long as we have known each other. We need to be sure it's us. Suppose the wrong word shows up on the paper, no information will be exchanged. We've always done it this way."

Both their heads went down as they wrote the secret password, the one only they knew. The word so far had never changed, and it's never said out loud. Then they both folded the paper in half. Exchanging paper, they both opened it simultaneously, glancing quickly at the word then putting the paper into their mouths as they both began to chew.

At the same time, they said, "Thank god we're okay."

"So fill me into what's been happening?" Relieved, Cyril sat back.

"Okay, let's start with work first. The satellite went into orbit just fine before your incident. That was your biggest concern back then. The launch was postponed for two days. They thought the oxygen tanks were leaking, but all tests were fine. Steam and I watched it take off. It was a night launch. It was beautiful. Also, Steam's baby in Alaska is finally empty. We're slowly refilling it with the overflow from the other holding facilities throughout the States. We've noticed the warmer climates not only have more orb sightings, but they're also filling up faster. At this moment, we only have two pods ready. We need at least four more—my god, I have so much to tell you! I'm trying to keep it all in order. Let's see, this I think you might find interesting. We got a call to pick up a package in Detroit. They said it was large. So after trying to trace where the call came from with no luck, we figured based on the line the call came in on, we should take the call seriously. So we sent a discreet team over to check it out. A handwritten note was left on the outside of the container. It was addressed to you. I have it in my satchel. Do you want to see it?"

"Sure, later, but tell me what it said."

"It was a simple note: 'Seal them up. Y.' Do you understand what it means?"

Cyril smiled as she thought about her last conversation with Yike. He knew who it was who took her that night in the hangar. "Yes, it's from Yike. They must be the Grays that took me that night he caught them. What did you do with them? Where are they?"

"We've been holding them for months waiting for you. We weren't sure what you wanted to do with them. Any ideas?"

It didn't take Cyril long to think about it. "Yes, I'd like to do with them what they did to me. Give them to Steam's research department to do what they want. Just don't tell me what happens to them. And remember my number one rule: nothing gets tortured."

"That's a good idea. Steam's been working on that chip you got from Yike. That will help his team break down some differences between their kind. He's finding out even the Grays come from different areas in the galaxies. The sojourning on each planet on Yike's list needs more details. It's not complete. But it's a start. These Grays will help with that. The information on that chip was very complex. We brought in all the head researchers into one room then sealed the room. Yes, it's all classified. They were only permitted to take notes. No copies were made. No pictures from the data were allowed. No, they have no idea where it came from. All they know is you want them to understand it, interpret it, and report their findings. They were given four weeks to submit their findings. Is that too much time, do you think?"

"No, that's fine. Does anyone besides you two know I'm back? I mean, they all think I never left, right? My memory, I mean."

"No, but at the party, someone might have noticed you were different. I don't think anyone will bring it up, knowing the stress of your position. We thought we'd leave that up to you how you want to come back into the fold. I'm just glad you're back." Cindy shook her head in relief.

Three little knocks on the outside of the door. Cyril turned. "Come in."

"What are you two plotting? Sorry about that earlier." Steam put his right hand to his heart. "I'm his doctor. I have to look out for his best interest. You weren't his best interest, you understand?"

Steam walked around to Mikel's desk and sat in the big old leather chair. He turned the chair to view the water. "So what do I need to know?"

Cindy gave Steam a smile that stopped Cyril. She kept it to herself only to examine it just a little further to be sure.

"I was just telling Cyril some of the things that have happened while she was gone. Let me rephrase that, while you were indisposed."

"Did you tell her about the vaccine?" Steam turned.

"We figured out why the people in the southern hemisphere's blood were not tainted. Everyone was given old vaccines, stuff left over from the prior year. It took us a while, but we're up and running now. So by next year, everyone should have the antibodies in their systems. We're trying to make it mandatory that everyone has to have a flu shot, so we're providing it free. Each government has covered its cost for their people. We're just leaving out a small detail." Steam smiled like he was proud of himself. "Your mom should be very proud that it's working."

Both Steam's arms crossed then dropped onto the desk as he got serious and looked Cyril in the eye. "Tell me exactly what Ezekiel said to you."

"Ezekiel! Now you only call him that when you're mad or worried. Which is it?"

"Both," Steam said without hesitation.

"As far as I know with what scrambled messages I could retrieve, my father and Sven are with Yike and Acid."

Cindy sounded surprised. "Acid is still alive. Wow, she must be at least eighty, maybe ninety years old by our standards of time."

"So what do you think they're doing to them?" Steam wanted Cyril's version; he had his own version already.

"Did you tell Cindy about the sunflower shells?" Cyril caught Steam off guard.

For just that moment, Steam gave Cyril a distorted look. "That was a cross-my-heart swear. What do you think?" The childhood game was a serious one, one each of them to this day understood and didn't take it lightly. A bit of distrust came in his tone. Then he smirked.

"Okay, stop it, you two. What about sunflower seeds?"

"That winter in Bonn, that summit I missed when I was taken. The person in the front seat of the car was eating sunflower seeds. When he opened the window to spit the shells out of the car, they flew back into the back seat, where I was blindfolded and tied up. The blindfold was pretty tight across my eyes. I couldn't see anything until I rubbed my head against the seat. That's when I looked down my nose through a small gap and saw the shells land on the floor."

"Okay, but that was how many years ago. What's that got to do with now?" Cindy asked.

"The night I arrived here at the Rock when I was getting out of the helicopter, the blue orbs stayed under my seat. I had to stop to see what they were trying to show me. There under the seat were two sunflower shells."

Steam interrupted, "That afternoon when Cyril returned, and you asked me what was in the sealed envelope I needed to have tested, I told you it was a cross-my-heart secret."

"Yeah." Cindy nodded yes.

"Well, can I tell her now?" Steam looked over to Cyril for permission to share the secret. Cyril nodded yes.

"She wanted me to run a DNA test on the shells. It came back. They were from her father. Now we're not sure about the ones in Bonn, but we are sure about the ones in the helicopter."

"Hold on, is this about finding out who eats sunflower seeds close to you?" Cindy looked at Cyril for an answer.

"Yes." She found the question so simple in Cindy's tone. Cyril asked, "Why?"

"Why didn't you just ask? I have full dossiers on everyone we make contact with. Your father started eating sunflower seeds when he tried to stop smoking cigars years ago. Do you remember how long ago that was? And how awful it was working around him? He was irritable, but he didn't smell as bad as he used to. It's annoying finding shells left everywhere. What's with men thinking someone is just going to come up behind them and clean up their mess. I hate those things. They're messy."

Steam smiled at Cindy for a moment. "So now that we have your opinion of men and sunflower seeds…" It was that same smile she saw from Cindy earlier.

"So you guys want to tell me what's going on here?" Cyril looked back at each of them.

Cindy glanced over; she knew what the question implied.

Steam looked like he had no idea what she was talking about. "What?"

Cindy looked over to Steam. "I'm going to tell her."

"I'm not sure right now is a good time. A lot is going on right now."

As if Cyril wasn't in the room, Cindy said, "She's my best friend. I've known her most of my life. She would want to know how happy I am and you being her best friend forever. I'm sure, yes. I'm positive she would want to know, and she would be overjoyed. Let's tell her."

"Holy shit, like you haven't just told me." Cyril's smile was from cheek to cheek. "How long? Tell me, how long has this been going on?"

Cindy smiled. "Well, we kinda knew for a while, but when we couldn't get two rooms when we were in Alaska, it changed everything."

"All the way back then and you never said anything? I thought I saw something a few days ago, but I couldn't be sure with all the chaos.

"And you, Mr. Single Guy with Secrets, I wasn't going to pry it out of you. But, Cindy, you gave it away. It was the smile. Please don't tell me you're in separate rooms here?"

"No, Anna's very open-minded."

Everyone in the room looked toward the kitchen as pots and pans fell to the floor.

"Who's cooking dinner tonight?" Cyril asked.

Cindy got up. "We better go find out. It better not be Mom!"

The Truth

"Are you coming down? Dinner's ready?"

"Come here…please!" Ezek's hand lay flat on top of the blankets. "I'm sorry."

"When were you going to tell me about my father and Sven?" A broken look covered Cyril's face.

"I didn't know how to tell you."

"When has talking to me ever been a problem?" Cyril walked over to the side of the bed when it occurred to her she had to find a way to know if it was him or not. He had never left before. He never posed a problem. He never had a problem talking to her inside or outside of their heads. So she decided to ask.

"There's a game Cindy and I play. We've played it for as long as we have known each other. It occurred to us one time long ago that if we were ever taken, how would we know the person who came back was the same person that left? So we came up with a method that, so far as we know, works for us. But we…you and I have nothing like that, so right now I'm not sure who I'm talking to."

"Why, is this all because I had trouble telling you about your dad? Really, or is this you being paranoid?"

"Good answer. The facts still remain." Cyril looked up at Ezek with a cold stare.

"What would you like me to do to prove to you that it's really me? Tell me, I'll do whatever you ask." Shaking his head, he saw the seriousness in her face.

He had always kept her word with Cindy a secret; it was something he read in her mind as never to be said out loud, so to him also he never mentioned it.

"Okay, how about if I tell you what the word is between you and Cindy. Will that be good enough?"

Cyril wasn't sure what to think; she was compelled to run down and ask Cindy, but at what risk? Would Yike do something so...she couldn't find the words. Would Yike? She had no idea.

Cyril sat at the edge of his bed and looked at him. He was different; the white in his hair, the look on his face. He appeared tired and stressed. For Cyril, it broke her heart and at the same time cautioned her. Red flags flew all around him. So she said, "Hold on, I'll be right back."

When she came back into the room, he said, "Can't I just say the word out loud?"

Cyril held her hand up to stop him. "No, don't say it. Don't say it out loud. It's not done that way."

"Here, write it down on the corner of the page."

Thinking how ridiculous it all was, he accommodated her. In tiny letters, he wrote the word then handed it back to her. She read it. It was correct, then to mess with him, she got a serious look on her face and said, "Tell me what you said that you would never tell me?" His head tilted to one side as he smiled at her. "No!" The covers to his bed went open to allow her in.

Cyril struggled for a moment then contained herself. She smiled then turned to leave the room.

"Come on, you're the guest speaker this evening. They're all waiting for you." She did everything she could not to jump into bed with him. Every fiber in her was turning back.

Virginia stood at the end of the long dining room table. Her hand displayed the armchair at the end. "Ezekiel, you should sit here." Straightening his shirt, he sat where he was told. Cindy came in carrying a large bowl of hot baked potatoes wrapped in foil. Steam came in carrying a huge wooden bowl with tossed salad and two kinds of dressing. Cyril held a platter of Brown derby garlic bread toasted just right on the top. She knew it was one of Ezek's favorites.

Allen went to the end of the table, displaying a large platter of barbecued steaks he had just cooked.

"Just point," Allen said to Ezek, as he placed the one he wanted onto his plate. Henry sat across from Virginia as he sipped his iced tea.

"Anna made a carrot cake for dessert." Virginia looked over to Ezek. "It's your favorite, isn't it?" She smiled at him.

Ezek just smiled and nodded yes.

Virginia said to Azalya, "Are you and Anna going upstairs to watch your program? Come down later and have cake with us if it's not too late."

Azalya took Anna's hand as she pulled her toward the stairs.

Virginia turned toward Ezek while she laid her napkin across her lap. "Will there be gory details? Should we eat first, or can you talk about it while we eat?"

"I'm starving." Ezek cut his steak then put it into his mouth. After a few minutes of eating, Ezek put down his fork. He looked over to Cyril. Everyone at the table knew he was ready to share his trip.

"Cyril, you have an interesting friend that cares a lot about you." Then he looked over to Virginia. "You also have a unique friend. One of the messages they wanted to be clear was that you are both loved. That I noticed was important to them that you understand that. As your friend, it was important to Yike that he cleared a few misunderstandings up for me. One."

Ezek paused as his hand went out toward his father. "He needed me to know he did not take my dad. But most importantly, he needed to rest my soul. Those are Yike's words."

Ezek gave his father a stare. "Yike showed me the moment my mother died. He let me watch it unfold right in front of me as if I were there. He needed me to know she was not harvested."

He looked at Henry and said it very clearly, "Don't ever say again she didn't know how to fly." He did everything he could to compose himself. Then he looked over to Steam. "He also needed me to tell you your mother was not harvested either. He tried to change her cells when he found out she had cancer. Apparently, you have the impression he was the one that caused it. Let me be clear he was not. He tried to save her and couldn't.

"But to the big question, let me just give it to you straight. Cyril, your father has tried to kill you a few times. And he has admired how smart you are even to his annoyance. The first time was when you and Cindy were in college. It was right after you got the first big contract. He knew he needed to stop you then. But Yike somehow got in between you guys. Have you ever wondered why it took you three days to cross the desert to get to Area 50? Just the fact that you knew about Area 50 made him crazy. It was Yike again. You two were never supposed to make it to Area 50. He had people all along the way to stop you." Virginia's hand went to cover her mouth in horror.

"That day when you shot the man on the hill, he wasn't there for me. He was there for you. He thought Tully was you. When he realized she wasn't, he decided to kill everyone in the house. He told your father so. He didn't want the trip to be wasted. Your father couldn't believe what he saw on the man's tablet, that you shot the man instead. The tablet the man had was lying in the grass. When you looked at it, it went black. Your father had already logged off. Your father was listening to every word. He saw you on the tablet when you went to check for a pulse."

"My god, Ezek, how do you know this is true?" Virginia took her hand from her mouth.

"Hold on, it gets worse. The blast in the desert you thought was from retaliation from the building. Sven didn't blow up, but you did. None of that is right. Sven was supposed to use the cloth on you. He just couldn't. No one was to touch that building that day, but you did instead. You knew what was inside. I'm truly sorry to have to tell you, but the blasts in the desert that day that killed Max, that was also your father's doing. None of it was from the Grays. Your father killed Max. He was trying to kill you instead."

Cyril sat there stunned as Steam and Twyce looked in horror. Then Ezek turned and took Virginia's hand. "Mom, that beautiful scarf, the gift from Mikel. Acid knew what had happened to you and who sent the scarf. She couldn't get to you quick enough. So she tried with the elixir she gave me. Mikel knew the flu vaccine you created was working and knew that if you weren't going to keep his secret, you too needed to go. The scarf was his weapon."

Ezek looked over to Cyril. "The only successful thing your father did to you was erase your memory. Yes, Cyril, Sven did it; but your father ordered it. No one on this planet has access to the compounds it took to create the black crystals except your father."

Cyril sat back in her chair and just stared at Ezek.

"You believe everything you're telling me, don't you?" Cyril said almost in disgust. Not sure of what she was hearing but putting the pieces together told her some of it might be true. This was her father. He talked about a man who practically raised him, a man who was almost a father to him.

"What's happening to him?" Shaking her head like trying to shake it all off, she repeated, "What's happening to him up there? What is Yike doing to him?"

He remembered what Yike said, so he said it aloud, "This is what he said: 'Let's fix this so you can go home. I will let him keep his memory, but he will not be able to share it with anyone. Nor will he be able to contact anyone outside his own body. He will not be able to do anything about what's happening to him. I think you call it a vegetative state. Inside he will be wide awake and see and understand his prison. He can scream and rattle the bars no one can hear. Cyril will hold no remorse toward my actions. You can explain to her this is for her protection.'

"I'm not sure if or when he will return him to you. I do know before I was permitted to leave, he was about to close off his memory. Similar to what happened to you."

Ezek looked over to Cyril. "I'm sorry. He didn't tell me. I'm not sure what Acid had planned for him either. As for the green orbs, I'm waiting to hear. That was something Yike found in my memory. Even he was surprised. Green orbs are inscribed on the inside of their crafts but never seen. So when he saw them in my memory, it stopped him. He needs more time to find the answer. So I should be hearing from him soon, I hope. I'll record my trip for the archives. I think I ate too much, and I'm tired. That's all I can pull out of my brain right now, okay?"

Ezek's fingers went through his hair; pulling it back, he twisted it.

No one said a word. Henry got up and went outside. Twyce followed him.

Steam asked, "Are you all right? Do you need something to help you sleep?"

Ezek looked over to Cyril. "No, I'll be okay."

Anna started to clear the dishes off the table when Ezek asked, "Where's Azalya?"

"She's asleep in her room. She's out like a light. She was tired. All this activity takes a lot out of her."

Virginia sat back in her chair, staring at Cyril. "I guess this means you can go to the summit in the spring. Do you know now what you'll tell them, now that there's no one to stop you?"

Cyril noticed a sour pitch in her mother's voice, one she scowled back at.

Ezek read Cyril but got nothing from Virginia. He heard the rage inside her toward her mother and realized the quiet war was not over. Cyril remained quiet as she thought to herself, forgetting that Ezek was walking inside her thoughts.

She had always wanted her words to be the truth; she was done being quiet about what was happening around her and all the secret projects the company was working on. No one had a clue about all the Grays asleep in pods in their thermosphere and exosphere floating alongside their satellites.

What would the public do if they were to see the inside of a harvest facility? Would they agree with her work? Would what she's done so far be okay? When she first saw Yike in her stardust moment, she recalled having to lie to herself to cope. So then, how could she make her truth become everyone else's? What would make that easy? Then it occurred to her when she looked through her father's eyes, as long as no one knows, as long as the quiet war remains quiet, her work can go on.

Her father wanted her to remain quiet; he wanted to take credit for the breakthroughs and discoveries acquired from all the Grays he knew. Simple applications to any Gray but complicated breakthroughs to mortal human beings. She needed more time to weigh the back-and-forth of it. Her head was spinning while her mother stared at her. Her look was not angry or sad. For a moment, Cyril felt responsible for everything that had occurred. That was the look her mother had on her face.

Ezek held his hand out. "Come with me." It almost sounded like an order.

Steam and Cindy went into the kitchen carrying bowls and platters. Cyril stared at Ezek's hand. This time he said it to only her. "Breathe, sweetheart, come with me."

Cyril took his hand like she had done a million times before. To Ezek, it felt like home. He walked her up the stairs down the hall and into his room, closing the door behind him. He turned while her thoughts were still swirling inside her head. He began to unbutton her blouse.

He heard her in his head, *None of this is my fault. You understand that, don't you?*

He listened then told her, *We're both tired. Let's give today a rest, okay? Please.*

Cyril stopped and looked at where she was at. *How did you manage that?*

What?

I like how you always sound so innocent.

She put her arms around him and kissed him gently. He leaned down to kiss her back as he scooped her up to put her into bed. He stopped to look at her, *Are you...?*

Am I what? She stopped to see what was next...

She held his face in her hands then simply said out loud, "Yes, I am." It was like the first time, not that first time but so many of the other first times with him.

It was discovering each other all over again; it was, as she remembered it, music.

A sharp noise came from the other room, causing Cyril's eyes to peel back as she lay trying to figure out where she was at. Ezek's hair went over her shoulder as his scent surrounded her. She felt his arm over her waist, and his hand gently held her left breast. She was tucked into him tightly. She wondered if he was alive; she couldn't hear him breathing.

Then in the distance, she heard ever so quietly a puckering, popping noise, almost like kissing. Then she heard it again. Giving Ezek a short push, she rolled over toward him. Her face into his chest, she said for only him to hear, *Listen.*

He said back in her head, *To what?*

The noise came from Azalya's room. They both bolted out of bed. Naked Ezek threw Cyril his robe; he put on his pajama bottoms as they both quietly left the room.

The light was off in Azalya's room, but the twinkling lights from her mobile illuminated just enough. There in the chair, watching in awe, was Yike. Down on the floor was Azalya and a Gray that looked just like Yike when he was that age. No words were exchanged out loud. Looking up with his deep purple eyes, Yike said, "This is my progeny. Its name is Wish."

Yike held his hand out. His fingers began to extend toward Cyril. "Here is the information you need about the green orbs."

The sharp tips of his fingers pinched the chip toward her. When she touched Yike to take the chip, he sent her a vision. It was her father sitting with the other Grays watching the wall reading something. Next to him was Acid. Then the image was gone.

Yike said, "I want them to be friends like you and I are friends. Like my mother and your mother are friends." Yike turned to Ezek, not asking for permission. He waited; then when he saw Ezek smile, the same smile his mother once got from him, he knew everything would be all right.

Cyril and Ezek sat at the edge of Azalya's bed and watched on. Yike watched as Wish and Azalya pointed at the mobile hanging from the ceiling. Everyone could tell a conversation was happening between the two. Azalya got up from the floor and took Wish's hand, leading him into the hall.

"Where are you going?" Ezek asked, looking at his daughter.

"Daddy, we're going downstairs to the kitchen." She took Wish down the hall. Wish looked back at Yike, almost like Wish was asking for permission. Yike didn't move as the two of them walked away.

Cyril asked, "What do you think she's up to?" They all looked at one another.

Yike said to both of them, "If she's anything like her mother, she's taking him downstairs to feed him."

It occurred to Cyril, Yike had referred to Wish as he. Before she could ask, Yike explained, "I want it to be a he." As he looked over to Ezek, he said to him, "You don't get to choose, and in a way, neither do we, but I can try to influence him." Cyril thought she saw a smile on Yike's face. The three of them followed them downstairs.

"Hi, Aunt Cindy. This is my friend, Wish."

Cindy turned around to close the refrigerator then slammed her back against the fridge door. She was staring intensely at Wish. Azalya went to the fridge door then looked up at Cindy and said, "My parents are coming. They know he's here." Azalya turned to Wish and asked, "Have you ever had steak or, let's see, try my dad's favorite cake?

It's got carrots in it."

Cyril saw the shocked look on Cindy's face as she walked into the kitchen. Cindy was still not able to move as she watched Azalya place the cake onto the counter.

"Cindy, would you like a piece of cake?" Cyril stared into her eyes to break her concentration, trying to seem casual as if everything was all right. Cindy walked around the counter to the other side of the island when she noticed Yike and Ezek coming into the kitchen.

"I'll have a piece of cake."

Ezek turned to Yike and asked, "Have you ever had carrot cake?"

Cyril went to sit at the island. "Have a seat." Cyril's hand went to move the stool so Cindy could sit next to her.

Cindy watched as Ezek went to get plates as Yike came over to sit next to her.

"Does this happen often?" Cindy caught her breath to look at Ezek.

Ezek turned as he put the plates on the counter, smiling at Cindy. "No. Never. Never happened before that I know of." He said it out loud. She could tell that what was unfolding in front of her was new.

"Cindy." Cyril touched her arm to get her to look at her, taking the moment away that Yike was sitting four inches away from her.

"This is Yike and his son, Wish." Cyril looked over to Yike as if she was going along with the idea Wish was a boy. For a moment, she thought she saw him smile back. Yike looked over, watching Ezek cut the cake and put it on to the plates.

"Are you having cake?" Ezek looked at Cindy, waiting for an answer.

"No, I'll pass." The words came floating out of her in a high pitch with a smile.

For a moment, Cyril looked up at the canopy and wondered how long she had been there. Rolling over to Ezek, touching him made him twitch hard.

Inside her head, he said, *How long have we been here? Where's Azalya?* He bolted out of bed, rushing into her room; he found her clutching her panda asleep.

He heard in his head, *Yike would never harm her. Did you think he had?* Cyril causally lay there looking up.

"How do you know that? Where do you get your information? He could have taken her." Cyril heard a fair amount of sarcasm and anger in his voice.

"Yike knows that to be my biggest fear. He won't let that disturb me. He is, after all, my friend."

Ezek noticed a calmness that came with her words. What she was sharing was the truth to her—something she could not doubt.

Fast footsteps were coming up the stairs, so Ezek waited to see who it was.

Rounding the landing, Steam said, "What the hell's going on here?"

Cindy held Steam's arm almost as if she was trying to stop him. "You all have to be checked."

When Cindy looked toward the window to hear the helicopter's landing, she turned. "Really, they just left."

Steam heard the relaxed, almost-happy way Cindy said it while she smiled at him. "Yes, and he just contaminated all of you. Where's Cyril and Azalya?"

"They're all right Azalya's sleeping." As he turned, Cyril stood at the door; she gave Cindy one of those familiar smiles. The same smile both had shared numerous times before after similar events.

"Okay, just a few swabs. Let me check you guys real quick, please!" Exasperated, he turned to hear Anna at the door, letting in the doctors and nurses inside.

After the nurses and doctors finished their tests, Cyril pried her hand open, holding it toward Steam. He stopped and stared for a moment while unfolding a cloth. "More information?" His head went down as he examined the small zip drive. He was surprised to see another one so soon.

"Yes, Yike said it's about the green orbs."

About the Author

Sherree Brose is a fiction writer. Her readers have called her Masterpiece, in-the-moment imaginative, intriguing, and compelling writing with a sharp female perspective. As a middle child, she got to view both sides of every story. Yet here as always, she searches for middle ground. Sherree spends quiet time writing and painting in her studio in Northern California.

CPSIA information can be obtained
at www.ICGtesting.com
Printed in the USA
LVHW100628290622
722260LV00006B/34

9 781638 813958